Bedside in Berlin

Bedside in Berlin

C.R. Page

Turn the Page Creations

This book is published by Turn the Page Creations.

Fullarton SA 5063 Australia

Cover designed and created by Alison Page Photography

ISBN 978-0-6454757-5-3

A catalogue copy of this novel is held by the National Library of Australia

First published 2023

To Hella and Marty, who not only inspired much of this book, but so much of my life. Rest in Peace.

12 March 2020

MARTA

An impenetrable wall. For a generation, that was what defined Berlin. Division wasn't unique to our city, but nowhere else had such a prominent point of reference for that division. West Berlin was completely encircled by the Wall, yet it was the people of East Berlin who were being contained by it. West Berlin flourished like few other cities as the world begun the boom times from the post-war global economic recovery. The Allies invested heavily in its growth, desperate to provide a beacon of hope and prosperity against the sprawling growth of Communism as it pushed further west.

Hundreds were killed attempting to escape across the Wall. I was amongst the success stories, making it out of the East thanks to significant assistance. I had the right people on my side to make it possible, but that didn't alter the fact that I was risking my life. "Shoot to kill" orders existed and applied to anyone caught trying to cross the border illegally. While the help I received made detecting me less likely, I would be as vulnerable as anyone else if I was caught fleeing East Berlin. I risked everything I had on that night yet looking back I realise how little that was. I had an existence in East Berlin, but I only had a life once I was across the Wall.

It is nearly sixty years since I made that journey. Now I am in the east of a united Berlin. Once again life has seen me as a prisoner behind a wall. I have even less chance of escaping this time. I am in a nursing home, an array of ailments ensuring my time is confined to either bed or a wheelchair. Even if my health allowed it, I still couldn't get out. It wouldn't be a wall holding me in, but a virus. There are grave fears that this virus will rip through our community, particularly the vulnerable such as my husband and me. So be it. We have had such full lives that whatever lies ahead of us is a fate we're prepared for. Henry and I never envisaged surviving this long.

Through all the good and the bad, Berlin has always been home to me. I spent years on the road, living out of a suitcase. For a decade I travelled the world as a figure skater, spending time in all the world's greatest cities. Many of these were defined by iconic structures, places and events. There were cities we considered settling in at the end of our careers. I could find houses, but never a home. It was only when we returned to the city of my youth that I knew I was where I belonged. There is nowhere in the world that compares to it. Berlin isn't about what you see, it is about what you feel. We don't hide from the past, we learn from it. The more that you learn, the richer you become. It is the lessons of our city's past that give us the richest culture you will find.

Of all that you have, you appreciate what you once lived without far more than what has been always yours. Berlin lived without freedom for so long that we now value it like few other cities can. What they take for granted, we cherish and celebrate.

For Henry and me, the magic of this city seems to have exhausted its value. When you are confined to a bed in a plain room, within a nursing home that you know you'll never leave, it hardly matters what lies outside your door. We could be anywhere for all the difference it makes, yet I feel indelibly linked to Berlin and take comfort from knowing it is outside my window. Whether Henry shares that view is another story, but this city has played nearly as great a role in his life as it has mine.

The Wall remained standing long after our careers in the entertainment industry ended. Choosing to live in a city encircled by a prison-like wall would seem unusual, yet it was a simple choice. There were no remaining ties here for us, yet we loved everything that West Berlin had become. I believed that the city unifying in my lifetime was improbable, but that wasn't relevant to our decision. West Berlin was where we wanted to be for what it was at that time, not for any hope of what it may become.

We settled in trendy Kreuzberg, not too far from the Wall. It was an ideal spot for us, so far as ideals exist. After living on the road, a constant home was a major lifestyle change. We ran businesses, held jobs and lived like average people, but it seemed mundane against the lives we had led. The same would have applied anywhere, but in West Berlin the adaptation to our new lives was the same thing that the city was undergoing.

I dreamed that one day the Wall would come down, and that I'd be able to walk freely down the streets of my youth. At that stage it was nothing more than a dream. The Cold War continued through the 1970s and early 80's without any sign of abatement. People on both sides of the divide were accustomed to the reality of our city and the impact was far less than when I'd left. For some on the eastern side, there was envy of the quality of life we had, but the propaganda machine was strong enough that many East Berliners had no appreciation of what they were missing.

When the Wall finally fell in 1989, Berlin partied like no city ever has. The worlds eyes were on us, for this wasn't a story about our city as much as a symbol of hope for the world. It was the defining moment in the end of the Cold War. The Wall divided the city of Berlin, but it served as the symbol of the global divide between East and West. The celebrations that occurred by the Brandenburg Gate were the centre-piece, but people around the world were sharing the euphoria.

The unified Berlin took time for the divisions to disappear. The physical barrier may have gone, but the difference between life in the two sides of the city had been so great, that it was impossible for every-thing to meld together quickly. What was apparent was the goodwill from many on both sides to come together. When all you have known is division, this unity doesn't come naturally for everyone. Distrust was everywhere, particularly amongst the older sections of the population. The idealism of youth ensured that many people were working on creating the utopia they believed was imminent.

Like most of my generation, it still took time before I felt safe to return to the old neighbourhood. When I did, it was cathartic in its own way, yet rather than bringing up good memories of my youth, it reinforced what I had always believed. I made the right choices all those years ago.

Berlin was destroyed in World War II. It was the global symbol of disunity for the next half a century. Thirty years later, it now stands as the worlds home of diversity, unity and hope. The brightest day follows the darkest night.

I can't help but imagine what it would be like to arrive in Berlin as a young person today. The opportunity to find yourself in a city as diverse and vibrant as this would offer limitless potential for what life can be. There are ghosts of the past scattered around the city. They don't diminish from the modern city, they enhance it, by ensuring a full appreciation of all we value most highly.

While I envy anyone who arrives in Berlin now, I wouldn't change what my life has been. Living through the worst of life allows for the truest appreciation of life at its best.

12 March 2020

AMBER

There is nothing like the day of arrival in a new city. It always generates a thrill that coincides with the limitless potential on offer from each place and its people. Every component is new and unknown. It is a feeling I am certain I will never tire of. However much I've loved the different cities I've visited, some of the gloss always fades with time. Perhaps familiarity truly does breed contempt.

Like the first night with a new lover, the initial movements through a city are sometimes awkward, but always exciting. As I move ever closer, Berlin takes the place of the most attractive stranger imaginable. My eyes have locked in on it, and I am filled with desire to discover it more deeply. Even if I fall madly in love with the city, the unavoidable reality is that it must have flaws. It is before these are found, that the stranger can appear perfect. This is the illusory feeling of perfection that can only exist before the full picture is seen. A city or a person, the reality is the same.

Since arriving in Frankfurt four months ago, Germany has proven to be an amazing experience that has enriched me more than I had thought possible. I had expected to spend no more than a month here, but as I arrive in Berlin, it will still be another month before I move beyond the German border. With the news that seems to be worsening daily about the new Coronavirus that is taking hold, I may be here far longer.

Nobody at home understood my desire to get on the plane and come here. I was reasonably well established at home in Toronto, but there was something about Europe that had called out to me for many years, and it seemed like the right time to discover it. To be honest, it was more about discovering myself than Europe. Life back home had thrown me into such a point of confusion that I felt I had to look from a different perspective.

Two years ago, I got engaged to Andrew and seemed to know exactly where life was taking me. I never felt like this had come through any definitive plans, I just seemed to keep falling into the pathways that life took me, whether it was work or my personal life. I hadn't sought to work in aged care, but an opportunity arose, and I took it. I didn't particularly enjoy it, yet once I was entrenched, I stayed. I suspect the same would have been the case with Andrew had there not been a precipitating event to change things.

I don't know what made me fall in love with Andrew. Well, I know now that I never really did. He was just in the right place at the right time. He wanted me, and I assumed that the right thing for me was to accept that. Everything about him seemed alright and at that point, I never understood that alright wasn't sufficient. Andrew obviously understood that, and decided the best approach was to cheat on me with my friend Rachel. To what extent I was to blame for this is arguable, but in the end, it proved best for everyone. Even better was the fact that I caught them in the act, so the charade that was going on was brought to a sudden halt. The biggest issue was trying to process my exact feelings about what I had seen. I didn't feel a sense of jealousy towards Rachel for stealing my man. I was jealous of Andrew for stealing Rachel.

I had never consciously felt any sort of physical attraction to Rachel. I never really felt physically drawn to Andrew or anyone else I'd been with. I'd yearned for companionship and a feeling of closeness, wherever it may come from. It had always been with men, and from my upbringing, that is the only way of life I knew. Any other feelings that may have fermented beneath the surface, stayed where I felt they belonged. Deep within.

I'm sure it's a familiar story for many young women. We believe what we are meant to feel. Even when it doesn't seem right, we continue. When what builds in our hearts as a true feeling seems like something wrong and forbidden, we suppress it. We convince ourselves that the feeling is something else. I had developed strong feelings for Rachel, but I convinced myself this was mere friendship, albeit at its closest. I never cried myself to sleep wishing she was sharing my bed, yet I look back with certainty. Any moment that the opportunity would have presented, I would have followed her into hell just to feel her lips on mine.

I didn't head to Europe on an adventure exploring my sexuality. It was merely another symptom of a young woman who never felt like she quite fitted in. At home, it seemed like I didn't fit in anywhere. I didn't expect that to be different in Europe, but that comes from a different source. In a foreign country, the outsider feeling is more circumstantial. Once in a land where nobody knew me, where I didn't speak the language nor understand all the culture, not fitting in would not be a personal failing, just a shortcoming of experience. I was resolute in my belief that this would make things easier to deal with.

I don't know why it is, but I've never been afraid of failure itself, but I've always been afraid of being seen as that. When I'm not noticed, results don't matter. I felt that coming to Europe gave me the opportunity to be anonymous while I discovered who I was. Through every failure I had here, none of the judgement I faced at home would be noticeable. One day I would return, Amber Megan, the person I had become of my own volition, not the Amber Megan I'd been moulded into by the judgements of others and my failed attempts to assimilate.

I didn't come here with an itinerary or a solid plan, but that was always a big part of the fun. Travelling on my own was always going to mean spending a lot of time in my room, planning what would be next on my agenda, so I didn't need it laid out in advance. I came to Germany first, mainly because of the exposure I had to the country when studying the language for a couple of years in high school. I never got too far with it, and remembered virtually nothing, so it didn't prove much of an assistance when I arrived. It did however seem a step less daunting than beginning somewhere like Spain or France, both of which I was keen to visit later in my trip.

I flew into Frankfurt in November but quickly moved on to Stuttgart where I got work at an aged care facility and stayed for four weeks. I had similar stays in both Munich and Nuremberg with a couple of weeks between these to explore what was arguably the more intriguing regions around them. Most recently I've spent two weeks in Leipzig and Dresden, not working, and able to enjoy the beauty of each city.

I have another aged care job lined up for me in Berlin, at a facility called *Senioren Fachpflegezentrum*. Working in these facilities with such limited German is a challenge, but largely we work in pairs and I'm always with a colleague who does the communication with the residents. In theory, they have the capacity to speak English with me, though in practice it hasn't always proven so easy. There seems to be little difficulty in them making their orders clear, though their understanding of any questions I may have is never so good. Whether it's merely my cynicism, it seems the ability to communicate has been the product of convenience. When it suits, they understand. Perhaps they think the same of me.

It's not ideal for me, the residents or the other staff, but there is a dearth of suitably qualified employees for this work. As a result, finding short term opportunities to cover absent staff isn't difficult. In Stuttgart I impressed enough to ensure I had good local references that gave me the opportunities as I moved on. I supplemented these with further good reports from where I worked in Munich and Nuremberg, and I was earmarked for this facility in Berlin two weeks ago. I had to cut short my time in Dresden to make it here. I would have liked to have stayed there longer, but I'm sure moving on will prove worthwhile.

The downside I have found working in Germany has been that I tend to be assigned a higher proportion of the more dreaded tasks. There are always residents who have experienced so much life that conversations can be incredibly insightful, fun and interesting. I miss these, as my partner gets involved with that, while I'm quite literally left with the shit. It's funding my time in Europe so I shouldn't complain. When I did find a fluent English speaker in the Munich home, it made the job so much more rewarding, though I only got limited opportunities to appreciate it. I can only cross my fingers that I find a similar resident at my workplace in Berlin, and hopefully I get a little more chance to build a relationship.

I start work Saturday, so I only have one full day to acquaint myself with the city before its head down, bum up, at the home. Working through an agency, I don't know far in advance what the shifts will be, but I have been told to expect five shifts a week for the next four weeks. I didn't ask beyond that period, as I thought that four weeks in Berlin would suffice. I know there's so much to see and experience in the city, but there's also a whole continent waiting for me to explore.

I had organised accommodation near the Warschauer Straße, no more than a ten-minute walk from where I'd be working. It was several kilometres from the Hauptbahnhof where my train arrived mid evening. While I usually try and dodge the expense, I feel too tired to juggle all my possessions on public transport, so I jump in a taxi. The city will no doubt become familiar soon enough, but for now, simplicity was key.

I don't know why, but with every new city I arrive in, I hold on to the fantasy that my accommodation is going to be a palace at a pauper's price. I knew the cost of this place was economical, yet I felt disappointed when I saw it. I shouldn't be, it's fine. I guess it's a reminder that life isn't everything I want it to be. If it was, then I wouldn't be looking for better, and that is the truest essence of why I am here.

It feels ridiculous to arrive in a city like this and spend the first evening curled up in your own room, but I am going to have such a full day tomorrow that I figure its best to call it a night before I begin.

A backpacker's hostel, a train station, a take-away kebab shop and a few streets that have connected them. At this point of time that is what Berlin is to me. I wonder if I've overextended myself with a month here. I'm not pretending that I've seen a cross section of the city, but I've seen nothing that compares to the instant feeling I got in Stuttgart and Munich. I need to be patient, and not think about these things until I've really begun to experience the city. Tomorrow is the true beginning of my Berlin adventure, and I will stop my constant analysis until I have a little more data to work with.

3

13 March 2020

MARTA

'Jesus Christ, just piss off and leave me alone.' Henry regularly spoke like this to the staff in the home. He believed those he was inflicting the language on would have had no idea what he was saying. Most of the staff knew enough English to understand, but they refused to give him the satisfaction of making him aware by reacting. Using it to their advantage, the main reason they claimed not to know English was to avoid unnecessary conversation with him. It was a two-way street. Henry had lived in Germany long enough to pick up a little German without trying yet was too pig-headed to use it here. When he was angry enough at anyone, he would move to his list of German expletives, but this tended to get no more acknowledgment from staff than when he swore in English.

Across the room I simultaneously berated him and apologised for him. It was pointless, for I would never change his manner, and the staff knew us well enough to expect nothing different. They all hated Henry but didn't hold it against me in any way. They considered me somewhat saintly for the patience I had, putting up with him for all these years.

'Shut up Henry. *Tut mir leid, Agnes, am Freitag benimmt er sich immer wie ein Arschloch*' I said to the staff member on the receiving end of his current tirade.

'*Ich dachte, es wäre alltäglich,*' Agnes replied suggesting that Henry was just as difficult as this whenever she had to deal with him.

Henry and I had been residents of the *Senioren Fachpflegezentrum* in Berlin for nearly two years. The adaption to this life was something that I transitioned to very easily, but my husband had never coped with. Our health had deteriorated progressively for many years, but it had eventually reached a point where living in our own home had become impossible. When the time came, Henry had been hospitalised, and I was left to make the choice of where we went. This home had been the only one with an available double-room we could share. After fifty-three years of marriage, there was no way I was willing to live in a different room from him. I had lived enough of my life with a wall separating me from who and what mattered most. Through all the good and bad, we were determined to stay by each other's side.

All the staff knew what they'd get from us. Pleasant conversation, cooperation and understanding from me, and the complete opposite from my husband. Many people would wonder what brought two such different individuals together, but in this profession, most people had seen the same thing often enough. They regularly dealt with people who had become shadows of who they had been throughout their lives. They understood that as sure as the ravages of time had softened me, they had hardened Henry just as significantly. Deep down we couldn't be more similar, but it didn't tend to show on the surface.

While the staff here dodge Henry as much as they can, they are fascinated by his life story. They prefer hearing about it from me, without his interference. When he is in the bathroom, they'll often look through my scrapbooks and listen intently to my stories. Why wouldn't they? Henry performed for millions of people across his career. What started as a booking for a few months in Europe turned into a career that had traversed the world for nearly twenty years. He was the best at what he did. Few people in life can ever reach the point of being the number one in the world at their specialty. I'd been a national champion figure skater, and a professional for another decade, but I was never close to the best in the world. Henry had that title.

The youngest of two children to Max and Rose Victor, Henry was originally from Australia. He'd left his homeland as a teenager when he and his partner Des had an opportunity to turn their part-time work into a professional career in Europe. They had anticipated it would be a short-term move, but they couldn't foresee the success they would have. Not only did their routines bring them success on the stage, but in the ensuing decade they each met the women they'd choose to spend the rest of their lives with. For Henry, this was me. Not only did he fall in love with me, but my city as well. Sixty years after he first visited the city to perform, he is still here.

Henry never sought to assimilate too greatly into Berlin, but it was a city that lent itself to that attitude. The main friendships he forged were with other expats, be they American, British or the few Australians here. He never sought to learn the language. He was the same young Australian that he'd been when he first arrived. It was never an issue until he reached the point where he was no longer in control of his own destiny.

For so long a city of oppression, West Berlin had become the bastion of freedom and inclusivity. Once united, the city took time to fully envelop that thinking, but today Berlin is a global city, home to people of all types, from all lands and with all beliefs. Some say it isn't truly representative of Germany. If that is the case, then I am more Berliner than German. Henry is equally a true Berliner despite being in no way German.

You never felt like an outsider in West Berlin, though as a city we felt like the outsiders together. An enclave surrounded by the Wall and the hostility of the East Germans beyond it, we felt no more a part of West Germany. The West German border was nearly 200 kilometres from West Berlin. Although we were closely aligned, we technically didn't belong to it. It was a progressive, forward-looking city. The individual was celebrated, not taught to conform. It was an attitude that Henry loved, and it is what made the city as much a part of him as it was me.

When we came into the nursing home, it was the first time that being an outsider in Berlin had a real impact. Once you are reliant on people helping you to the toilet, your independence was gone. Without independence, you had to conform. There wasn't a set of rules or demands that were set in place, but depending on others meant having them on your side. The staff were never going to renege on their responsibilities, but they were always going to prioritise the people who showed them appreciation. Henry was always going to stay bottom on this list.

Neither of us had ever been the type to look too far forward. We lived exciting lifestyles in our younger years, focussed always on the present.

'Life isn't about living the most years, it's about living the best years,' Henry said when a doctor told him to consider how he was living many years ago. It was always our attitude. We never envisaged this point of life. I guess many people don't, but it becomes a natural transition as the years pass. As much as I don't like it, I feel that this home is the natural transition for me. For Henry, it is now that he wishes he had family close by. Nobody enjoys life at this point, but those with loved ones making regular appearances have a lot more to get them through.

We had hung on as long as we could in our own home before reality could be avoided no longer. *Senioren Fachpflegezentrum* was far from ideal to Henry, but he would have been more miserable anywhere else that was available. I was no happier, but at least more accepting. If for nothing else, it felt like a homecoming. After fifty-five years I was finally back to where it all began. Just a block from Karl Marx Allee, I was again home in East Berlin.

For me, a new stage of life had begun. For Henry, life as he was willing to interpret it, was over.

4

13 March 2020

AMBER

I don't know which layer to strip back first, but with guidebook in hand and little more than a quick read last night, I set off towards the heart of the city.

Berlin is famous for being the 'least German city' in Germany. What defines a city as German comes down to perspective, but it highlights that Berlin is in many ways the odd one out. As someone who has felt that way for my whole life, it may prove to be the perfect fit for me.

Like any great city, Berlin has its share of attractions, but compared with the likes of London, Paris or Rome, there is less here to put on a short itinerary that would stand out to everyone. The city has one of the most unique histories in the world, particularly in modern times, and most of the standout sights such as the Berlin Wall, Checkpoint Charlie and the Topography of Terror, all take you back to that history. Berliners don't hide from their past. They don't celebrate it, but they acknowledge it and use the lessons from it to build a better future.

'You can understand most cities without going there because they're defined by particular sites,' my brother Craig said when he returned from Europe a few years back. 'Not Berlin though. It is a feeling. A place with all the reminders of the horrors that life can bring, and then uses these to build a society more progressive than anywhere I've seen. By understanding the dark side of life, it is now so embracing of the light.

It is a city of celebration, of diversity and of freedom for individuality. You can't understand Berlin without going there and embracing it.'

The Berliner Fernsehturm, or TV tower, stands out head and shoulders above the city and is my guiding point as I walk into town. I don't know where I'll end up and I don't really care. Feeling the city, as I've been told to do, is not about ticking off items from a list. That said, there is no way I'm not going to see all the most recommended points of the city, but they aren't luring me the way that they do in most cities. I am here for long enough that I don't need to see anything other than by the natural flow. Where I end up today doesn't matter. Time is on my side.

My route into town is along Karl-Marx-Allee and as the name suggests, this section of East Berlin highlights the socialist style of architecture at its finest. An incredibly wide boulevard that would have been used to showcase the might of the East German state in its heyday, it is lined with eight-story apartment buildings that would have housed workers in relative uniformity. Of course, most of the real uniformity for the working classes would be far from such a scenic spot as this, but like any system of government, the socialists wanted to have a snapshot they could show the world which highlighted the strengths of their way of life.

I reached Alexanderplatz and decided that such proximity to the city's ultimate viewing point was a message worth heeding. I've never been completely comfortable with heights, but the whole point to being in Europe was to step away from what is comfortable and choosing what I knew to be right for me. With very limited knowledge of the layout of the city, there was no better time to see it from above and gain my bearings from there.

The last time I had faced my fears on an observation deck so high above the ground, was in New York City. Up there it was a case of identifying as many as possible of the hundreds of famous sites that were spread across the city. Berlin may have less obvious points of reference to focus on, but I felt that would make the experience more valuable.

Without having a pre-conceived notion of what to be looking for, it was far easier to take in the overview of the city and allowed for a greater appreciation of the beauty beneath.

The magnitude of the city is the first thing that stands out. Berlin is three times bigger than Munich and eight times bigger than Paris. Appreciating the size can only really be done when you can see it all at once. It also seemed to be covered by many natural wonders, from lakes and rivers to parks and forests. I'd read that Berlin was a very green city, but I was yet to get a great appreciation of this until seeing the city from up here.

As I looked to the west, I immediately recognised the Reichstag and its dome. Apparently, the glass dome was a feature added to symbolise the transparency that a government needs to show, a reference to the infamy of history. Just by the Reichstag I can see the Brandenburg Gate, the symbol of freedom that the world came to know at the fall of the Wall. From that point on there was little I recognised, but one of the standout features was a stunning cathedral right in the foreground. I'd made the decision already that I would head that way when I got back to the ground.

I spent nearly an hour surveying the city. The discord in architecture between East and West was stark, so even after thirty years, the divide in the city is still evident. I'm sure that the aim of the city's planners is for people to only see one Berlin. Perhaps the city's desire to ensure the past is seen as an example for the future is what leaves this legacy.

Back on the safety of solid ground, I took off towards the Cathedral. I have no religious beliefs or affiliations, but I tend to love places of worship. When they were built, they were generally designed as a sign of the people's devotion to their higher power, so they are usually the most elaborate structures within cities. It is less the case back home, but through Europe, Asia and the Middle East, the grandest structures are most commonly places of worship. I was fascinated by the Frauenkirche in Munich and the Dresden Cathedral, now the Berlin Cathedral had me spellbound, particularly set against the River Spree running alongside.

The cathedral sits on what is known as Museum Island. Across from the cathedral sits the Altes Museum, then the Neues Museum, the Pergamomuseum, the Alte Nationalgalerie and the Bode Museum. In the other direction is a whole other set of museums. A small island in the Spree, it is a place that could take several days to discover in depth, but for now I am content appreciating the buildings from the outside.

Maybe my love of old buildings connects with how I got into aged care. Old is fascinating, whether it is buildings, people or anything else. Age brings character and I suppose it is that belief that makes me feel so attracted to Europe. When I chose to take off from home, I had people suggest heading to Australia, but it was always Europe that held greater appeal to me. To be honest, the prospect of travel anywhere excited me, but the history and culture of Europe made it my ideal destination.

Back at the cathedrals front, I can walk along the Unter den Linden to get to the Brandenburg Gate, but the afternoon is getting late. I want to go out and experience a small tase of Berlin by night, so decide to have a break and rest up for a while first. Tomorrow is day one at work and I need to be at my best. There is little point to overdoing the first day on a stay as extended as this.

Downtown Berlin would normally be much busier than it is today, but the impact of this new virus is keeping a lot more people inside. There are no restrictions in place, but there is enough being said to have people nervous and that is changing behaviours. The trains are nearly empty, and quite a few people, me included, are wearing face masks for extra protection. It seems crazy in a way, for the mask would be relevant on a crowded train, but there's enough space that any point to the mask is lost.

Back in my room on my own at the hostel, I enjoy the feeling of being alone. I'm relieved that the city is quieter at this point. It may seem a contradiction to bound from one large bustling city to the next when you yearn for quiet, but life is rarely black and white. I love the atmosphere, but there is only so much of it I can handle before I love escaping it even more.

I thoroughly enjoy spending time on my own, but I hate being lonely. It may sound counter intuitive, but I only ever feel lonely around other people. As a rule, the bigger the crowd, the lonelier the feeling. You feel anonymous and irrelevant to the scene around you, and the gaze of others straight through you. That is where genuine loneliness stems from.

I want to overcome that. I want to be able blend in. Crowds may never be comfortable, so I might be in Berlin at the exact time to get what I need. Small steps towards being seen and being me.

It's all part of my journey.

5

13 March 2020

MARTA

'We never should have been in this shithole of a place.'

'We didn't have a choice,' I said. I knew Henry wasn't talking so much about the home we were in, but the choice of being in Berlin. We had nobody here, and at this stage of life the importance of family was far more relevant than when we'd decided to settle here. Henry's family lived half a world away and we only saw them every couple of years. Whereas most residents in the home had weekly visits from loved ones, visitors to us were few and far between.

Henry made the decision, as much as he would say it was my choice. Berlin had been my home growing up, but it had also been the place I fled as a young woman seeking a life that wasn't available under the East German regime. I was equally nervous and excited about coming back here. Enough time had passed that my escape from the East was very unlikely to threaten the way we lived in West Berlin. It was a vibrant, progressive city in the 1970s which was perfect for us at that time. When you make plans in your late thirties, it's hard to envisage what your needs will be in your late seventies.

Henry first arrived in Berlin in 1954. Little did he know that a few kilometres away, in the Soviet controlled part of the city, a young girl was dominating the youth ranks of Berlin figure skating. At age thirteen, I was in the audience when Henry returned to Berlin at the end of the year, in The Victors first ice-skating show. I paid little attention to the acrobats who were little more than a distraction amongst the wonderful skating that came before and after their cameo. A little over a decade later, I was not only working in the same production as The Victors, but I was also Henry's wife.

***

'I've got no other options,' Max Victor explained to his wife Rose. 'Contracts are in place. I need to send The Victors to Europe and Henry is the only person I've got who can step into Allan's role.'

Allan Raymond and Des Stipe had been performing as The Victors for three years. They worked at numerous venues around the city of Adelaide through that time, but the opportunities were too few to sustain a long-term career. Comedy-acrobatics was a specialist field, and the real opportunities were all in Europe and the United States. As much as this had been their ambition, when the opportunity arrived, it was too much for Allan who quit.

'Henry is better than Allan ever was anyway,' Max insisted.

'But he's seventeen. He can't be trusted at home on his own for an hour, let alone having him travel to Europe. It is a recipe for disaster.' Young Henry had given his mother thousands of examples of why he couldn't be trusted, but she was never going to win the argument. No parent can stand in the way of their child's career dreams, even if the timing is not what they would have chosen. Rose had even less chance of winning the argument, as Henry was not only following his dream, but Max's dream as well.

The deal was in place for The Victors to work as a guest act in a cabaret show for three months at a range of cities through Europe. Max's plans were much greater than that.

'You've got a decent run earning good money, but it's only going to get you so far. If you really want to make the big time, you need to be able to perform on ice.'

'I can't even stand up on ice skates and I doubt your son is any better,' Des said. 'I'm not risking my life doing these routines with him shaking beneath me.'

'You've got three months before you leave. Henry's ready for the stage, and if you both use the time wisely, you'll be just as adept on ice by the time you leave. It's then going to be the following season before you need to be performing on ice. Trust me, you push yourselves and I'll get you long term work over there for money that'll blow your minds.'

Des was several years older than Henry, and many would argue infinitely wiser. Whether it was his general character or the exuberance of youth, Henry felt certain that he was up to the challenge. There was little in their routines that would need Des to have anything more than competence on the ice. If Henry could do his bit, Des's skills shouldn't have been a problem.

Several years earlier, Max had a gymnasium built in their backyard. He conducted his teaching in there after previously having the family's living room almost destroyed by overly exuberant young acrobats. For this period, he was willing to sacrifice the gymnasium's primary purpose by installing all the necessary infrastructure for a small ice rink. Des and Henry did most of their training outdoors and the older partner quickly built sufficient confidence in Henry.

'You know, this might all just work,' he said.

It did. By the time they left Australia they were both more than competent on the ice. Although not ready for performing on it, they continued to work on this throughout their season with The World's Greatest Vaudeville Show. The tour saw The Victors play sixty shows in fifteen different cities, starting in London and finishing in Berlin. It was after the second show there, that they had a visitor at stage door who was going to shape their direction going forward.

'Can you do the same routine on skates?' Marcel Beauchamp was the European director of World on Ice. They'd always had an acrobatics act in their show, but their previous act had taken an offer in America at the end of last season and wouldn't be returning. He'd seen enough from The Victors show to decide they were ideal, with the ability to work on ice the only obstacle.

'Sure,' Henry said.

'Maybe,' Des added. 'We can skate, but we've never worked on ice.'

'We've trained enough though,' Henry said, determined not to let the opportunity slip before they'd given it a chance. Henry and Des had the most perfect connection when they performed, yet there were great differences to their characters. Henry felt he could take on the world, and nothing could ever stop him. Des never lacked confidence, but always sought to avoid reaching beyond his grasp. They'd been thrown together through circumstance, but these differences were the key to their success. Without Henry, Des would never have pushed enough to achieve his potential. Without Des, Henry would have taken risks that couldn't come off, leading to inevitable failure.

'Our base is in Bremen,' Marcel continued. 'We start rehearsals in November. We'll fly you across and you can spend a week with us and see how it goes. If you are capable of what I've seen here in the different setting, then we'll talk contracts.'

They kept the night quiet, despite the excitement of the offer. After the following nights show finished the season, Des was a little more willing to indulge his partners desire to hit the town and celebrate. Henry had only just turned eighteen. At that age, no young man half a world away from his home and celebrating a career achievement like this was going to be interested in a quiet night out. Most of the company they'd been touring with were equally keen to let their hair down, so a big night was guaranteed.

Des had already shown an interest in a British girl named Barbara that was part of a dancing troupe within the show. She had seemed similarly interested in Des, but nothing had happened between them. After noticing them chatting at the bar early in the evening, Henry couldn't see either of them soon after, and assumed that was a good sign.

Henry had similar intentions. There was a French magician in the show, and his assistant Jene-Marie, had captivated Henry. Armed with an overwhelming confidence from his success on stage as well as a half-dozen brandies, he was ready to step in front of the many other suitors seeking to woo the French glamour. When she invited him back to her room, he was more than ready to have her perform a little magic on him.

They had a few days remaining in Berlin before World on Ice were flying them to Bremen. Although their time in Bremen was designed to work on their act, they wanted to be as prepared as possible in advance, wanting to create the best first impression on arrival.

'Whatever they call it, this is more of an audition than a rehearsal. They can put any act in our place if they're not convinced we're up to the job, so we need to arrive there ready,' Des said.

As tempting as it was for Henry to be enjoying some time out in Berlin, they used most of their time on various rinks in the city. The role of the bottom guy in a balancing act is partly about strength, but principally about balance. While they weren't doing full routines on public rinks, he was doing the various lifts with all the security and stability that he'd have shown on stage. He knew he was ready, and once Des agreed, there was no question that they were going to make it.

Barbara had stayed in Berlin with Des, and while Jene-Marie was gone, Barbara's colleague Michelle had taken her place at Henry's side. There were to be many more Michelle's in the next few years. While Des was falling in love with Barbara, Henry was far more intent on experiencing everything he could without the restrains of a permanent relationship. In many ways, he was a standard young Australian tourist in Europe, and he wasn't going to miss out on anything that was on offer. It never came at the expense of his professionalism, but when it was time to party, he never held back.

They found enough time to enjoy some of the restaurants and bars of Berlin each evening. Michelle wasn't completely winning him over, but the city was.

'I'd be happy to stay here forever,' he told Des. 'I don't intend sacrificing what we've got now, but if we don't end up making it in any of the touring shows, there's plenty of work here and a hell of a lifestyle.'

Henry knew that if they landed the job with World of Ice he'd be back for a week over Christmas.

Barbara was hoping to land a role in the chorus of the show, being an adept skater. Michelle had no such desire and was heading back to London, which suited Henry. There would be plenty of options to take her place.

It only took a day in Bremen before they had proven their capabilities. They were signed for the 1954/55 European season. 78 dates, 30 cities, 14 countries starting in their new favourite city of Berlin. As Max had suggested before they left Australia, the money was massive, and provided they entertained the crowds, there was no reason to see it stopping there.

The Victors were a featured act, separate from the main show. Their routine was to provide a break of a little over five minutes for the main company to make the elaborate costume changes prior to their return to the ice. There were four of these featured acts throughout the show. As the newcomers, they were the first to appear, but last on the billing, promoted as Australian Acrobatic Sensations: The Victors.

In 1954, Berlin was divided, yet movement between the East and West was allowed. While the shows were at a stadium in the West of the city, a significant proportion of the audiences were crossing from the East, despite the ticket prices being beyond the means of most East Germans. My father was a politically engaged East German who hated the prospect of his daughter being exposed to such a Western experience, but my mother was determined to ensure I got to see a show she knew I'd cherish. In the ongoing fights between them, my father usually got his way. On this occasion my mother refused to yield.

That night the seeds were sown in my mind. I didn't want to become another East German athlete, forced into a program that would be built around bringing glory to her homeland. I'd seen the career I wanted on the ice that night. I would continue to work as hard as I could, and progress along the current trajectory. I hoped that by the time I grew up, we would have one Berlin, and one Germany.

6

13 March 2020

AMBER

Amongst Berlin's greatest claims to fame was its prolific nightlife. While the clubbing scene had never been my thing, I enjoyed the buzz of cities at night. The lights of the city from a high vantage point, the adrenaline of the youth in the streets out for a good time, and the ability to sit somewhere quiet and stylish when you need an escape from the noise. That was an ideal night for me. Ahead of my first day in the job, I wasn't going to be out for long, but when your first night in a city is a Friday, how can you not take a glimpse of the city at night.

'Where are you headed?' asked Erik, who was working at the reception desk at the hostel. He always seemed happy to defer all other tasks in preference to chatting with anyone who passed through. He'd checked me in, and I guess, checked me out when I arrived last night. What had only needed to be a couple of minutes had taken closer to half an hour by the time he gave me his life story and got a few key elements of mine.

'Into the city. I start working tomorrow so don't want to do much. Just want to get a feel of the city at night,' I said.

'There is more exciting nightlife out this way than you'll find in the city. Downtown is driven by the tourist market. You want a genuine taste of Berlin you'll get more of the flavours nearby here than downtown.'

'I'll bare that in mind for when my tastebuds are ready for more.'

'If you are going by train, you will see what I mean. Some of the biggest and best clubs in Berlin are right by it. Matrix Club, Suicide Circus. It's a great area. Nothing open for a few hours yet but look when you're coming back.'

I smiled and got moving before he had time to extend his advice too far. I accepted his point, but with a month in the city, the standard tourist fare seemed like the place to start before getting into the real city. The TV tower wasn't the domain of the locals, but it had been the right choice for me this afternoon. I would take the same approach this evening. Tomorrow, when I begin work, I begin to live like a local. It makes sense that I shall then start navigating the city like one. Even then, I'm not sure if the biggest clubs in a famed nightlife city would quite be my ideal spot.

It was only a five-minute walk to the station, and I was back where I'd alighted just a few hours earlier. Once again, the reminder of the impact of current news was evident when the train arrived, with the sparseness of passengers in the carriages. A few more people got on at subsequent stops before I got off at Friedrichstraße, the stop between Alexanderplatz and the Hauptbahnhof. Without knowing much of the city's layout this seemed the most central stop.

My rumbling stomach meant that before I did anything else, I had to find dinner. I've always hated eating alone, for the feeling of standing out in a restaurant setting. Good food is associated with a social occasion. Part of what makes a great meal and justifies the time and expense of a good restaurant is the interaction with people whose company we enjoy. Without that companionship, why would someone choose a meal that is closer to an event? It is far more common in those situations to choose speed, simplicity and economy. Walk past a fast-food restaurant and someone eating alone doesn't stand out. I end up choosing these uninteresting options more often than I'd like. I wanted to be breaking that habit, but like everything I sought to do differently, it was always a case of one step at a time for me.

Walking down the street, I immediately had the city's diversity reinforced. Mexican, Italian, Japanese restaurants were all in the first block, but all of them looked busier than I wanted. After the quietness on the train and in the station, I hadn't expected anywhere to be so busy. Perhaps people were looking at the risk and reward of different situations. Public transport was always a place to fear for the spreading of germs. People were starting to seek alternatives. They obviously enjoyed their restaurant dinners too much to give these up for an inferior alternative.

A takeaway kebab shop looked like the ideal easy option. For once, I walked past the easy option, determined not to revert to my standard approach to change, which was always built around saying that I'd start tomorrow.

Seeing a little cocktail bar further up the street, I steel myself to go inside. It's way too early for a place like this to be busy. The place was less than half full, a combination of couples and a few larger tables. There was a cosy spot in a corner not too far from the bar, so I took a seat and prowled the menu, ordering a cocktail and a pasta dish. Before the meal came, I watched a band setting up, the entertainment for when crowds started pouring in, by which time I would be long gone.

I may have stood out sitting on my own, but it seemed like everyone else was too interested in their own night to be worried about me. One of the guys in the band came over and chatted, but as I was still savouring my spaghetti, he gave up on his chat-up routine quickly.

The moment my plate was cleared, another guy from the band took a seat and asked if I wanted a drink.

'I get free drinks, may as well make it worthwhile,' he said. He introduced himself as Otto, the quality of his English immediately evident despite insisting he was a local, born and bred. He was the bassist in the band, and after accepting his offer, I enjoyed chatting with him. Not that there was anything particularly interesting to him, but spending so much time alone led to an extra appreciation of any interaction with others.

Otto probably had hopes far beyond what he was going to get. He had to leave me to tune-up before their set, ready to play for me as much as the audience. By the time they started their first song, I was out the door. I may have been keen to try new things and find myself, but that didn't mean finding a bassist with no intentions beyond the night. Maybe at another time I may have let things play out differently, but with the first day at work tomorrow, my evening was going to stay true to a simple path.

Further down the street I passed another couple of bars that were far busier, but I wasn't ready to stop. If I planned to keep the night short and still see a decent cross section of the city, I needed to keep moving.

At the end of the street, I saw an impressive old building. After a while I found that it was the Pergamonmuseum which I'd seen only from the other side. I was back at the edge of Museum Island despite thinking I was walking in the other direction. I was undoubtedly a long way from knowing my way around as yet. The obvious option of taking out my phone and using the map didn't appeal to me. It was just part of my stubbornness, but I always preferred working my way through these challenges.

It was almost by accident that I stumbled across the Unter den Linden, the main street of the city. Finally, the Fernsehturm was no longer blocked by other buildings, so I had my bearings back and headed away from the tower. A wide boulevard, the street started with majestic structures including the Berlin Opera House and the Humboldt University. As I progressed, the street turned more into tourist central, souvenir shops dominating the scene, interspersed by restaurants all geared for overseas visitors. That street changes again a block from the end, where the street is open only to pedestrian traffic at the approach to the Brandenburg Gate.

You can't come to a spot like this and not take a leaf from the stereotypical tourist. Selfies to send home to friends showing me at such a historic place was essential. I didn't normally like to look like a tourist, but most of the people around me were just that. Naturally anywhere that enough tourists are congregating, people looking to profit from them will follow, yet this didn't seem anywhere near as evident as I've found in other places. I was free to bask in the magnificence of the structure, contemplate the history it has seen, then move on.

I was torn between stopping for another drink and heading home, and it was only the appearance of a cool looking bar just around the corner of Friedrichstraße that made my mind up for me. Cool for me may not be what most people my age would choose. This place wasn't overly crowded, but had enough people there that I could blend in. There was a jazz band on that caught my ear from a few doors down, and though it was getting later than I'd planned, one drink wouldn't hurt.

'Are you Canadian?' a voice asked in a familiar accent as I ordered my drink.

'Yes. Where are you from?'

'Montreal,' the woman said. 'You?'

'Toronto.'

We talked for a few minutes, but I didn't escape Canada to meet Canadians. There was little else that would connect me to this woman as we had quickly discovered, so I was happy not to join her when she returned to her group. I settled into my standard spot in a darkish corner. I loved the music, so I didn't need any other interaction. Most of the people there considered the band as background music, but I could see they appreciated someone who was genuinely intent on listening to them. The singer was great, whatever it may be that she was singing. The German lyrics meant nothing to me but proved that good music transcends language. Unfortunately, they finished their set long before I'd finished my drink, but a couple of them came over to my table on their break.

'*Sprechen Sie Deutsch?*' the drummer asked.

'*Nein,*' I replied in the most extensive level of German I had.

'English?' the singer, who appeared to be his girlfriend, then asked.

'Yes. I loved your set.'

'*Danke*. How long you in Berlin?

'A month.'

'Maybe. Maybe you won't get out.'

The threat of the virus was dominating the media, so it was something I'd already considered possible. I wanted to feel at home enough here that if anything was to happen that forced my stay to extend, I could do so happily. Random conversations with musicians in jazz bars wasn't likely to do this, but the more people you interact with, the more chance of finding people who you genuinely can feel comfortable around.

'I'm sure there are worse places in the world to be stuck in,' I said.

'They didn't say that a generation ago,' the drummer added, now showing that his English was more fluent than his girlfriend's.

'When you can leave any time, nobody wants to. When you're stuck somewhere, everybody wants to get out,' I said.

Of course, if the virus locked down Berlin, it would be the same anywhere else. I wasn't going home whatever happened to borders. I hadn't ever set a time limit on my stay in Europe, but if the work continues to be available and the borders do close, I don't care if it's a year or two, I'll gladly see it through. Of course, I do want to see more of the continent, but I already feel that Berlin is offering me most of what I hoped to find.

The couple, returned to the stage and re-joined their bandmates for the next set. They had told me where the group, Das Unity Quintett, play every Wednesday night, as well as their other gigs over the next week. It is good to know that if I've got nothing and nobody else, there's somewhere I can go and see familiar faces, as well as listen to some great music.

Tomorrow a new work assignment begins. The work may be the same as what I did back home, but when you're the new kid on the block and the one who doesn't speak the language, you cop the shittiest parts of it. The residents are the same everywhere. Some are pains in the arse. Some are wonderful. Here, most of them can't understand me and I can't understand most of them. For the difficult ones, they remain equally as difficult, but it means I never get the best of the good people. Who knows? Maybe there'll be someone who makes the job a little more rewarding.

Knowing my luck, I'll probably get lumped with the most difficult person in the place.

7

14 March 2020

MARTA

'These arseholes are going to kill me.'

I heard this sort of thing from Henry often enough that I didn't give such rants a second thought. He had deteriorated so much in the past couple of years, and it seemed as though his coping mechanism was to blame everyone and everything.

'What do you want Henry? What in the world can I, or anyone do to make things better in any way?'

'I don't want anything. I just want them to leave me alone. All of them.'

'They only come in when you ring the bell,' I said, defending the staff who did just as much for him as they did for me, despite the very different feelings they had towards each of us.

Henry groaned, unable to further his largely incoherent argument. He knew that there were no words of explaining what he meant. He knew he needed care and attention, but he found it degrading. He was a man who'd had it all. He had experienced life at its absolute optimum and now he was permanently confined to a bed. He never believed he'd survive to this point of life, and as much as he fought to do so, he now felt more regret for achieving this. He knew what life was meant to be, and this could not be further from it.

I had been similarly as strong and successful. The parallels in our lives were many, both in our prime and now. Both of us had reached a point where our bodies were no longer capable of functioning in ways where we could live on our own. For a couple of years before we came to the home, I was already largely incapacitated. Henry, already weakened and struggling, did everything for me. For all that the staff here may see of him, he was constantly compassionate and selfless, doing everything at home to ensure our independence for as long as possible. Perhaps without the anchor that I was, he would have been able to avoid this fate for a couple more years. Would it really matter though? Fate catches up with us all, eventually. Neither of us ever believed in living as long as possible but living as much as we could. We'd stayed true to this throughout our lives.

When we came into the home, I understood what it was like to be completely dependent on others. While Henry had been exposed to it enough caring for me, he wasn't prepared for being on the other end of things. Initially he was still able to do more for himself than I could, but that was followed by the inevitable decline. The more his dependence increased, the more depressed he became. He hated the lack of dignity he felt. I, however understood the natural flow of life. I knew that the body deteriorated with time, and this was life in the only way it could now be. It offered none of the pleasures and the wonders we'd known, but it was part of aging.

'I never thought I'd get old,' he said. 'I wish I never had. There's nothing worse.'

'There's only one way of avoiding it, and that isn't better,' I said.

'Isn't it?'

I didn't have to worry about his intentions. He may have hated this existence, but he would fight for life just to spite the world he complained about. Continuing for my benefit was a big part of it. We've both always preferred the thought of dying before the other. I couldn't face life without him, and I know he couldn't without me. Because of that love, we'd each do anything to survive for the other one.

Memories were the only great pleasure at this point of life. I reflected every day on the various great moments I'd experienced and the fullness of the life I had led. I didn't need to live great new moments when I could relive great old moments. It didn't compare, but it was the only option of retaining sanity now.

I was born in the town of Thorn in September 1942. Now known as Torun, the city was returned to Poland at the end of World War II. Like most Germans, we were forced out of the city and back across the western border. We moved into government owned housing in the east of Berlin, and being so young at the time, this is where all my earliest memories stem from.

Home life wasn't happy. Mum and Dad had very different views. In those days, that meant Dad had his way and Mum was left unhappy. After the war, Berlin was under the control of four different countries. The East was controlled by the Soviet forces, while the West was split between an American, a British and a French quarter. On arrival, few people were looking to leave, but with time that changed significantly. West Berlin was a growing, prosperous city. While the Soviets were ensuring the rebuild of East Berlin was progressing quickly, they were also ensuring that the fruits of this were headed back to reparations for the war. Dad was adamant that this was right, and in the long term that would prove the strength of the East, and it would see all of Berlin united under it. Mum was more focussed on the current time and our family. She'd have taken us to the West in a heartbeat given the chance.

My brother Lars had discussed leaving Germany for as long as I can remember. America, Australia, Canada and South Africa were all mentioned as possible destinations. While his choice alternated regularly, the desire for a new beginning never left him.

Blonde hair and blue eyes. he couldn't look more like Hitler's poster child. That may have been an asset if he'd been born a decade earlier, but in the 1950's it was a liability. He was a symbol of all the past. Of loss. For every bit of pride our father had in Germany, Lars felt shame.

'You are so naive,' Dad said to him. 'Believing you can leave here for some utopia in the West. You think being a German amongst our enemies will be better than at home?'

'I will always be defined by who I am, not where I am from,' Lars replied. 'Most of the world don't mark enemies based on birth certificates, but on attitudes, and they won't find an enemy from mine. You just take whatever the government inflicts on you without ever stopping to think about what is right. And to think *you* call *me* naïve.'

The growing conflict between Lars and my father accelerated his desire to leave, with South Africa eventually being settled on as his choice to move to. He told me to start thinking about where I'd go when the time was right.

'Whatever he tries to tell you, there will never be a future here. All this principle of the wealth being shared. There is no wealth. The war reparations we owe the Soviets means there never will be. All we will share in East Germany is our poverty. You want a life, you too will need to leave.'

Skating had become my escape in my childhood. By 1953 I had been skating with the Dynamo Berlin club and was amongst the top skaters in East Germany for my age. By fifteen, I had left school, committing to full time figure skating in the clubs' elite program. I was already determined to move to the West and turn professional once I reached eighteen. To me, skating was performance rather than competition. When you compete as a skater, however good you perform, your results are dependent on the performance of your rivals. You profit from the failures of others.

'You will not be turning professional,' Dad insisted. 'Your talent needs to achieve something, not just to have people clapping then forgetting you. This country hasn't had it easy, but it funds you and it trains you so that you can bring glory to it. You should be aiming for the Olympics. Not just to make it there, but to win gold for Germany.'

It was hard to believe, but while Germany was divided in so many ways, we were to compete in the 1960 Olympics at Squaw Valley in the United States under the name of the United Team of Germany. A compromise anthem was used, a compromise flag flown, and compromise selection policies were used across all sports. I had finished second in the national championships in 1960, which in theory should have been enough for me to make the Olympic team. With no systematic reason behind it, the decision was made to send three women figure skaters all from West Germany to the Olympics, a compromise that gave the East more spots elsewhere in the Olympic team. This was little consolation for me, or Nikki Schneider, the woman who beat me for the national title.

My father remained insistent that I continue on that path. At European and World Championship level we competed under the East German flag. I had qualified for the 1961 World Championships in Prague, but again fate intervened. The Sabena Flight 548 crash saw the entire United States figure skating team killed a week before the championships. The event was rightfully cancelled. By 1962, my position on the East German team had been taken by the young superstar Gabrielle Seyfert. Whatever talent I had, this younger skater was a level beyond. I knew by this time that reaching the top of the amateur ranks was an unattainable dream. When he saw what happened at the East German National Championships that year, even my father was ready to accept this, and gave my blessing to turn professional. His one condition was that I stay in East Berlin.

My first job was with the Zentral Zircus before joining the Berolina Eis Revue. Both were small companies, gaining me experience, but unable to take me to the next level. Getting where I aspired to meant leaving East Germany, but that was virtually impossible. The East German government had erected the Berlin Wall the previous year, in response to the number of people leaving the city topping a thousand each day. The state had argued that it was designed to keep the fascists out, but the movement it was stopping had all been the other way. Now, without special government approval, leaving for the West was impossible, and the prospects of me getting such approval were slim.

'You can't stay here Marta,' my mother told me, repeating the advice my brother had given years ago. From a career perspective, she was right. There was no future here, but too much time had passed for such decisions to be in my own hands. Aside from that, I had a loyalty. Not to my homeland, but to my mother.

Out of the blue, I got a contract with Paris Sur Glace. I didn't expect to get the necessary governmental approval, but ironically it was my father who aided me, with his established loyalty to the state allowing a visa to be issued, despite his personal wishes being opposed to the move. The conditions were strict and the demands on the company were strong. Any thoughts I may have had in taking the opportunity to defect would carry significant dangers to my family as well as to myself. I accepted that my time in France would not extend beyond the three months. There was little doubt that when I returned to East Berlin, the experience I had gained would have equipped me to be leading one of the local companies.

My father was resentful of me leaving, and equally angry at my mother for encouraging it.

'There are opportunities here. We have a responsibility to be building East Germany, not to be entertaining fascists,' he said.

'We have a responsibility to help our daughter pursue her dreams,' Mum argued.

'We are part of a society. That comes first.'

Dad didn't speak to me once he knew I was going to Paris. He knew it was short-term, but it was still an act of hostility in his mind. He had become more obsessive with time, and his role as father was one that had become increasingly insignificant to him. He forbade mention of Lars ever since his son had left the country. His relationship with Mum was at breaking point, and I considered it more than possible that by the time I returned, they wouldn't both still be under the same roof.

Paris Sur Glace was an amazing experience. Working with professionals and playing in front of full houses across France was incredible. Playing in a show like this gave me a clearer picture of what was involved in genuine professional shows. We had a cast from many different countries with different languages being spoken. I learnt not just about the profession, but about life. The clearest lesson was just how suppressed we were in East Berlin.

As the season was coming to an end, I reflected on the many people I'd met. Many of these were people with the power to hire and fire, and they were important to have on your side in this business. I'd won over the right people, though it wasn't likely to help me much in the short-term. Stuck in East Berlin once the season was over here, I couldn't know when circumstances may change in my favour.

Shortly before leaving Paris, it was someone from outside of the industry who would prove to be the most significant person I met in my time here. Cedric Lemaire.

8

14 March 2020

AMBER

Frida Schoenberg was hardly the kind, welcoming type that helps ease the nerves one naturally has on the first day in a new workplace. She certainly seemed to fit the stereotype of being efficient and to the point and I guess that was necessary in her middle management role within the aged care facility. Frida reported directly to the General Manager, Hans, but as he didn't speak any English, he transferred the responsibility of performing my induction to her. Her accent was strong, but I had no trouble understanding her.

'*Your language barrier is advantage. You not vaste time with conversations. Just verk.*'

I nodded rather than replying verbally, avoiding making unnecessary conversation with her, given the focus she had just placed on the topic.

'*One resident is Australian. Only speak English. He create problems sometimes and other staff not vont to deal vith him at all. You vill talk vith him.*'

Great. She wants me to talk to someone who will be abusive towards me. She just insists that I avoid talking to anyone who will treat me with respect. I hate the principle behind that, though in practice it is no major concern. I am here to earn a wage that allows me to keep my journey going longer. I'm not here to be enjoying myself but to do whatever they need from me. Other than income, the only thing I really seek to gain here is additional experience. Maybe the test of dealing with a resident other staff struggle with will enhance my reputation and assist me going forwards.

Having spent the first hour and a half going through my induction with Frida, I had missed the initial contact with each of the residents in the area I was responsible for. I was introduced to my partner, Klara, who seemed a similar though slightly younger version of her boss. She also spoke no English at all, so after listening to a conversation between her and Frida that was quite obviously about me, I got a sharp '*Guten Tag*' and little more.

As we began to attend to the first calls from residents, I saw how the dynamic would work. We walk into the room, I get introduced in German and struggle to understand what is said about me and then we deal with whatever issue has arisen, generally with me doing the major grunt work. So be it, that was what I'd become used to.

The third room we entered was the one I had been spoken to about. Henry and Marta Victor, the former acrobat from Australia and his wife, a former professional figure skater.

'Hello, I am Amber,' I said to Henry.

'I don't expect to hear that around here,' he said, referring to my accent. 'Canadian, right? Whereabouts are you from.'

'Toronto.'

'You're a long way from home,' he said.

'So are you.'

'Nah. I've lived in Berlin long enough that I am a local. Australia may be my origin, but it hasn't been my home for sixty years.'

'They say home is where the heart is.'

'Well, I guess home is in the bed next to me then.' For everything I'd been told, it seemed like he was an old romantic. It was hard to reconcile what I was seeing with what I had heard, though I sensed it mightn't take long before the illusion was shattered.

'Home is wherever you want it to be,' he continued. 'At this point I couldn't give a shit. Stuck in a facility like this until I die, it wouldn't matter what city I was in. At your age it's the opposite, you could be in any city in the world, and you can enjoy life. Why Berlin?'

'I'm travelling across Europe. Been pretty much all over Germany. Hamburg's next before I head west to the Netherlands. I work in places like this to earn enough money to keep the trip going.'

'Well, that is a hard-earned trip then.'

Klara called me across to Marta who needed the help of us both to get to the toilet.

'Hello Marta, I'm Amber.'

'You just had the longest conversation Henry has had with anyone other than me in a long time,' she said to me.

'The language barrier makes it hard sometimes,' I said.

'Henry's attitude makes it hard sometimes too. Language is just an excuse, particularly for you English speakers. The rest of us learn to deal with language issues earlier and more often.'

Once we'd got her into the bathroom, Klara shooed me back to Henry. Clearly the positivity he showed from the moment he heard a native English speaker was something they wanted to foster while they could.

'How long are you here?' he asked.

'I have a four-week contract working here. I'll probably stay a few days beyond that. I've already been in Germany for nearly four months which is far longer than I'd intended. More work has come up than I expected, and I didn't want to turn it down.'

'*Sprechen sie Deutsch*?' he asked.

'*Nicht sehr gut*' I answered, explaining that I had only the most very basic German. 'I get by in this work without speaking German because we work in pairs. All of the contact that the residents have is with my partner, and I just need the most basic understanding of my partner to do what is required. It isn't ideal, but I'm good enough at the job to compensate for the understanding.'

'It's good to hear language I can understand. I played Toronto several times. All long before you were born.'

'So, you really did travel the world. I envy that.'

'It's a big world. We didn't see all of it, but most places that you'd want to see, we saw. We usually had a long enough run in cities that we had a chance to experience what the tourists did, but also to experience a whole lot that they never would,' he said.

'I hope you'll share some of that while I'm here.'

'You never know,' he said somewhat dismissively. He seemed to be enjoying the conversation, yet almost with a sense of bravado he didn't want me to know it. He'd become so accustomed to the role of grumpy old man, that stepping away from it left him like a child giving up his security blanket.

'True,' I nodded, removing the requirement for him to extend the conversation any further. Klara needed my assistance with Marta and that had to be my primary focus.

'What is your name,' I heard him yell from behind the door as we assisted Marta from the bathroom. I knew I'd introduced myself the moment I walked in as a discreet way of highlighting my language and accent to him. I guess he's not used to paying attention too often.

As we returned to the room, I reintroduced myself and told him I'd be back later, but Klara and I were on our way to assist another resident who needed our help.

For all I'd heard, I didn't think Henry was going to be a problem. Far from it. I think he will be the most fascinating resident I've had across any facility I've ever worked in. Both he and Marta seem like they have lived the most incredible lives. They'd seen the world in a much more in-depth way than I could ever hope to, and for someone who is fascinated by what life can be, I wanted to hear as much as possible that would inspire me. I'd be taking every opportunity to return to room 2B11 and get to know more about Henry and Marta.

The shift ended up being far busier than I had anticipated. While being busy makes the time move faster, when you already have plans for your down time, the longer it takes for such a time to arrive, the more frustrating it becomes. I delivered meals to Marta and Henry, and came back to collect them when finished, but they were both hit and run trips as there was so much else required as high priorities.

Handover time was at 10pm and it was closing in on that before I got back to them.

'Hello again Henry.'

'Who are you?' he said. 'Just joking. I haven't lost my mind even if every arsehole in this place seems to think I have. All it takes is for them to provide someone who speaks my language, and you can see I'm alright.'

'Of course.'

'So how did you end up here Amber?'

'Considering how fascinating the life stories of you and Marta are, mine isn't worth talking about,' I said looking for an excuse to avoid discussing my least favourite conversation topic, myself.

'Everyone's got a story. Because we live our own story every day, it doesn't seem so interesting to us,' he said. 'Doesn't matter how or why, you're in your early twenties, Canadian, yet you're working in an old farts home in Germany. There's got to be a story behind that.'

'A story maybe, but it doesn't have to be a good one.'

'Unless you tell it in bloody German, it has to be the best story anyone has told me in a long time.'

I sat beside his bed and told him about the break-up with Andrew, the feelings of uncertainty I had about the next stage of life and that I felt seeing the world was the best way of starting to see where my place within it should be.

'The more you see, the more you realise there is to see,' Henry said.

'Yes, but that's a good thing isn't it. Don't you think the journey is worth taking?'

'Who knows? It isn't where you go as much as who you are with.'

'So does travelling solo defeats the purpose?'

'No. It's the best option really. When people are home, they tend to live with their eyes down. When you travel, everything is new, so your eyes are up. You take everything and everyone in, you discover their stories because you are open to them. The people intertwine with the places. Berlin isn't special for any monument you see, it is special for the people. Berliners are a unique breed, and when you spend time here you learn something new, something different and something special that helps shape you. Stay here long enough and it will lose its lustre. Every place I've ever stayed too long has, but as long as you travel, you always rekindle that feeling in each new destination.'

'I am already getting that, especially thanks to you,' I said.

'Don't be fooled. There is as much to gain from anyone you meet. You may be working here, but you're a traveller. Never miss out on all the benefits that provides. Always keep your eyes and your mind open.'

'So, if places are all about who you meet, I take it your favourite place is where you met Marta, right?'

'Did you and your fella have *your song*? I bet it wasn't the first song you ever heard together. A place, a song or anything else, it isn't what comes first, but what has the most impact. We didn't meet here, but Berlin was special to both of us for different reasons. For me, most of them were positive. For Marta, that wasn't always true.'

'How so?' I asked.

'Well, she met me, right? That wasn't going to happen if she didn't get out of East Berlin, and that meant giving up plenty. And taking an incredible risk.'

9

12 January 1962

MARTA

It was with a feeling of dread that I returned to East Berlin. I hoped it would only be temporary, as the experience of France had exposed me to a snapshot of the life I wanted. I didn't want to wait for little more than politics, but I knew there was no alternative at this point and unhappily boarded the train.

Seeing my mother was the one highlight to my return. I loved her deeply and felt a sense of pity that her life had followed such a course. Growing up during one war, bringing children into the world during the next, the world around her had been unforgiving. She lost one parent in each of these wars, never knowing her father at all. Lars had left for South Africa three years ago, and if I did leave the East permanently, what would she be left with?

'Did Dad not want to come?' I asked her after meeting her at the station.

'Your fathers' movements are no longer my concern,' she said. 'He has left us.'

'Left us?' I didn't know how to interpret her words. Had he left our family? Had he passed away?

'It has been coming for many years. It's what I wanted, but he wouldn't give me the satisfaction of giving me what I want, so I made him think it would destroy me if he left. When he believed that, he did it, his usual spite coming to the fore.' She wasn't trying to poison my view of him, for this was exactly as we had all seen him from the time we were born.

'Not if, when,' she said to me, when I asked her how she would get by if I, too, was to leave. 'When you get out, I will be happy. The day I gave birth to Lars, my life forever onwards was always going to be secondary to the lives of him and then you. My happiness comes from your happiness, my pain from yours. My dreams are your dreams, and I can only feel fulfilled in the knowledge that you are both living the lives you should be leading.'

'If you can't be there to see it, how will you know?'

So long as a way can be found for a person to get out, ways can be found for information to get in,' she said. It may have answered my question, but not the point behind it. Was it sufficient for Mum to know that we were living the lives we wanted, while she suffered a lonely and impoverished existence here? She wasn't likely to say otherwise. Conversation was irrelevant. Whatever was said, there were two inescapable realities; for my sake she wanted me to go and for her sake, I wanted to stay.

Whatever either of us wanted was only so relevant. Since the Wall was built, the options for leaving were minimal. The Visa I'd had for the Paris trip was unlikely to be repeated, so leaving meant escaping. Many attempted this, but few succeeded, and the price that was paid was designed to stop others contemplating taking the same risks.

About 100 metres inside the Wall was a secondary fence. The zone between the two structures became known as the death strip. It was designed to ease the ability of officials to detect trespassers, and importantly to have clear line of vision to fire upon anyone they did detect. While some who attempted to flee the East were jailed, the authorities were more than happy with a more definitive result. Anyone seeking to leave was considered a traitor to the nation. Death was an appropriate punishment in their eyes. I could envisage my father supporting this view.

There were numerous novel approaches that people had taken to try and escape. Hot air balloons to go above the wall, tunnels being dug to get under it and vehicles being driven to try and go straight through it. If it could be imagined, it was attempted.

Any possibility of me joining the long list of people to attempt to flee East Berlin was going to be dependent on someone else assisting. I was aware that this assistance would be coming for me, nowhere near as fast as I wanted it. I knew had to be patient.

***

A month into my stint with Paris Sur Glace, I'd had a visitor come backstage. He brought me a large bouquet of flowers. He spoke to me in German and begun by telling me he was a friend of Nicolas Alleyne, the president of the European division of renowned show, Ice Follies. He wanted to invite me for a drink somewhere that we'd be able to talk in private. I was automatically cynical that this was most likely an attempted seduction and nothing more, but I decided to give him the benefit of the doubt.

Identifying himself as Cedric, he stated that he worked for the French Embassy in West Germany. He asked what my intentions were after my season with Paris Sur Glace was completed.

'My Visa only covers this season. My return to East Berlin is locked in.'

'Yes, but what about the longer term. Would you consider joining Ice Follies if we could get you out of East Berlin?'

I had no idea how to respond. Naturally, that was my dream, but one that had seemed impossible. Maybe not impossible, but close enough without the help of the right people. If this man was who he said he was, then perhaps he was the answer. It was impossible for me to be certain that he wasn't an East German spy seeking to find my intentions and set me up for the drastic consequences that would follow if I'd been earmarked as a traitor to the nation.

'We have got people out. We have names on a list of more who we will get out. You can be on that list if you wish,' he said.

'If my name is on a list, then all that it takes is for the list to be known by the wrong people and I endanger myself and my family.'

'This is true.' He paused, knowing the distrust I had was well founded, not based on anything to do with him, but the reality of the iron curtain. A Frenchman may well be perceived as an ally to someone looking to cross to the west, but it was well established that the Stasi had informers in the west. I couldn't say anything definitive.

'I would love to perform in the West, that is why I am here now. I am here with the permission of my government. I have no intention of becoming an enemy of that same government.'

'I understand. Your father would be proud. Your mother would be disappointed.'

I was shocked to hear them mentioned. It was an accurate assessment of their wishes for me. This wasn't a throwaway line. Cedric, and whoever he worked with or for, had plenty of background on our family.

'There are hundreds of thousands of people who want to flee the East. If we only have the capacity to help one a month, it's not going to be a random approach. There is someone on each side of the Wall wanting you out. Nothing will happen fast, and nothing will happen without your consent. When you go back, your mother will explain what she knows. Then your mind may be changed.'

***

I'd been home for more than a week when Mum told me about the plan to get me out of the country. We'd gone out for a walk to the Volkspark, and when in an open area, she said that it was only in place like this that we could talk safely.

'I don't know for certain, but I think there is every chance that our home is bugged. If the Stasi hadn't already done it, your father would have presented the case to do so.'

'You can't blame him for everything,' I said. I didn't doubt that she was correct in this instance, but I'd noticed the trend in everything she said. For her own sake, I didn't consider it helpful long-term to continue thinking in that way.

'I know his stance on me and on the concept of people leaving. He knows what I want for you, and I suspect he would do anything in his capacity to stop it. Right or not, the idea of taking every possible precaution is something you need to learn. Be incredibly careful what you say, where you say it, and who you say it to. The greatest enemies often disguise themselves as friends. From there they can gain the information that can hurt you the most.'

I told her about the approach from Cedric Lemaire in Paris.

'Yes, that is what I've brought you to safe ground to discuss.'

'He came to me as a friend. How do I know that I can trust him, and that he's not undercover for the Stasi?'

'Because I tell you.' She explained that the season in Paris had always been a precursor to a permanent opportunity in the West. Ice Follies had their European base in the West German city of Stuttgart but the levels of distrust from the East German government was greatest against its nearest neighbour. My company in the East wanted me to gain the experience and insight of a Western company and had put me forward for that opportunity. This brought me to the attention of Ice Follies. They then used their connection through Lemaire to ascertain how best to get me permanently West. They profiled the family, and it was before I ever went to Paris that they had preliminary conversations with Mum about my long-term prospects.

'I was approached in the street and asked to meet someone the following day. I was told that if I wanted you to have your dreams met as had been the case with Lars, then I should go to the meeting and not breathe a word of it to anybody. I was very sceptical, but for them to reference Lars, I knew I was dealing with spies one way or the other, I just couldn't be sure which side was approaching me. The man I met, explained that if he was working for the East, he needn't have approached me, as they had an ally in your father to work through. It didn't give me certainty, but it put my mind somewhat at ease.'

The East and the West each had many people working for them on the other side of the Wall. The French Secret Service had assisted the transfer of several people but had maintained sufficient discretion to avoid problems having arisen. The task of getting anyone out of East Berlin was sufficiently risky that they only acted when a range of circumstances had been met. Ice Follies had agreed to sponsor the mission of my defection, providing funding to the French to cover the expenses involved. They also provided a guarantee on my security as well as a long-term contract for me to work with them.

I wondered why my father's links to the government hadn't stood in the way of this opportunity coming up.

'He probably helped.'

'But don't you think he might be working for the Stasi?'

'He isn't smart enough for them. They want information. They want discretion. These things require a set of qualities your father never had. He's just an insignificant supporter. The Western powers might have thought you may be an asset to them by passing on any information he had. They quickly learned that not only was he too insignificant to have anything of value, but he was far more loyal to the state than to his family.'

I couldn't imagine what my parents were like before the war. For as long as I had been alive, they seemed as divided as the city we lived in. It seemed hard to believe there was ever a time that they'd been in love, but if time can pull a city apart, it makes sense that it can do the same to a couple.

Despite her convictions, his close support of the government made him the embodiment of what the East stood for. He was never going to comply with anything that would aide his own flesh and blood working against these ideals.

The French Secret Service had devoted resources to my parents, an agent having no trouble in finding the loyalist nature of my Dad and the contrasting attitudes that Mum had. Mum wasn't political at all. It wasn't a belief in the rights of wrongs of the West, but the standard envy that seemed to permeate people on our side of the wall.

Dad was the embodiment of the East. Ask no questions, accept what he was told. Mum wanted better, not so much for herself, but for her children, and the generations to follow. From the time we were born, Lars and I were encouraged to dream big, then to work towards those dreams. Every day that I went to the rink to train, it was inspired by dreams. The dreams were about performing, but that didn't fit the narrative that suited the government. Competition. Winning. Bringing pride to the state. It was a long way from my dream, but in the East, it became my responsibility. As the passion died, I stagnated. I had failed to make the Olympic team in 1960, but still I was kept on the same pathway.

Mum hadn't left Dad to help get me to the West, but the timing was opportune. They no longer had anything in common but a shared resentment of each other. Eventually Mum believed that it was best for her, and more importantly me, that they separate.

Without Dad as part of our family unit, the request to get me out no longer had an impediment. The French knew that Mum would be a willing ally in aiding my move. There were no guarantees given, and no indication of timing. It may never happen at all, we were warned, but it also may happen at a moment's notice. There were a range of circumstances that dictated every action.

'Do nothing to arouse suspicion,' Cedric had said when we met in Paris. 'Show anything bar loyalty to your State, and you will be watched. From there, we have no chance. Your stint here automatically keeps you on their list of potential defectors. Your return implies a loyalty, but it will take time for that to be taken with certainty. Make sure you appear to share your father's beliefs. Stay close to him. Ensure that it is clear that any love you have for your mother does not extend to sharing her views. All of this will speed up the process.'

I explained this to Mum and asked how I was to do this with Dad gone.

'Part of your job on the ice is to play a role. To make the audience buy what you sell. You need your father to be your audience and put your acting to the test. You don't need to establish the perfect father-daughter relationship, just have him believe that you share his faith in the East German state. You've learned more of your craft in the West, and you are back to strengthen the East with this expertise.'

'To be honest, I'd be happier never seeing him again.'

'When this is all done, you never will. Sometimes you must accept whatever means delivers you to the end you want.'

For twelve months I followed everything to the letter. I was a loyal East German. I worked hard, I kept a low profile, and I rekindled a relationship with my father. He showed pride, but only after time, and it had little impact as I knew that this pride was in a character I was playing, not the real me.

I was starting to lose faith that my day would ever come. As I heard of the fates of people trying to cross the wall, I began to question whether I was willing to take my chance if it ever came. I knew the people who would be helping me would have far better methods than those we heard about. They didn't rush things, however frustrated I felt by that at this time. If it came, I would be ready to jump at their command. I needed to be free.

10

15 March 2020

AMBER

Spending the time yesterday listening to Henry and Marta had me determined to put a pair of skates on and venture on to the ice for the first time in years. It may be unusual for someone from Canada, but I've never been much of a skater. Despite not being full of wonderful memories on the ice, hearing their wonderous stories had me envisaging a type of magic I wanted to feel. Although I was working in the afternoon, I felt compelled to spend part of my morning turning these thoughts into realities. If nothing else, then at least I would have a real conversation piece for Henry and Marta this afternoon.

I got the train to Hermannstraße in the south of the city and walked to the Eisstadion Neukölln. I'd read this was the best outdoor rink in Berlin and it was far enough away that the prospect of embarrassing myself in front of anyone who may recognise me, seemed non-existent.

The delusions of grandeur that had filled my mind last night were long gone as I put my hired skates on and very shakily made my way on to the ice. My hopes were now set to the much lower level of adequacy. It didn't take long to realise that mere adequacy was likely to prove beyond me. It had been a long time, and my rustiness was making that timeframe seem even longer.

As I very slowly and cautiously moved around the ice, I reflected on Henry and Marta. There was a photo on their wall of Marta in full costume, a grace and beauty radiating from someone with both the skill, and the confidence to perform difficult manoeuvres with seemingly no effort. Alongside that had been a photo of Henry and his partner Des, in their routine. It must have taken incredible commitment, determination and stubbornness, to transition those acrobatic routines from floor to ice, with no background in skating. Looking at Marta and Henry now, confined to their sedentary life, it was hard to correlate the people in their stories with the people I was attending to. Therein lies the circle of life.

Most of what Henry had told me had prompted more questions than it had answered about the realities of their lives. The prospect of learning more was going to ensure my enthusiasm to return to work each day, but I wasn't so sure if it would lead to me continuing my attempts at skating. I'd started to feel a little more confident but that proved to be my undoing. I moved towards the centre and immediately found myself on my backside.

'*Geht es dir gut?*' I was asked by someone checking I was alright.

'*Ja. Danke.*' I replied.

'You speak English, yes?' My feeble attempt at a simple German phrase obviously sounded unconvincing to German ears.

'Yes,' I replied paying more attention to her now, at the promise of conversation that I would be able to understand. She had a strong German accent but spoke quite fluent English. She was also strikingly beautiful. Long blonde hair, blue eyes, feminine, curvaceous. I had noticed her before I went out on the ice and with her now beside me, I felt the fall had been a blessing in disguise. Admittedly, it was a somewhat embarrassing way of making an introduction.

'You don't skate much right? Where are you from?'

'Canada,' I said, 'so you'd expect me to be better. Everyone skates back home, though I guess I'm proof you should never say everyone. If you only just saw me once I had fallen, you wouldn't know how bad I was.'

'Maybe you'd already caught my eye,' she said.

What did she mean? It sounded somewhat flirtatious, but I couldn't imagine a woman like this saying anything like that to me. Such openness in an environment like this was rare, so I understood that it was highly unlikely that she had meant quite what I had hoped, especially considering the potential for misunderstandings when people speak in a language that they're not completely proficient in. Most likely, she meant that my utter awkwardness had caught her eye. I had more reason to feel embarrassed than flattered.

'I'm Greta' she said.

'I'm Amber.'

'So, what is a non-skating Canadian girl doing on the ice in Berlin all alone?'

'Good question. I don't have such a simple answer though, I'm afraid.'

'Well why not come to some more solid ground. I will buy you a coffee and you can give me the not so simple answer. *Ja?*'

I doubt I would have said no to any question she asked me, but the combination of coffee, warmth and an escape from the ongoing embarrassment of my clumsiness on the ice ensured there was no hesitation in my response.

'Take my hand' she said, 'and it will be easier to make it across to the exit.'

Again, I needed no further invitation. Greta could well have been a modern version of Marta, such was her ease and comfort on the ice. I imagined Marta when she was a similar age. How glamorous she must have been in the elaborate costumes she wore? Greta may not be the national champion figure skater, but she wouldn't have been too far behind in the glamour stakes. Why she was showing such attention to me, made little sense. I know that anything that seems too good to be true usually isn't, so I remained sceptical. Just in case this was one of those exceptions, I wasn't walking away just yet.

As we sat in the warmth of the café, the irregularity of the scene struck me. I was always the one who listened to the lives of others. I was always the spectator, never the spectacle. Here I was with a beautiful woman who was insistent on making me the focus of the conversation, yet through it all I retained a level of comfort that I usually lacked in social situations. I didn't mention Andrew but alluded to the fact that my time in Europe was an escape from things I didn't want to face. I talked glowingly of my time in Germany and explained how life in Berlin had started. I went into great detail about Marta and Henry and how the stories of their past had led me to the ice today.

'You didn't think you'd be replicating elite skaters straight away?'

'No' I said, my eyes rolling a fraction as I spoke. She may have already picked me as clumsy, but I didn't want her thinking I was stupid as well.

'I just wanted to feel the stories they were telling me. You know sometimes when you hear a story, you picture it so vividly because you can understand it. I don't need to be able to skate well to relate to their stories, but I think it was Henry's scenario, converting a standard acrobatic routine from land to ice with no previous experience on skates that screamed out to me. I know that must have been difficult, but how difficult? I think I have a better appreciation of that story through coming here today.'

Finally, the tables turned sufficiently so that I regained my favoured role of listener as I managed to get Greta telling me a bit more about herself.

'I haven't worked out what I want to do with my life,' she said. 'I was always asked what I wanted to do when I grew up and I said I never knew. I still haven't worked it out. Some would say I still haven't grown up. I'm a bit of a dreamer but the dreams keep changing. I wanted to be a speed skater, a tennis player, a singer, a jockey. I would become obsessed with my latest passion before my obvious lack of talent put me in my place.'

She had grown up in Leipzig but moved to Berlin three years ago. She came here looking to find herself, in much the same way that I had sought through travel. She didn't specify a precipitating moment that led to this, but then I hadn't revealed that about myself.

'My family never really accepted me for who I am. I was always the black sheep. My brother and sister were the typical 'dream children' that parents want. In every way, I was the opposite,' she said.

'How so?' I asked.

'They were better students than me. Elena was a talented dancer, Matheaus a footballer. Most significantly they are both married now with children and once they knew that wouldn't happen with me, I went from merely being the least favoured child, to the one they didn't want to know at all.'

'You have no contact with any of your family?' I asked.

'A little. I haven't seen my parents since I moved here. I'm still in touch with my siblings, but only occasionally. We were never that close, but they have some appreciation of blood ties.'

I felt it was better to get away from that topic and switched to life in Berlin. She told me that she worked in a supermarket in the south of the city, just near where she lived, in a unit on her own. How she could afford to live on her own on a part time wage surprised me, knowing already that the cost of living here was high. Everything about her appearance screamed affluence, so I felt sure there had to be more to her story. Maybe if I wasn't so enthused by her, I'd have been more inclined to ask questions, but attraction rarely leads to the best decisions. At this point I was enjoying sitting across from her and listening to her voice. Anything she said was almost secondary.

'Do you want to have another attempt on the ice?' Greta asked.

'I would, but I must go shortly. I'm working this afternoon,' I said. I wished I didn't need to leave, but given this was only my second day there, I really had no alternative. I didn't want to be walking away from her at this stage. I clung to the hope that something which sprung so easily and randomly, would work out of its own volition, if it was genuinely meant to be. When she asked to swap phone numbers, I felt more confident about that. I wasn't getting presumptuous about the nature of her intentions, for I knew that I needed friends in Berlin as much as anything else.

We walked to the station together. She was heading home and caught the same train, but only as far as Hermannplatz, several stops before I was getting off. As we got closer to her place, I got the kind of questioning I wanted.

'When is your next night off?'

'Thursday,' I said.

'I'm working in the daytime, but do you want to go out that night? Let me show you another side of the city.'

I didn't know what she meant by the other side. It didn't matter, the answer was naturally going to be yes.

'7pm Thursday. I will see you at Alexanderplatz.'

She farewelled me as she got off the train and gave me the most beautiful smile. It would serve as a memory that would stay implanted in my mind until I saw her next.

It was a rush, but I made it to work on time, and once again found myself paired with Klara. The shift seemed to drag more than last night, no doubt the morning fuelling the desire to be somewhere else. Once dinners had been completed, there was a standard busy period that seemed to carry on far longer than I'd like. Eventually things settled and I had the opportunity to spend some more time with Marta and Henry.

'You're not going to believe what I did this morning.'

'Surprise me,' Henry said.

'Went skating. First time in years.'

'How long until you turn professional?' Marta asked.

'I don't think so. It wasn't pretty.'

'I doubt being pretty was your problem,' Henry said. It felt like he knew the real reason my skating exploits were so happily memorable, but I managed to avoid blushing at the compliment, or the other thoughts rushing through my head, and continued.

'Stop flirting old man,' Marta said. I didn't really think he was. His moments of feeling positive were rare, and I think he just sought to play on that feeling.

'True Henry, I was pretty. Pretty awkward, that is.'

'I had to become a professional on ice in virtually no time when I was about your age. How old are you?'

'Twenty-five,' I said.

'Shit. In that case I did it many years before I was your age. The point is, I looked as awkward as you would have. Most skaters develop a career after they've built it as a passion. I was one of the rare people who had a ready-made career that just needed the skating to leave me ready. If not for that, I probably never would have put a pair of ice skates on. Why you would do so now makes no sense.'

'I blame you,' I said with a laugh. 'Everything you said yesterday just had all these thoughts of the magic of your life and I just wanted to feel the sense of that.'

'My life has been like everyone else's. Shithouse and wonderful. All just depends on which moments you look at or which minute you ask me in. Either way, ice skating has been an insignificant part of it. Not like her,' he said, pointing to Marta.

'I think you should do it more,' she said.

'Who knows. I just might.' I didn't really want to have the conversation back on me, so I decided to ask more about how she managed to get out of East Berlin.

'Don't tell her,' Henry said. 'You know they're bugging our room.'

I wasn't sure whether he was serious or not. I couldn't believe he was right, but whether he was seriously delusional, or merely playing up the magnitude of their story, was something I was sure to understand better with time.

'I'm already back in East Berlin. There's nowhere else to take me.'

Henry groaned and shook his head. Marta explained that she'd been paranoid of retribution in the early days after her escape.

'The reasons for those fears have been confined to history. There is little chance of anyone connected to my escape still being alive today. Nobody left to care what the truth was.'

'You don't have to talk about it if you don't want.'

'It doesn't bring back the happy memories that ice skating does, so it isn't something I talk about so much,' she said. 'But everything that followed for the rest of my life could never have happened without that day.'

11

16 July 1963

MARTA

To anyone observing, it was just another day. I left home at the normal time, walking to the skating hall, training the normal session before setting off on the normal route home. When the investigations begin into what had happened, it would be these details that would be looked at. Nobody would have been looking by the time I diverted to a different route, fifteen minutes down the road.

I had received the letter the previous day. A man walked straight into me on my walk home from the rink. Rather than apologise he put an envelope in my hand, and in a French accent, told me not to look at it until I was safely inside at home. I was to read it with my mother, for she would be able to assist with understanding the code. The envelope had Polish stamps on, and the letter written in Polish, all precautionary acts in case of interception.

'There isn't much to understand,' Mum told me once we read it. 'I was told the plan a year ago. All that is hidden in this letter is confirmation that tomorrow is the day, and all is to proceed as originally indicated.'

I didn't sleep last night. How could anyone in such a situation? I would be saying goodbye to my mother forever. My home, my possessions, however meagre they may seem. Mum's paranoia of the home being bugged meant we couldn't address these. I couldn't say goodbye.

I had to make it appear that it was just another day, ensuring that no suspicion arose if we were being listened in to. I knew what I had to do, but whether I could manage it was another story.

I held Mum closely and cried. In her typical stoic manner, Mum continued to talk with no emotion, on seemingly irrelevant matters that wouldn't require any response from me. How she could retain such composure was almost frightening. I would be attempting to cross the border tonight. If I succeeded, she was unlikely to ever see me again. If I failed, she wouldn't see me either, but for a far worse reason. I knew I had to carry her attitude within me. I needed the same hard, un-emotional manner. Not only did I need it on display all day at the rink, but I would need it throughout the saga that would follow. If this was to be the last time I ever saw my mother, it would be that characteristic burned in my memory, and a feature that I would spend the rest of my life trying to emulate.

It felt like the longest day of training I'd ever done. As much as my mind was a world away, I stayed good to my word, showing the com-posure of a true professional. In conversation through breaks, and on the ice, nobody could have seen any difference in my demeanour until late afternoon. At that point, as the plan dictated, I indicated that I felt unwell. Discreetly, and not to an extent that would impact me at the time, or my ability to walk home as normal, but one that might make my absence tomorrow prompt less consideration.

I walked from the ice rink in the normal direction, ensuring that anyone who knew me, saw that all was normal. It was only a few blocks from home that I diverted to the planned route. My mind was filled with a myriad of explanations I had prepared if anyone should ask where I was headed. Naturally enough, this was a waste of time. I barely passed anyone on my journey, and certainly nobody who would have any idea who I was.

I reached the wooded area surrounding the Fauser See, right on schedule. Although still daylight, a set of headlights briefly shone on me. I understood the signal and continued to walk. The vehicle passed me doing a lap around the parkland, before again coming into my view, after I had turned into a quiet street by the edge of the woods. This time the car stopped, a door opened, and I got in. Within ten minutes we had arrived at a safe house in Freidrichshain.

My life was in the hands of others. All of them were unfamiliar to me. I'd had to trust everyone involved was on the same side. The East and West were on the brink of a third World War, and I was now right in the middle of the diplomatic game. Both sides had double agents. If anyone involved in my defection proved to be working for the East, then I'd already lived my last free day. Provided that wasn't the case, and we manage to clear the border checkpoint, I was hours away from a different level of freedom.

The French Ambassador's car arrived just after 7pm. The plan had been to keep the pick-up as quick as possible, so the car and its occupants were fresh in the memory at the checkpoint from the interaction heading into the East. This shouldn't be important, for Cedric Lemaire made these journeys multiple times a week. Operations like tonight's were rare, but every time he crossed the border, it went to building the cover that made the exceptions possible.

I was taken into the garage and shown the car. On the surface, there was nothing to see, but the car had been rebuilt for this purpose. No vehicle could pass through the border without being thoroughly checked, irrespective of ambassadorial privilege or how familiar the car was to the border guards. Harbouring an escapee wasn't as simple as covering them with a sheet in the boot or the back seat. Cedric showed me how it would be done.

'Under the bonnet is a false panel. In front of that is a compartment that you will be curled up inside of. It will be very uncomfortable, but we will be at the checkpoint twenty minutes after you're in place, and we will have you out ten minutes after we clear the checkpoint. The checkpoint can vary, but worst-case scenario you'll be confined in there for just over two hours.'

'I would have thought that the worst-case scenario is that we get caught?'

'True, but we choose not to entertain those thoughts. We put such a plan in place so that we avoid that.'

He explained the various modifications that had been made to clear space, including the removal of the fuel tank, replaced by a smaller canister containing just enough fuel to make the short journey.

'Am I going to be safe in there? I won't burn?'

'No. The padding on your side of the metal divider will protect you. Don't forget, you are not the first person to travel like this in this vehicle. It has always been successful.'

Cedric and the driver assisted me into the spot. There wasn't an inch of room to spare, which is why they were so strict that I could bring nothing with me. The commitment to leave involved an acceptance that everything and everyone had to be left behind. Mum aside, that was easy, but the struggle I had in leaving her was why I broke the 'nothing rule' to bring a couple of photos of her with me. Those photos and the clothes on my back were now all I owned in the world.

'See you in the West,' Cedric said as I saw the last bit of light before the metal panel was drilled in, finalising the discreetly modified vehicle that would hopefully deliver me to freedom.

I had never been claustrophobic, but nobody could feel comfortable confined to such space. There was no air flow into the compartment, so it didn't take an anxious person to start struggling for air. I had to remain calm though. Movement, however small, could alter the balance in the vehicle and add suspicion. We were set up to succeed, but failure was just one false move away.

I felt every turn and instinctively knew when we'd pulled up at Checkpoint Charlie. Before too long I could hear the dogs barking, the orders of border guards reigning out, and the calm composed words of Cedric keeping control.

My heart rate rose to a level I'd never known. How fortunate it was that I was confined in such a small space, for my anxiety would have given me up if I was in any place where that was possible. I've spent a lifetime learning how to suppress nerves, and to perform routines perfectly when fear of the moment challenges me. That was no preparation. This was life or death, and nothing could compose me through that. Cedric was accustomed to it, and for him, such a situation was the equivalent of me performing a basic routine on ice.

We were stopped for roughly half an hour. I never stopped shaking. They never seemed to be getting close to finding me, but I couldn't understand why it was taking so long. Seconds seemed like minutes, minutes seemed like hours. The relief I felt when the engine turned back on, was like nothing I'd ever known. A little more than five minutes later we had stopped again, and despite a moment of panicking that it was too soon to have reached safety, Cedric's voice composed me, confirming the ordeal was over.

I had spent less than two hours in the car, but once they managed to assist me out of the vehicle, I fell to the ground. My legs were swollen, my back was aching, my nerves were shot, but overriding all of this was the belief that I was safe and free. The heavy rain soaked me, yet I could barely feel the impact.

'You'll find the back seat a little more comfortable,' Cedric said, helping me up and guiding me to the open door.

I expected to feel ecstatic when I reached this point, but I felt nothing. I was being welcomed into a new life, but that meant the old life was over. It had been all that I wanted, but now that it had come my way, it was hard not to reflect on the good things I had given up. They may have been greatly outweighed by the positives in front of me, but as we drove to the safehouse, I couldn't stop thinking of my mother.

12

16 March 2020

AMBER

Marta's escape from East Berlin had taken place at Checkpoint Charlie, the most famous of all border crossings. After hearing about it yesterday, there was no question of where I felt the need to head this morning.

I shouldn't be surprised, but it was the most disappointed I have been by anywhere in Germany. Cheesy, kitsch and fake, it was sad to see a place of such historical significance being treated in such a way. Every element of the spot was geared towards being ideal for tourists, but it is a sad indictment on those who lap it up. From the actors playing the military police to the overpriced souvenirs in adjacent shops and the unauthentic photos of soldiers and the replica of the border station, it was disingenuous to everything this place was.

Normally Checkpoint Charlie is overrun by tourists. Trying to go into the adjacent museum required greater patience than I possessed. Taking advantage of the current sparseness of crowds, I paid the admission fee, regretting it from the moment I entered. Like the outside, there was little to see here. Given the city had so many free museums that have so much history, paying for this is a tourist trap. I'd like to say I never fall for these, but today has proven me wrong on that count.

Tourism is never one dimensional. Some people would find Checkpoint Charlie simple and accessible. They don't need to learn and understand the history, they can pay for a photo with someone in uniform then buy a piece of the Wall. Who cares about genuine when you can post on social media that you're at a pivotal place in history? Sadly, few of them would have the slightest understanding of that history, nor a desire to change that.

I don't normally feel this way about the most touristy sites. I visited Neuschwanstein Castle and Dachau Concentration Camp when I was in Munich. Both attracted huge crowds of tourists, and while opposite in the types of facilities, they both retained a level of authenticity. I got plenty from both experiences.

It may be more pantomime than history, but travel is more than what you see. I closed my eyes and focussed on Marta's story of escape. Being here, however removed it may be from the terror of 1963 made me feel so much more connected to her words.

***

I'd had to rush but managed to make it to work just in time. For day three, I had a new partner, named Hannah. She seemed to be yet another similar character to Klara and Frida with any element of personality well hidden beneath a strong and tough exterior. She did speak a little English, not much more than I spoke German, but perhaps enough that we'd work together comparatively well.

We worked our way across our section of the building to greet everyone under our care as was routine at the start of a shift. I was eager to make my way back to Henry and Marta's room and tell them about my morning.

'Maple syrup time, eh,' Marta called out, as we walked into the room. I walked past Henry who had dozed off to sleep and made my way across to his wife.

'Guess where I went this morning,' I said to her.

'Where?'

'Checkpoint Charlie.'

'I'm sure you got a better view of it than I did in 1963, though I doubt that your day will end up as memorable.'

'Maybe not,' I said. 'I remembered every word of your story as I looked at the exhibits in the museum, particularly one with a car that had been remodelled to hide a person in the trunk.'

'I have been there and seen it. Very different vehicle to what we used, ours being an official consulate car. The amount of space would have been similar. It's not a ride I recommend.'

'Sometimes circumstances dictate just how uncomfortable we are willing to be.'

'This is true,' she said.

'We need to keep moving, but you've got Hannah and me today. I hope to come back soon and talk to Henry.'

'Good,' she said. 'It is so rare that he has any sort of conversation with anyone other than me. He's really enjoyed you being here the past couple of days.'

'I enjoyed it to,' I said. 'You have both had such fascinating lives and I loved hearing about it. I am sure we've barely scratched the surface.'

Hannah didn't seem impressed by the additional time I spent with Marta and looked impatient as I made my way to join her for the next rooms. I wasn't surprised. Working in Germany, I had seen the dynamics of the workplace. Professionalism and efficiency were prioritised above being personable. My understanding of the personal service element may be distorted by my language skills, but it still seemed very different to what I was used to in Canada. At home, our role was closer to a customer service role, where making the residents happy was central to our job. Here the emphasis was greatly different. Not better, not worse, but something that I was taking time to adjust to. There had been examples of colleagues spending extended time with patients during shifts, but with the language barrier I faced, it had never been me. With Henry and Marta, I could take on this role. I just needed to build a better understanding of just when and how this would be considered appropriate.

'How long in Berlin?' Hannah asked me as we got back to our station at the completion of our initial rounds. As I knew from my feeble attempts speaking German, tense was often more of a challenge than vocabulary when speaking a foreign language. I couldn't be sure if she was wanting to know how long I had been here, or how long I was intending to stay.

'Maybe a month, but I'm not certain. I arrived on Thursday and started here Saturday for a four-week placement.' I had no intention of explaining why, but yesterday morning had me contemplating the idea that I might be keen to stay far longer.

'Good,' she said. I knew this was not necessarily meant as a positive comment, but a standard way of acknowledging the previous statement while seeking to finalise the conversation. She added to my uncertainty about this by remaining seated, looking at me, as though waiting for me to provide something else.

'How long have you worked here?' I asked, seeking to deflect the attention. It was worth trying to begin learning a little more about one of the people I'd be working most closely with for the next month.

'Six years' she said. I had guessed she was mid-forties but didn't want to make assumptions. She had short dark hair, hard features and not a sign of femininity about her. I was curious if she had the capacity to smile, such was the permanently sullen look on her face. How much of it tied into the workplace was hard to know, but when that is your only contact with a person, you tend to see it as a reflection of their overall being.

She told me she had grown up in the small town of Gunzburg, roughly halfway between Stuttgart and Munich, but had moved here at age twenty to move away from a life that didn't feel like hers. It seemed similar to Greta's story, as well as my own. I started to wonder just how typical this mindset was. I had felt like my journey of discovery was something unusual. Perhaps it is just a routine part of life.

There was also a part of me that started to wonder a little more about Hannah. Here I was, just a day on from the first woman to ever show an interest in me and I had an inclination that Hannah may just be headed in the same direction. I hoped that wasn't the case. I didn't want to have any sort of awkwardness in the workplace.

I had to be misreading the situation. There is no way in the world that I'm the type of woman to get that attention, wanted or otherwise, so frequently. I am plain, however much anyone says otherwise. Short, average build, and glasses, there is nothing about me that stands out other than my bright cherry red hair. That was a recent change, covering my natural light brown so that I had something distinguishable about my appearance. I'm not unattractive, but I was always the girl who got the attention of the boys once the pretty girls were all taken. It made no sense that I would suddenly be getting more attention in Berlin than I'd ever had anywhere else. Maybe I was carrying myself more confidently, the new person I was trying to be managing to shine through despite the insecure feelings I was still carrying within.

We got a call from a patient which ended the first little session of getting to know each other. A bed-bound resident needed assistance going to the toilet. This was a big job, getting her from the bed to a chair, then a chair to the toilet seat and after leaving her for a couple of minutes, repeating the task in reverse. It was a ten-minute job that we'd repeat twenty times across a shift. Naturally we'd get back-to-back calls for the same job for the best part of an hour before there'd be a period of relative peace and quiet. When we got to that point, I decided to uncover a little more from Hannah about Henry and Marta.

'So why does everyone refuse to speak English around Henry?' I asked.

'He difficult. He rude. He gets angry at us. He swears at us. He makes no effort with anyone, so we make no effort back with him. We are professional, and do everything we need, but nothing more.'

'Maybe if people made an effort with him then he would be better in return,' I said.

'We do everything he need, and he need plenty. When he make an effort, we make an effort,' Hannah said.

I knew people who fit this description from various homes I'd worked in, and I could understand the perspective that Hannah mentioned. I also knew that there was a long way between the best and worst of most people. The chances of seeing the best of anyone came with giving them the best of yourself. Naturally this environment is one where you're dealing with people at a stage of life where things aren't always going to be good, but attitude and approach can minimise the negatives and maximise the positives in each day. If I could aide Henry with that, then I'd be doing my job well. Not only would that earn me kudos with management, but it would make doing my job easier, make life feel more pleasant, and have me leaving work each day in a better frame of mind to go out and enjoy exploring the city.

Henry's bell rang almost simultaneously with another resident, so Hannah was happy to leave him to me while heading further down the corridor. We had constant communication if the other was needed, but at least with Henry the call needed nothing more than me.

'You better watch out for that woman your partnered with,' Henry said. 'She's a lesbian. She's into good looking young women like you.'

'Oh, shut up Henry, you *Arschloch*,' Marta said. 'She can look after herself.'

'Easier done when you know who to look out for.'

I wouldn't have expected someone who'd worked in the entertainment business to have that type of attitude. Surely he'd worked with the most diverse group of people over the years, and most likely established good friendships with all types of people. I'd already told them about the split with Andrew and had considered telling them more about myself. This was a reminder not to let myself be too open. He may just be trying to protect someone he may think of as naïve, rather than a genuine rejection of Hannah's sexuality, but it did leave me feeling a little disappointed.

I certainly felt no semblance of attraction to her. Why would any of that be an issue though? I had worked with enough heterosexual men in my time who I wasn't attracted to. There was never any awkwardness.

The fact that they were heterosexual men didn't mean they were attracted to any woman, so why should it be that a homosexual woman would automatically be attracted to any woman? People don't stereotype majorities, but as soon as a minority raises its head, people seem to jump at the opportunity.

'So, was there something you actually needed?' Although I was frustrated by his attitude, I didn't want to be sliding down a pathway that would impact the dynamic we'd been building. The best hope I had of this was to move on to territory we'd both feel more comfortable in.

'I was just sick of talking to Marta and hoped I'd get some better conversation.'

'You see what I put up with. Fifty-six years of marriage. Ask any of your colleagues here, and they will tell you that I deserve a medal,' Marta said. I was sure they would all agree, and I'd seen enough to think they were right. Henry was no longer paying attention and appeared to be dozing off again.

'Sometimes you probably feel as imprisoned as you were in the car that night.'

'My journey across the Wall was meant to be to freedom. I quickly learnt that you don't need to be behind a wall to have your freedom withheld.

13

17 July 1963

MARTA

Living in East Berlin, the perception of the other side of the Wall was one of freedom. Making it across to the West offered a very different reality than what I expected. As I woke for the first time in West Berlin, I was more of a prisoner than I had ever been.

After we crossed the border last night, I'd been driven to a safehouse that the French government owned. I was told that this would be home for me until I was transferred to Stuttgart, where I would begin with Ice Follies. I was introduced to Bettina, the housekeeper who I was told would be looking after me through my stay. Cedric advised that he would be returning in the morning as there were several matters that needed to be discussed.

'I trust you slept well,' Bettina said, finally waking me mid-morning, worried at just how late I had slept. Given the physical and mental ordeal of the previous day, I felt sleeping for a couple of days would be justified.

'Monsieur Lemaire is waiting for you.'

I wouldn't be here without the assistance of Cedric and the Embassy, so I accepted my responsibilities lay with them. I quickly dressed in yesterday's clothes, the only possessions I still owned, and joined him downstairs. He was with another man who he introduced as Horst.

Horst lived in the house that I was sharing and was the man responsible for me in my time in West Berlin.

Cedric began with a range of small talk, hoping I'd slept well and showed a genuine sense of relief that my ordeal was over. I gave him the answers he'd want, but in my mind, I knew only a phase of the ordeal had ended. I didn't have freedom. I had nothing to my name, so I couldn't walk out the door and begin a new life. Plans may be in place, but I have limited knowledge of these. As I was to find out, the plans weren't as firmly in place as I had thought.

'You will not be joining Ice Follies. There have been complications in the past couple of days.'

'What have I gone through all of this for?'

'It's alright. You have a role in the chorus for World on Ice. Very similar show, similar length season. They are based in Bremen, so that is where you will be heading from here.'

'What happened?'

'Word got out within the company that an East German would be joining the cast. We had an intelligence report suggesting this information had been passed back to the East and the company wanted to distance themselves from it. Luckily, it's a small industry, and we were able to organise a new job.'

'Won't the same thing happen?'

'No. You'll be an official West German citizen before anyone knows you are part of World on Ice.'

'They'll still know I have defected.'

'Which isn't an issue. There are former Eastern skaters in most shows. Any company would be happy to have Marta Roloff in their cast if she was available, but no company wants to be known as aiding the defection. That is how the Ice Follies situation would have looked, whereas this move, weeks after you cross the border, will look more like opportunism from World on Ice.'

If at any point I was questioned about how I crossed the border, I was to say I had escaped through a tunnel that I had found by chance.

Several tunnels had been dug under the Wall, and while the East German authorities had found many of these, more were constantly being constructed. It would never be believed that I had miraculously found one without advice from someone, but that didn't matter.

'It is very unlikely you will ever face such questioning from anyone connected with the East German authorities, but there is no doubt you will be asked by people you meet. Avoid the topic as much as you can, but if something needs to be said, our role must never come out.'

'Am I safe in West Berlin?'

'There are many Eastern agents here, just as the West has many agents across the Wall. For all our resources, it took a year to get you out. Once they close in on you, the information will get back to the Stasi, but their prospects of taking any action in our part of the city is negligible. You aren't important enough to take that level of risk for.'

'If I don't matter, why did you get me out?'

'The East let you go to Paris to do a show. You may have been given the impression that this was to help develop you professionally for the sake of East German entertainment, but we don't believe their long-term plans for you had anything to do with skating. We decided it was far better to let you skate and stay out of the politics that they would have been earmarking you for. We did need to spend a year tracking you, making sure that you weren't yet working for the Stasi.'

'Working for them? Are you kidding. They are why I wanted to escape.'

'We don't take chances on good intentions,' he said.

All the talk of agents and spies had me concerned that I was set to pay a higher price than had been negotiated for this move. Everything that was discussed was simply passage across the border for a career as a skater. No price. No questions. The understanding that both Mum and I had, was that any price was financial, and this was being met by Ice Follies. Perhaps it was too good be true, and as my mother had always told me, if it appears that way, it usually is.

'What happens now?' I asked. 'I have nothing but the clothes I wore yesterday. What do I do?'

'Your time in West Berlin is designed to rectify that. A West German passport and associated paperwork has been organised for you. Money has been set aside for you from your employer and you will use this over the next couple of weeks to accumulate what you need.'

'Can I go wherever I want?'

'Only after a few days have passed. It will take a couple of days before the authorities across the border question your whereabouts. We don't want you to be seen before then. Once they know you have fled, we want them to be examining the widest possible time frame.

'Once that time passes, you must only go out with Horst's accompaniment. He is here to help and protect you. I am sorry if it feels like you don't have the freedoms you expected, but this is for your own best interests. Soon you will be with your employers touring Europe and enjoying the freedoms you've dreamed of, but only once it is safe. The more closely you follow Horst's instructions, the faster that will be.'

I wanted my mother to know that I'd arrived, but Cedric reminded me that I was to have no communication with her, nor anyone in the East.

'Thankfully the war at hand is one fought with information as the primary weapon, rather than bombs, but it is still a war, and you are a potential weapon.'

'I am not part of that.'

'You are. Not intentionally, and only in a small way, but you are still caught up in it. You will get the chance to communicate with both parents, but only in writing, and only with the words that we provide you to write.'

'Spreading misinformation?'

'No. Just well-tailored truths.'

'Why?'

'Once the Stasi know you have escaped, they will be watching your family very closely. They know that every successful escape is dependent on assistance, it is merely a question of whether that assistance has come from their own side, or ours. We need to ensure that they're thrown off the scent. An understanding that you got out through the French ambassador will make future escapes using our method impossible. Not to mention all the other impacts on relations between the two sides.'

'How will they know I've escaped, not just disappeared?'

'The East Germans make it their business to know everything about everyone. Your mother will report you missing, which is part of the plan to protect her. We want the Stasi to believe your escape was a shock to her. If she doesn't report it, then it will appear that she is hiding something, and she will be arrested on suspicion. The Stasi will feel sure you have escaped. Their spies in West Berlin will find you, but the authorities leave them with little capacity to act here. They will merely report back, and it all ends there. How they react to those who have aided you is another story, and the reason why we must control the messages back across the Wall. Your father's politics are known, but we also need to protect him.'

'I had virtually no contact with my father. I met him a few times after returning to Paris. He will disown me when he knows I've left. There is no point communicating with him.'

'They will likely suspect him.'

'He wouldn't have helped me in any situation, but certainly not in this. He would see this as betrayal.'

'The perfect cover story.'

'No, it's real.'

'The best person to engineer an escape is someone against such an action. That is how the Stasi think and it is why your communication to him could be invaluable in his protection.'

'I have no interest in protecting him. Just my mother.'

'You must understand how ruthless they are. In the years to come, your conscience may struggle with knowing you didn't help him, whether he deserved it or not.'

I nodded. I was relieved to have him out of my life, but that was the ideal result. I didn't wish ill on him, and I certainly did not want to be the cause of any suffering. I just wanted freedom from him like I wanted freedom from his side of the Wall.

'We'll tailor things appropriately,' Cedric said.

He moved across the room where he picked up some papers before returning to me.

'There is one person you will be able to communicate more freely with now. I have a letter here for you.'

He handed me an envelope, and as I opened it and noticed the date it was written, nearly five months earlier, I knew from the handwriting who it was from.

Dearest Marta

If you are reading this, you are safely out of East Berlin, and I will be incredibly relieved when I have confirmation this is true.

I was devastated to be unable to say goodbye to you, but every step of the way, I had a plan to be following, for the safety of us all. I knew that the plan would eventually lead you to freedom in the West, and with it, the opportunity for the two of us to reunite. I know it may take time, but we will find a way.

It breaks my heart that I shall never see our mother again, but I know that it must be this way. She helped me get out, and her next mission was to do the same for you. Her life revolved around us and making our lives all they could be. How painful it is to have accepted that gift and been un-able to provide my thanks. I'm sure you now feel the same, but rest assured she knows. There are webs that have been weaved which we can never fully appreciate. What Mum knows and how she knows it, is something that I cannot explain. Some things in life we need to know, while others require faith. This is one such example.

You are going to find there is much to adapt to. You cannot get by without other people but place your trust in the wrong ones and the results can be catastrophic. It is no accident who aided your escape. Follow any

instruction they give you, and soon you will be appreciating the freedom
that awaits you in this next stage of life.

Until we see each other again.

All my love, Lars.

'How did my brother know where to send this?' I asked.

'How do you think you came to our attention?'

'He is behind all of this?'

Cedric shrugged his shoulders. 'It is always best that no more people than necessary are aware of all the details. What matters is that you know he is safe and living his new life. You are almost to the same point, but just need to follow every instruction Horst gives you until you are in Bremen.

'Unfortunately, this will be the last I see of you. Who knows, maybe one day you'll be performing in a city somewhere around the world and I can be entertained by you. If, however, you ever see me, be it in the streets of Berlin or backstage in New York, you must treat me as a stranger. The French Embassy must never be linked with your escape.'

There are times in life when all of us feel small and insignificant. Contemplating the time, money and vast array of people who'd been involved in getting me out of East Berlin, I knew I couldn't be as insignificant as I'd often felt. While the powers that be in both the East and the West may consider me a pawn in a bigger game, I was simultaneously a more precious piece in other's games. My mother, my brother, the World on Ice company. All of these had been involved and none of them had anything but my own personal and professional best interests.

I said farewell to Cedric and thanked him for all he had done. Horst explained that he would be departing as he'd arrived, through a back exit that wound its way towards a French run shop a block away. No passer-by working for the East was ever going to see a Frenchman in Horst's proudly German home. Once again, all part of an illusion. Horst himself was known in the East for his role in aiding and abetting escapees, but it was critical that who he was working with and for, remained secret.

I would be forever indebted to all who had assisted my escape. My repayment was to stay silent and to follow instructions. There was no question that I would be doing both things to the letter.

14

17 March 2020

AMBER

After my best night of sleep since arriving in Berlin, it was mid-morning before I got out of bed. On afternoon shift I have no opportunity to do much after I finish, so any exploration of the city I do, comes before work. My slow start to the day meant that today's discoveries would be limited.

For everything that Berlin has to offer, it will always be known for the Wall, and everything associated with it. On my fifth full day in the city, it seemed remiss that I was yet to see anything of the Wall. I was rectifying that now, with a walk down to the East Side Gallery.

I hadn't realised how close I'd been staying to the Wall. Every time I had walked to the Warschauer Straße station, I would only have needed to walk another five minutes and I'd have seen it. This time I did and was soon at the river facing two choices. I was at the start of the famed section of the Wall, but my attention was grabbed by the amazing looking Oberbaum Bridge. I didn't have a huge amount of time, but enough I figured, to walk across the bridge and back before walking the length of the gallery.

Walls divide. Bridges unite. The Oberbaum Bridge had been both. In the divided era, the bridge was effectively part of the Wall, a checkpoint existing along it, but only for use by West Berlin residents crossing to the East. Now it linked Friedrichshain, where I am staying, with

Kreuzberg, one of the trendier suburbs of Berlins inner south. The two suburbs now form a single borough, a classic example of how the city has celebrated unity.

While trains run on the upper deck of the bridge, down below is a pedestrian path alongside the dual carriage road. Halfway along, I stopped to appreciate the view down the Spree towards the TV tower and the main heart of the city before turning back and admiring the bridge. It was built in the 19th century and features two gothic style towers that look like the city gates that you find in many old European cities.

I was tempted to continue on and wander through Kreuzberg but as I got to the end of the bridge, I decided that was best left for another day. I'd come for the East Side Gallery and to leave myself sufficient time to see it all, I needed to head back.

There are sections of the Wall that were left standing in various spots around Berlin, but the East Side Gallery is far and away the largest of these. Stretching more than a kilometre, this section of the wall had murals painted on by more than a hundred artists from around the world. Although not the largest outdoor gallery in the world, the history surrounding it makes it arguably the most significant.

Without a drop of paint, the Wall presented history, but brought to life with the array of art that was now upon it, there was something special about the East Side Gallery. It didn't offer the protection to the art that most galleries did, and in the spirit of the Wall when it surrounded West Berlin, much of this section has graffiti impacting the original artworks. The first mural was a combined Palestinian and German flag, with the Star of David between them. There was a whole lot of text on the side which unfortunately I couldn't understand, but I assume the divergence of images was a warning of division, the Star of David representing both the oppressed in the Second World War and the oppressors in modern Palestine. Regardless of who is wrong and who is right, surely the past provides stark enough lessons that they don't get repeated. Division and physical barriers are never the way forward.

A similar theme recurred across many murals. Messages of unity and peace were at the heart of much of the art, but variety did exist. Shortly after the start, I saw the most famous of all works on the gallery, the kiss between Leonid Brezhnev and Erich Honecker. Since arriving in Berlin, this image seemed omnipresent. It was a painting that reproduced a famous photo taken of the political leaders of the Soviet Union and East Germany, locked in a fraternal kiss at the 30th anniversary of the foundation of the German Democratic Republic. The image was reproduced on t-shirts, coffee cups and every other imaginable souvenir, and in the city centre it was rare to walk far before seeing it yet again. I had no idea why the image was so iconic. The original photo captured it at an exact moment and angle that it looked more passionate than such a kiss would be expected, but so what?

'My God, help me to survive this deadly love,' said a man who had seen the confused look on my face as I tried to interpret the text accompanying the painting. There was Russian text above it and a line in German at the bottom, and while I had the general gist, I appreciated the clarification.

'Thank you,' I said. The look on my face may have been just as confused as I contemplated the words, for he continued.

'Love isn't meant to be deadly, right? The relationship we had with the Soviet Union had the element of love and death. The Soviet support was critical to East Germany, but it came at a very high price. The quality of life on this side of the Wall was so far behind the West as the Soviets ensured that any resource of value went towards war reparations. The people suffered, those who could fled, and in many cases paid with their lives. The propaganda told us that the Soviets were our saviours, but the reality didn't quite match that.'

'You were an East Berliner?'

'No. I was East German, but from Dresden. I am just on holidays, but I have been here many times. It was no different at home to here, but when you can see your neighbours living a different life, the impact seems so much greater. In Dresden we only knew one reality. In East Berlin, a different life was in view, rising above the Wall.'

The man was middle-aged, too young to have known pre-war Germany, but old enough to have lived through most of the divided era. I thanked him again for his insight as he continued his walk, headed towards the point of the gallery where I had started.

I stopped and looked for a long time at one painting, titled Curriculum Vitae. It had every year from 1961 to 1989 painted across it, and a red rose for each person killed trying to cross the wall within each year. I noticed that there were ten roses across 1963, the year Marta escaped. How grateful I am that there wasn't eleven.

The painting also has a poignant reference at the bottom. East German refugees had triggered the building of the Wall, while East German refugees also eventually triggered its fall. The human reaction to a crisis often creates a different and greater crisis. When typing a document, we click the undo button, and it is as though the error was never made. In life, past mistakes carry a permanent reminder, with scars that never heal.

One of the paintings featured a representation from the Pink Floyd film, *The Wall*. While that was the story of isolation that didn't directly relate to the structure in this city, it inevitably was linked here. A concert version was held soon after the Wall fell, so it was a natural fit for this gallery.

Some of the murals were less obvious in their references to the history. While most had a focus on Berlin, the Wall and the themes of unity and peace, some stood out for their aesthetics and could have been placed anywhere else with the same impact. Perhaps I just wasn't up to the interpretation in some cases.

Eventually the art changed to advertising and without realising it, the backdrop was no longer the infamous concrete structure, but deserted buildings that stood adjacent. I was past the end of the longest remaining section of the Wall.

The era of division will never be forgotten. As much as history books can tell the story, this form of representation tells the story in a more confronting way. Many of the works didn't resonate with me, but isn't that life? We all respond differently to each way a story gets told. The fact this gallery ensures that some people learn the reality of the times, justifies its retention. I don't need to have seen this to have an understanding, for living in this city for any period of time ensures it, but when the lessons are important enough, they should be taught in every possible way.

I had time to return to the hostel before work, walking back past the Mercedes-Benz Arena. If they were fifty years younger, this would be where Henry and Marta performed in Berlin. It was a modern entertainment centre that hosted sport and concerts, now the main indoor arena of the city. I saw banners promoting coming events, though I wondered if these would take place given the issues with the virus. Now wasn't the time to worry about that. I was intent on getting ready and making my way to work early. The best entertainment available to me was the stories from my two favourite residents, so why not make the most of the opportunity.

***

Henry and Marta were locked in a slanging match as I walked into their room.

'What is the problem, Henry?' I knew he was more likely the cause, but he was also the one who most needed an ally. By staying on his good side, I felt I was better placed to be helping Marta.

'My bloody wife is a constant problem.'

'Is that so?'

'Doesn't give me a moments peace.'

'Do you want me to take her outside. I can take her around the block, get some fresh air, give you some peace.'

'Hell no. She isn't getting any perks that I don't get.'

'You want her at your side?'

'Of course.'

'But she is so painful.'

'Don't you dare say a bad word about her.'

All my time working in aged care had taught me a little psychology. People like Henry would be constantly looking for a fight, and their poor wives would be the easiest target. The moment they perceived the slightest semblance of an attack against their wife from anyone else, they would turn around and defend their loved one to the hilt. It was only then that their true feelings would be on display.

'I think you're an incredibly lucky man to have her, don't you?'

'You know life is all about balance. All the suffering of old age is what I get for all the good luck I've had in life.'

'And what is the best luck you've had in life?'

'Marta, of course. My wife, and my life. The day I met Marta I became the luckiest man in the world, and I'm willing to put up with every bit of shit this world has in store for me. Doesn't mean I won't complain, but even after all these years, she is still my reason for living.'

In one moment, Henry had redeemed himself. The constant complaining, and the outdated attitudes may be part of who he was now, but underneath it all was someone capable of delivering one of the sweetest explanations of his love and gratitude that I had ever heard.

'I'd love to hear how it all began.'

15

28 June 1964

HENRY

'Who is that?' I asked Des as my eyes locked onto a spectacular set of legs belonging to someone on the ice. With so many new cast members, my attention was being spiked constantly, but nobody had my attention as strongly as this.

'I don't know, but I'm sure you will make it your business to know before too long.'

We had arrived in Bremen ahead of our fourth season of World on Ice, but the first back in Europe. The company had its base here, and most of the cast had been here for six weeks of rehearsals. A new season meant a new show as well as many new cast members. The Victors performance was a piece of around five minutes early in the second act of the show. Unrelated to the main show, we'd been able to do our own rehearsing when and where it suited. Our arrival in Bremen was only a few days before the first full dress rehearsal which required us on sight, predominantly to know our places for the finale.

The previous few months had been a whirlwind. We'd done the Ed Sullivan show in New York back in February. I was sitting in the green room having a coffee. I was never keen to get into costume too early, but Des was already preparing in the dressing room. An Englishman joined me, asking if I was an acrobat.

'Yeah, that's right.'

'I saw you a few years ago in Hamburg. Really enjoyed your show.'

'You've got a good memory. You're on the show tonight?'

'Yes.'

'What's your act.'

'I play guitar. I'm George'

'Henry' I said shaking his hand before it finally clicked who he was. I dropped my head and apologised that I hadn't recognised a Beatle. They were playing several songs on the show, which would have a couple of significant impacts for Des and me. Firstly, we were guaranteed to be performing for the biggest audience we'd ever had. That said, when anyone reflected on the show, they weren't likely to be remembering us, whatever we did. Beatlemania was an unparalleled phenomenon and everyone else on the show tonight would fade into obscurity for the many millions of viewers across America.

We did a perfect routine but the warm reception we received was more likely the excitement of what was to follow us than a deep appreciation for our work. It appeared insignificant compared to the screams that greeted the Beatles, before, during and after their performance. We ended up meeting all the band, having a few drinks after the show. In our line of work, meeting famous people wasn't unusual, so the experience probably meant less to us than it would to most other people. When relaying the story to Pam, the woman I was seeing at the time, her anger at missing out on the experience proved that. She'd wanted to come to New York with us, but I told her our bookings were fixed for just Des and me. When we returned to the company, Pam had already taken off back to her Florida home and I never saw her again. To be fair, that was destined to happen soon enough anyway.

At the end of the tour, we holidayed in Spain and Portugal with Des's partner Barbara and my new girlfriend Sarah. The plan was to be combining holidays and rehearsing, but there was very little rehearsing done in the first few weeks. By that time, I no longer had a girlfriend, the excesses of my behaviour driving Sarah away. Without the distraction of company, I was ready to increase our preparations for the new show, but Des was still in the mode of celebrating freedom.

Back at work and single, my first attempt at chatting up this glamorous figure skater got nothing more than an instant snub, so still not knowing who she was, I relied on a third party to get my first insight into her.

'Strike out with Marta, eh Skippy,' Collins said. Derek Collins was a Canadian skater who had been with the company far longer than us. Derek and I got along well even though the name Skippy pissed me off. I used to call him Maple Leaf, but when that didn't bother him, I always referred to him by his surname. His father had been in the military, and that background seemed to trigger a frustration with me calling him Collins.

'What's her story?

'Marta Roloff,' Collins said. 'Former national champion skater in East Germany. Defected earlier this year and the company picked her up. Next week will be her debut for a Western company. Probably focussed so much on that and on avoiding the Stasi that you could be any man on earth, and she'd still be ignoring you.'

'So, she snubs everybody?'

'Nah, she's alright. Maybe she's heard enough about you and feels like she needs to avoid you. She also doesn't speak much English, so maybe she didn't understand what you'd said. She would have had reason to expect the worst from you, so probably assumed accordingly.'

We left Bremen for the first dates of the tour in Hamburg, and by this stage I was getting the occasional bit of eye contact and acknowledgement from Marta, but nothing to suggest that there were any prospects of us becoming closer. She intrigued me enough that I wasn't going to write off the chances too soon, but I also wasn't going to devote too much focus to her.

Ask most men in their early twenties why they want to be entertainers and the answer is simple. Women. The money was good, seeing the world was fantastic, but that was all secondary and it was the constant stream of beautiful women that made my lifestyle ideal. There were always women, and the ease with which I'd find another, made me take this for granted. Once you take people for granted it rarely follows that you treat them well. I don't think I was ever too bad, but I can understand those who ran away. I used women for sex, they used me for my status. In most cases we deserved each other.

The after-show partying was as much a part of the entertainment business as the show itself. A few years into our career, we were veterans of the scene enough to be at the centre of whatever was going on. Marta was a different story. She'd grown up in the strict discipline of the East, and it was the professional career path that had seen her move to the West. She retained the principles of her upbringing, and steered clear of the post-show celebrations, looking after herself to ensure she was at her best the following day, ready to work harder on developing the perfection in her performance.

Early in the season I got a bit of an update. She did know me, just unfortunately she knew me as "*the rude and arrogant American acrobat.*" Before too long I managed enough contact with her to get my reputation upgraded to "*the rude and arrogant Australia acrobat.*" It didn't augur any better for me, but if nothing else, she at least knew one extra thing about me.

When anyone is exposed closely enough to an environment, there tends to be influence spreading both ways. The environment can adapt in some small way to the individual, but the individual will adapt far more to their environment. The other women in the chorus drew her into the social circle. She began going out after the shows, and bit by bit she learnt that life in showbusiness wasn't purely about dedication to the craft. Those who made it worked hard, but that didn't mean there was another side of life to make the most of.

Marta started seeing me differently with time, developing strong respect for the work ethic that had me on the ice just as much as she was. Neither of us confined our training routines to what was demanded of us. We were both driven by a desire to perfect our skills and would never stop short of what we could do through a lack of work. She admired this, even if she was quick to mock my relative awkwardness on the ice. To be fair, she was one of the world's most elegant ice skaters, while I was incredibly limited. Our routines were dependent on confidence. Doing them on ice when it was so foreign to us had been an incredible test. I think my ability to do that was admirable, but to a purist like Marta, it was comical.

Our routine was designed to entertain, and comedy was as important as the spectacular. As Marta had been amused by our clumsiness, we began to accentuate this within the routine. We had initially tried to work as closely as possible to our original stage performances, but this element of working on ice had given the potential for a new angle. Our act wasn't dependent on it, for it was our balancing work that remained the memorable component to the Victors, but anything that would earn the appreciation of the crowds gave us an edge. The complex acrobatic elements seem more dangerous and more impressive when just standing upright couldn't be taken for granted.

As Marta began spending more time socialising, she began to see more of me. Having always been the life of the party, I was beginning to hold back just a little to give a more sensible impression to Marta, while she began coming out of her shell a little more with time. She still spurned my advances, yet it began to seem more like that was an act. Eventually I broke her defences, and she was ready to give me a chance. We began dating in late 1964. As uncertain as she always claimed she had been, she fell for me quickly.

Marta was a strong and tough woman. She had escaped from East Germany in the most amazing circumstances and had been ready and willing to leave her family and friends forever more to do this. She missed them greatly, but never regretted the decision she made. It typified who she was, that she could be simultaneously crushed in spirit yet display a solid nature that hid those feelings from the world. I slowly began seeing more of what was within her and not only did I admire it, but I also felt it change me. The man who'd been known for having a girl in every city was now completely happy to be settled with the same woman in every city.

We did have challenges. Marta and I were both quite dominant personalities, so when we had a disagreement, it ended up blowing into a genuine fight. As per the contracts we had with the company, we still had our own hotel rooms throughout the tour, and it proved to be that we often needed them. As a skater in the chorus, Marta was often in a different hotel. We'd share my room, but we were always on the edge of a fight that would see her storming back to her base. Ironically, these fights seemed to strengthen our relationship. We had something special, but it was simultaneously highly volatile.

We had planned a holiday in the Caribbean for the end of the season, but after the worst fight we'd had, the last thing either of us could bare was the thought of being with each other another minute. She flew to Paris with a few of the other girls from the chorus, while I headed to Spain ready to forget her and party as hard as possible, considering this the ultimate cure to getting her out of my head and my heart. It always had worked for me in the past, but the greatest clue of how life had changed through my time with Marta was how completely un-satisfying my time in Spain felt. Marta had apparently felt the same way, and within a week we met up in Marseilles, the memories of the fight virtually non-existent. Several years would pass before we again spent a week apart. I knew then that this was it.

16

AMBER

There is a fine line between nerves and outright fear. As a naturally nervy person, I find the line is easily crossed. For the past couple of days, I have been nervous about the thought of tonight, but I am way past that now. It is now nothing short of debilitating fear.

This is what I want. People normally pursue what they want without reservation, yet I'd spent the day questioning whether I should back out, such was the tightness in my stomach when I thought of the night ahead. I feared how I'd look, what I'd say, what I'd do depending on how the evening went. The more exciting the thoughts of what may happen, the more scared I got of how I'd fail to cope. It made no sense, but I couldn't shake it.

Around the world, there could be a million people going on first dates tonight, but I took no solace from the relative insignificance of my situation. It meant enough to me to render the rest of the world irrelevant in my mind.

Greta pursued me. She showed the interest, so I shouldn't need to feel afraid. An interest formed in a moment can disappear once a clearer picture emerges, and I was fearful this would be my fate.

A first date is like a job interview. You place your credentials on the table and hope they meet what is being sought. In this instance, I was like a kid out of school being interviewed for a chief executive's job.

I'd been picked by the interviewer, so I needed to believe I belonged, however inadequate I felt.

Greta was beautiful and confident. This was probably a standard night for her, but it was a genuine beginning for me. I hated that prospect. Getting anything I want in life, requires passing through steps that I fear. I had to face it. I kept reminding myself that anything worthwhile doesn't come without some form of struggle.

I wasn't going to make a great first impression. Backpacking doesn't leave the scope for a large array of outfits for every occasion. Rather than dressing for the occasion, I, like always, would be dressed for practicality. Jeans and a jumper were the only alternative from what she'd seen me in when we met.

As I boarded the train, my thoughts skipped ahead to the end of the night. What if she invites me home? I was scared that she would, but just as scared that she wouldn't. My entire mindset about this trip was to broaden my horizons and take chances rather than avoiding them, but as soon as the opportunity has arisen, it's terrified me. It doesn't matter how much you tell yourself you want to change, it doesn't happen easily.

There was a voice inside my head that told me to stay on the train as we arrived at Alexanderplatz, but the louder voice made me alight and follow through as planned. I was early, which I'd decided was essential given the uncertainty of the exact meeting spot, but the downside was that it gave more time for the anxiety to build. Had I overplayed this in my head far too much? I was new to this, could I have misjudged the situation? Was it a date? How could I be sure it wasn't just two new friends catching up for a drink? I needed to compose myself and let the night play out whichever way it does.

It was still a couple of minutes to seven when I saw her. As she saw me walking towards her on the steps in front of the fountain, she stood and smiled. Every bit as beautiful as what I remembered from the train.

'Sorry, I hope I'm not late,' I said despite knowing that I wasn't.

'No, I was early. Too keen for my own good, right.' She kissed me on the cheek, nothing more than a standard European greeting. 'You look great.'

'You do too.' I wasn't sure if that was the right thing to say. She looked amazing, but I sure as hell didn't, so I wondered if it was a cynical comment from her. If so, my response could have come across inappropriately. Thankfully, her smile said otherwise.

'So, what do you say we go for a drink. We can work out dinner options from there.'

'Sure.' It hadn't mattered what she suggested, the response would have been the same. I would love to have the ability to be decisive and take the lead, but that had never been me. Now was most certainly not the time to begin. I preferred the idea of leaving everything in Greta's hands, and at this stage it seemed like she was comfortable taking that role too.

We made our way to a cocktail bar which was the perfect place. Just enough atmosphere to be able to fill any awkward silences, but little enough noise to not inhibit conversation. There was enough on their menu that I would have been happy to stay here to eat. Wanting to avoid the view that I couldn't think for myself, I offered this as a suggestion, and she agreed.

There was an awkwardness I felt sitting across the table from her. I struggled to hold her gaze, looking down every time she looked at me. I could easily lose myself in her blue eyes, but I couldn't envisage her seeing the same beauty in me that I saw in her. As we ate, I captured every opportunity to take in as much of her as I could. The tiny slithers of food that she placed on her fork before raising it to her mouth and quickly digesting each bite before returning to the glass and taking another sip. Whatever intoxication I felt from the alcohol was secondary, for I was getting drunk on the company.

'Do you feel like dancing?'

'Sure.' It wasn't my thing at all, but I was maintaining my commitment to following Greta's lead.

We walked out into the brisk evening, and she recommended we head to Kreuzberg, which she said was the best part of Berlin's nightlife.

'It's a half-hour walk if you have the energy, or we can get a cab.'

'I'm happy to walk off the food and drinks. No better way to see more of the city than on foot.'

It wasn't so much the city I wanted to know better, and I felt that before we ended up in a loud club, it would be good to walk and talk without distraction. We walked along Alexanderstaße, crossing the River Spree, and as we rushed across the road to beat the traffic, she grabbed my hand to make sure I moved in sync with her. It was perfect. No need to think, just allowing the moment to happen.

The neighbourhoods we walked through were full of diversity, and the people out on the streets seemed to reflect all walks of life. I didn't want to make eye-contact with anyone, fearful of the judgement that some might have in seeing me walking hand in hand with another woman. Why should I be? Greta had no fear, and that confidence was part of her allure. I wanted to be like that. I couldn't be everything she is, but I don't know if that's necessary. Her confidence doesn't come from a belief of being better than anyone, it's from being proud of who she is. That much is something I can aspire to.

As we got to Oranienplatz, a small square a few blocks from our destination, she turned to me and pulled me close. Whatever concerns I may have had about the judgement of others flew away as she kissed me. I felt like I was melting on the spot.

'You've never kissed a woman before, have you.'

'I'm sorry.'

She chuckled. 'Don't be sorry. I feel very privileged.'

She kissed me again before we moved on, walking along Oranien-straße until arriving at a small bar. It didn't look that appealing, but I didn't care. I didn't envisage staying too long, for it was clear we were both already thinking about the next stage of the night. We had a drink at the bar before stepping on to the dancefloor together. I can't imagine how awkward and uncoordinated I looked. It didn't matter, for I was lost in Greta's eyes. As far as my focus lay, there could just as easily not be another soul in the club.

A slower song came on, and she pulled me in closer. I felt her breath on my skin and with it a feeling that excited me more than I'd ever known. Displaying this in a public location was both frightening and alluring. As much as I knew this was a safe place, stepping into the unknown never comes without apprehension, but this was being drowned out by the passion of the moment.

'You want to go somewhere quieter?' she said.

'I would.'

'Why don't we go back to my place?'

'Yes.'

I didn't care about the unfinished drink I'd left on the table. I wanted to be alone with her, and I didn't want to waste a moment.

She organised a rideshare car to pick us up. We sat in the back together, and as she stretched out her arm, her hand found mine. It was less than ten minutes until we were at her place, an apartment in Reuterkiez just across the road from Hermannplatz.

It was a beautiful apartment, elaborately decorated and furnished, and I wondered how someone of her age could afford such a place. She had a casual job in a supermarket, yet her home looked more in-keeping with the model I believed she could have been.

'Gorgeous place. You live here on your own?'

'Yes. Would you like a glass of wine?'

'Um, sure if you're having one.'

She disappeared to the kitchen as I took in my surrounds. As nice as it all was, there was little evidence of her personality on display. No photos, no personal effects, but I guess that stood out to me due to my home having always been quite opposite.

Greta returned with two glasses of white and sat close to me despite the size of the lounge.

'When you look forward to something, it often fails to live up to your hopes, but tonight has been just what I hoped it would be,' she said.

'I feel the same.'

'I'd been worried you wouldn't turn up.'

I sensed a redness start to show in my cheeks and confessed that there had been a moment of uncertainty.

'Not that I didn't want to. Just, I don't know, nerves.'

'Nerves aren't a bad thing. You're only nervous about something if you really want it. I'm nervous now.' This wasn't reflected in her actions, as she leaned in confidently and kissed me. We wouldn't have reached this stage if she had anything to be nervous about. I am certain she knew that as sure as she would lead, I would follow.

Despite all my fears, I couldn't feel more alive.

17

14 April 1966

MARTA

Despite all my fears, I couldn't feel more alive.

Experience had taught me that seeing loved ones was something that couldn't be taken for granted. I didn't know whether I'd ever see my parents again, but there was no such issue other than distance and expense stopping me from a reunion with my brother. Henry understood my desperation for a reunion and paid for our trip at the start of the break between seasons.

As we prepared for the trip, my excitement began to devolve into anxiety. It had been such a long time since I'd seen any of my family. Would the bond from our childhood remain? Would he be angry that I'd left our mother to a lonely future? He'd told me it was the right thing to do, but would time have changed that view?

We were due for a major change in our lives after this trip. Several months ago, The Victors had signed on to the American tour of World on Ice for 1966/67. While my two-year contract with the European tour had been completed, I felt a loyalty to those who aided my escape.

'It's just as good an opportunity for you as it is for us,' Henry said. 'You always told me you wanted to work in the States.'

'But I still owe the company here.'

'It's the same company. You wouldn't be leaving them, just moving to a different part of it.'

Ernst Thelan was the European tour manager. When Horst had accompanied me from Berlin to Bremen after my escape, it was Ernst who became responsible for me. It was public knowledge that I had come from East Berlin, but all the details of how this had happened remained in the strictest of confidences. Only Ernst was aware of the whole story, having been involved in the plan from its initial formation. As uncomfortable as it made me, I asked him about the prospects of transferring to the American company.

'Once we finish this season you are a free woman. If you do want to go to the States, I can organise a transfer. Of course, I would love you to stay, but I know there are other factors involved,' he said, in reference to my relationship status. 'If you do stay, there will be more solo work next season. As the new kid on the block over there, the Americans are going to have you at the back of the line.'

As important as developing my career was, Henry had become the central figure in my life. I didn't have faith in our ability to make a long-distance relationship work, so I knew that if I didn't follow him to America, it would be the end of us. When confirmation of a place in the American tour came through, the decision was easy. Henry hadn't made me any promises, but he was determined that I join them in America. Whether it was the best decision for me professionally, love was more important.

Prior to the American season, the company was doing a tour of the Far East, including Henry's homeland of Australia. The Victors had never performed professionally in Australia, and though the show wasn't visiting his hometown of Adelaide, they'd both been excited to participate. While their act would be headlining, there was no place for Barbara or I to be performing in the modified version of the main show. We weren't required to report to headquarters in America until September, meaning we were free to join our men for the tour. Henry and Des were due to report in Tokyo in May, leaving us with just a few weeks break. Henry was determined to make the most of it and insisted that visiting my brother was the best thing we could do.

Lars met us at the airport, and although neither of us were generally great at showing emotions, the excitement we both felt seeing each other after more than five years of separation was overwhelming. We ran into each other's arms and Henry must have wondered if I was quite the strong unemotional woman he'd come to know over the past couple of years.

Henry and Lars hit it off immediately. Lars was an amateur body-builder, and for the bottom man in an acrobatic duo, Henry saw a deep connection in his own regime to that which Lars followed. For all the discipline both showed towards their craft, it didn't limit their ability to party hard, and for our entire time in South Africa, their workouts were secondary to their long drinking sessions.

A week into our stay, Lars had to head to Port Elizabeth for a couple of days. I wanted to join him, but he insisted we'd be better off spending that time on our own exploring more of the beauty of Cape Town. As a trio, we'd done little sightseeing, spending most of our time on the beaches and in the bars. He gave us a list of sites to see, most notably Table Mountain.

'I only came here for your sake,' Henry said, 'but I couldn't be happier that I did. Not only do I love the place, but getting to know your brother has been amazing. I feel I know you better through know-ing him.'

'I feel I know myself better through being reminded of where I've come from. Family makes us, and he's more a part of me than anyone.'

'He's going to be a perfect brother-in-law,' he said as he got down on one knee and took a box from his pocket. 'That is of course provided you say yes. Marta, will you marry me?'

I didn't have to think at all. My decision to follow him to America was based on a belief that he was the one, and formalising it was exactly what I wanted. The man who I'd been told couldn't be tamed was ready to commit.

High above the city, the view of Cape Town was as stunning as you'd find anywhere in the world. Following Henry's proposal, it felt like I was floating above the world. The trip to South Africa had been designed to rekindle the past but had ended up as a precursor to my future. The joys of freedom that had begun with my arrival in the West had become far more special than I had ever imagined.

'Anything happen while I was away?' Lars said on his return. He hadn't been to Port Elizabeth but had given us the time to ourselves knowing what Henry had planned. He was incredibly excited for me, and with the strength of his rapport with Henry, he was certain I'd made the right decision.

'I never had an intention of travelling to America, but I will make an exception for your wedding,' he said.

'We're getting married there?' Following the overwhelming joy of the proposal, Henry and I hadn't discussed a wedding. I had no desire for anything more than simplicity.

'Most likely. It's going to be home soon enough, so why not?'

I hadn't thought of America as being home. I always envisaged it was a base for a time, but I wanted to believe we'd eventually settle in a free and unified Berlin. Whether such a Berlin would ever exist was uncertain. I had to accept that what matters in life is not where you are, but who you are with. If I was with Henry, where we lived wasn't important. Beyond that, if Lars would be there for our special day, that would take care of my only wish for the wedding.

***

Three weeks later after the first show in Japan, I realised how wrong it was to believe that perfection in life could ever be more than fleeting. A telegram came through from South Africa. Lars had gone to Port Elizabeth for a bodybuilding contest. On the highway headed back to Cape Town, he had been in a head-on collision. He was killed instantly. I was born surrounded by horror during World War II, but this was the first time I had ever been so directly impacted by tragedy. My brother, my hero, so recently returned to my life, killed in his prime.

18

19 March 2020

AMBER

The natural light of mid-morning seeped through the gaps in the curtains and allowed me to feast on the sight of her naked body as she walked towards the bathroom. I was awake, but only felt certain after pinching myself and realising it wasn't a dream. None of it had been, yet the past sixteen hours had been more idyllic than I thought reality could deliver.

I was working this afternoon, so the fantasy was about to end, or at least be put on hold temporarily. As much as I hated that thought, I wanted last night to be the beginning of a new reality. Of course, it could never be recaptured in quite the same way. The nervousness that ran through me made every moment more exhilarating. There can be ways of making anything better with experience, but there is nothing that comes close to the adrenalin of the unknown. That memory, more than anything, is what I will hold on to.

'What time do you have to go?' Greta asked as she walked back into the bedroom.

'I probably should already be gone. Soon though.' I'd done the calculations of how long I'd need, knowing I had to go back to the hostel before I went to work. Whatever natural urges I had to elongate my stay had to be overcome. My responsibility came first. I'd see Greta again soon enough, but trouble at work would compromise my stay in Berlin.

When she climbed back into bed and asked if I could call in sick, it was difficult to say no. I stayed strong, and she accepted it after providing one last temptation with a long kiss.

After organising a ride-share service back to the hostel, we made plans for tomorrow. I wasn't working until the overnight shift, so Greta said she'd show me more of the offbeat parts of the city. This is the great advantage of travelling once you know locals. The greatest examples of the real city can't be found in brochures, but in the backstreets, and it is only a local who can cut a swathe through to deliver you the best of it.

She came to the door and gave me one last passionate kiss, and the whirlwind of emotions that had filled last night and this morning came to its inevitable end. That was fine by me, for we'd be back together this time tomorrow.

*

'You look happy,' Henry said as I walked into my favourite resident's room early in my shift. 'Did you get lucky?'

Was I that easy to read? I could feel myself starting to blush, so I had to deflect the comment somehow.

'I'm always happy Henry, you know that.'

'You don't always go that red though, so I reckon I'm on to something.'

'Leave her alone Henry,' Marta said, jumping to my defence. 'He gets jealous. He needs to think back too many years to remember when he was capable of that.' She was as sure of what I'd been up to as what her husband had been, even if she was less inclined to seek information on it.

I was comfortable with myself. Well, to some extent I was, but I was still fearful of judgement and had no intention of telling Henry and Marta about Greta. Even if my blushes gave too much away, there was a limit to what I'd tell them. I appreciate them both, and I don't want that dynamic to change, so in the circumstances I feel like less is more.

They've had such fascinating lives that I want to be listening to them, not telling my comparatively insignificant stories.

Last night may have been the greatest leap forward I've ever had in becoming the person I believe I am meant to be, but it is a personal step. These two have had moments that tie into history, culture and the attention of the masses. Whatever the magnitude last night carried to me, it is something that only one other person can ever appreciate.

'What was this guy's name?' Henry was refusing to let up.

'Henry. He's an old guy in a nursing home who doesn't know how to behave himself. Asks too many questions and ignores all the directions he's ever given, whether by his wife or the staff. Even his favourite English-speaking Canadian who isn't going to tell you about any other guy.'

'What do I have to look forward to if I can't live vicariously through you?'

'That's *my* job. To listen to your stories and live through them. They are far more exciting than anything that has ever happened in my life.'

'He doesn't let up, does he,' Marta said. 'But he'll fall asleep again in a minute and you'll be spared.'

I had to leave them as the call bell rang from another room. After attending to the resident, I ended up getting a similar grilling from Hannah.

'No need to speak same language. I understand you from your face. If that's not enough, then how often you check your phone is biggest clue.'

Greta and I had sent messages back and forth before I started work, and I hadn't had a response to the last one I'd sent more than an hour ago. It didn't need one, but I think the pull on my heartstrings over the past day had left me with a constant desire for more. Clearly Hannah was wise enough to know what that was all about, but I wasn't up for telling part of the story when I was determined to keep most of it to myself.

'No. Just a whole lot of plans up in the air. The way things keep changing with this virus means it is hard to be sure what tomorrow holds.'

The Coronavirus outbreak was a handy piece of interference. What I had said was true, for every day there seemed to be another step being taken towards restrictions on day-to-day life in the city, just as it was globally. The local government had today announced plans for a thousand bed hospital specifically for COVID-19 patients on the grounds of Messe-Berlin. Numbers aren't that high here, but clearly all the forecasting points to it becoming catastrophic before too long. Other parts of Germany have brought in numerous strict regulations, but we so far have avoided that.

One thing that has changed, in our workplace at least, is the banning of visitors. To an extent that makes life easier, particularly for me with my inability to communicate easily with them, but there are times when visiting family assist the residents and therefore reduce the demands on us. Now there seems to be diminishing downtime on each shift.

Starker impacts on us were coming, as I learned when Frida came to see me during my break. She'd already spoken to all the staff at the beginning of the shift but wanted to be certain I'd understood. All being spoken in German, I hadn't, but part of the gist had been explained by Hannah as the day at gone on.

'Vart you do on your time is your business, but if it impacts verk, it is an issue,' she said. *'Vartever the restrictions are, ve need all staff to protect themselves. Please vear masks venever you are in contact vith other people.'*

I hadn't worn masks anywhere but work and on public transport. The reduced numbers of people in most surrounds had made it seem irrelevant, but I understood the reasoning. As much as nursing home protocols can vary from home to home, city to city and country to country, the impact of viral infections is universal. The residents are all particularly vulnerable, and while most places have had to face these issues with colds and flus as a matter of course, this new virus was impacting to a whole new level.

I agreed to her request. She continued by saying that if at any stage I had even the slightest symptoms, I was not to come to work. As this instruction was explicitly conveyed to all staff, it meant the likelihood of absenteeism was very high, and they would only be able to survive the impending period with additional flexibility shown by all staff.

'V*e vill need people verking longer shifts and at times verking with limited breaks between shifts. From tomorrow ve vill have two twelve-hour shifts. These cover one and a half standard shifts. You're on tomorrow night from 10pm until 6am, but under the current situation, you may be called to start at 6pm, or to verk through until 10am the next morning.'*

'Really?'

'It is only a precaution if ve are down too many staff. Ve hope not to put anyone on for these additional hours, but ve need everyone prepared. It shouldn't happen tomorrow, as ve are unaffected at this stage. If it does, I vill pick others first. Just understand, this could change at any time.'

She saw the look on my face, that once again was easy to read. I needed the work to pay for my travels, so more hours would normally be welcome. Full-time work was enough to achieve this. I had a city I wanted to explore. More importantly, I had a special person I wanted to spend as much time as possible with. As easily as I dropped into the fantasy, I knew that it was unlikely to turn into anything greater, but I wanted to make the most of what it was for now. I didn't want work making that impossible, but I understood the bigger picture, and knew I had to fit in with their needs.

'Hopefully this never becomes necessary. Ve have got through the difficulties of vinter unscathed this year, but ve need to be prepared for vartever this new virus gives us. We cannot let it get into the home.'

I got back to work determined to keep busy so I could avoid thinking any more about the possible compromises in store. Time passed quickly, and before I'd had a chance to get back to Marta and Henry, there was only half an hour left on my shift.

'You're still awake,' I said, surprised to see both sets of eyes focus on me as I walked back into their room.

'Sleep, wake, sleep, wake. At this point our bodies don't care whether it's day or night, they just do what they want when they want.'

'Your body does nothing you want,' Marta said.

Henry gave his standard groan of disapproval, however much he knew she was right.

His mobile phone was sitting on the edge of his bed, just out of reach. As I picked it up, I could see that he had missed a couple of calls. Based on everything I'd learnt so far, I was surprised there had been anyone trying to contact him.

'My sister. I still speak to her a few times every week. A world apart yet we still have that closeness. Do you have any brothers or sisters?'

'One brother, Craig. Even when we were living in the same city we probably didn't speak that much.'

'The older we get, the more we depend on those who knew us when we were young. You might find the relationship with your brother gets stronger over time.'

'Maybe.'

'Lorraine and I are a wonder of genetics. So opposite, yet that same upbringing has given us a connection that has always been strong enough to cope with the differences and the distance.'

19

10 July 1966

HENRY

This is the first time I've played professionally in Australia. Our show is a novelty down here, unlike the staple it is in the entertainment industries of America and Europe. The lack of exposure the Australians get to such shows is helping to make us stand out and generate strong ticket sales. Des and I have featured heavily in the marketing campaigns. Although we're far more unknown here than overseas, the ability to refer to us as locals helps generate interest. A couple of days ago we did a photo shoot on the roof of the Southern Cross Hotel in Melbourne. Des was more than a little nervous, but he couldn't complain when he saw the front page of yesterday's newspaper, with me holding him aloft over the ledge, fifty metres above Exhibition Street.

We are only playing Sydney and Melbourne, but I have got a brief opportunity to head home to Adelaide. After doing two shows yesterday, Des, Barbara, Marta and I have spent the night driving to Adelaide as today is my sister's wedding day.

Lorraine is eighteen months my senior and has been in many ways the most important person in my life. She couldn't be more different to me, yet we were very much a team. I was always in trouble growing up which strained the relationships I had with my parents, but Lorraine was the one person who was always on my side. As different as our lives have become as adults, this much hasn't changed. She spent a year in

London while I was working in Europe, and we caught up as much as possible before we got her a backroom job with World on Ice, and she toured for another year with us. It wasn't her world, and she headed back to Australia in 1961. Although it had been five years since I've seen her, we've never lost that closeness.

When Marta got the news of her brother's death six weeks ago, it brought the importance of my sister closer to home. With every tear Marta shed, the stories that followed of their childhood reminded me of the relationship Lorraine and I had. I feel sorry for siblings that don't have this. When you've learnt the fundamental essence of life together, it should be a connection that never breaks. Distance had altered the relationship, but never broken it. The tragedy of Lars had broken Marta's heart, and it had softened mine as I looked forward to seeing Lorraine on the most important day of her life.

Lorraine is marrying a man named Ian. Naturally I have not met him, but I've heard enough from her and from my parents to get a reasonable indication of what to expect. From what it sounds like, Lorraine has searched the world for a man who is the most opposite possible person to me, and in Ian she appears to have found this. She wants children, she wants stability, she wants a house in suburbia behind a picket fence and the stock standard mundane life of middle Australia. I'm sure he'll be the right sort of person to provide this. I probably won't be his cup of tea and he won't be my glass of brandy. Neither of us need to be. Lorraine is the common ground, and all that matters.

It's also a big day for Marta. This will be the first time she meets my parents and Lorraine. We live distant enough lives that I doubt there'll ever be a close bond formed, but there still is a feeling of significance meeting the family of a partner. When Lorraine last saw me, I was still with Judy, a woman from Manchester who I met on tour in the US. We were together for several months, but whether it's the benefit of hindsight that makes me say it now, I never really felt too confident about where that was heading. With Marta it has genuinely felt right all along, despite the fights we've had at times. She is strong willed, just as I am, so there are inevitably moments of conflict, but these pale into insignificance alongside the magic we share.

Having a wedding on a Sunday is almost unheard of here, but Lorraine was desperate to have me there and it was the only way this could be coordinated. We had another fortnight in Australia before more shows in Southeast Asia and then back to the United States. There were no decent breaks in the itinerary, so all we had was Sunday and Monday off, giving us time to drive over.

As excited as I was for Lorraine, I knew the downside of the day was going to be the additional unwanted attention I was going to get. It was more than a decade since I'd been in Adelaide. On Ian's side, everyone would be pointing me out and staring at the novelty value I brought. On my side I'd be dealing with constant bloody harassment from old aunts and cousins who didn't want to know me when they considered me a troublemaking rogue as a teenager. I haven't changed a bit but because I'm now a celebrity troublemaking rogue, they'll all be fascinated.

I didn't know how best to prepare Marta for the day. With Lars recent passing and the inability to see her parents in the East, family was now nothing but a memory for her. While I retain the connection with mine, distance has made them irrelevant to my day-to-day life. Today she has to face them all, plus a whole lot of extras who are connected in various ways. I don't know which one of us will have the greater challenge, but Marta adapts well enough to any type of company that I am sure she will have no problems.

Dad was out the front on our arrival. No doubt he wanted a brief escape from everything going on inside the house. Many years ago, he built a gymnasium in the backyard of the house for teaching acrobatics, and that's where the reception will be this evening. Catering for sixty people in that gym will be a hell of an ordeal and I'm sure he is in no hurry to get back there.

The ceremony is across town at a church in Norwood. We're a Catholic family though you wouldn't know it. Mum believes in blaming

God whenever anything goes wrong but wouldn't put a moments faith in anything beyond that. Dad considers his religion part of an identity rather than a belief. Proudly Catholic, but today will be the first time he's stepped into a church since forcing us to go as children. I wouldn't even call myself Catholic, but Lorraine is the one who still shows the teachings from childhood have stayed with her. Ian isn't Catholic and apparently that nearly stood in the way of the marriage. Not his or her beliefs but the principle of how they'd bring up children when the time came. Lorraine was someone who always sought to avoid fights, but when she stepped up, she always won.

'Here we are,' I said to Marta. 'Welcome to my childhood.'

Marta seemed quite amazed at the size of the place. Growing up in Soviet controlled East Berlin couldn't have been more different to leafy inner suburban Adelaide. Whereas she walked miles to train in her teens, I walked into the backyard. By local standards our house wasn't that special, but it did have enough trimmings of my father's success to allow us a good quality of life that would have seemed incomprehensible to Marta.

It was already a full house on our arrival. It took half an hour for the basic introductions for Marta, particularly through the difficulty some of them had with her accent. Mum was in such an excited state about the day that it was as though all was forgiven with me. Dad focussed more on Marta, I think wanting to talk about the different acts he was working with and where he thought they could end up. He also wanted to learn more about her pathway into the business.

We were driven to the church slightly before Lorraine and the rest of the family. When we got there, I introduced myself to Ian. He was probably entitled to look a nervous wreck at that point, but I don't know how much more assured he would have looked any other time. He fit the image I expected, but I'd save any major evaluations for a more appropriate time and place. When that will be is another question. They are coming to Melbourne for their honeymoon, and we will no doubt see a bit of them over the next week but after that it may be a long time.

I don't see Ian heading to where we're likely to be and I don't see us coming back to Australia anytime soon.

I don't have a negative view of Adelaide or Australia, but it feels like a single bed after you've been sleeping in a king-size. I feel like I've just returned to 1946, only I'm not a child this time. I've outgrown the life that I would have had here, and I don't see how I could step back to it.

'When is our turn, Henry?' Marta asked me as we took our seats in the church.

I knew this was the likely result of us being here. Nothing puts the thought of getting married into a woman's head like being at a wedding. I didn't see the point to marriage. We weren't settling down and our lifestyle was not going to be like a standard married couple. What we would gain by having a marriage certificate seemed inconsequential, but for all of that, I was certain about us as a couple. I had no fear of committing to her for life, hence the proposal. With nobody else in her life in a formal sense, I understood why the status would mean so much to her. I was ready to give her what she wanted.

'You want all of this?' I asked at the end of the ceremony.

'Not this' she said raising her eyes to the people standing in line waiting to give their first greeting to the newly married couple. 'That,' she said, in reference to the newlyweds kissing then stopping and holding up their ceremonial marriage certificate.

I let out a mild groan that typified my responses in these exact situations. She knew what it meant. I was on the same as page as her, but I wasn't willing to admit it. I wasn't going to be deflecting any attention away from my sister on her day, but our day wouldn't be too far away.

One by one the cars departed the church and made the five-mile journey back to our home. Marta and I were in a car with mum and dad at a point in time when I would rather have been alone, but so it needed to be. Tonight, we were not going to be allowed to share a room thanks to the strict archaic attitudes of my mother.

'You can do what you want anywhere else but not in my house,' she said, blissfully unaware of the many teenage girls who I snuck into the same room years earlier. I'd be in that same single bed tonight, with Marta next door in Lorraine's old room. The newlyweds would be staying at a hotel in town tonight before heading to Melbourne tomorrow. They were coming to the show on Wednesday night, and we would be seeing them after the performance.

The reception had its moments. Ian gave a brilliant speech and really went up in my estimations. Maybe I was drunk enough by that stage that it sounded better than it was. I did find it a little exhausting putting on a show for the people who were treating me as a celebrity rather than the brother of the bride. The food was very good. Marta and I eat out in places all around the world, so we've become almost qualified to work as food critics. I could envisage us as restauranteurs once we're too old to perform. That is probably what leaves us paying close attention to every aspect of food service and preparation when we're in environments like these. As good as it was, we both had ideas of how much better we'd have done it.

As the happy couple left for their downtown hotel, the crowds started leaving. Marta and I stayed out back continuing to drink with Des and Barbara. Eventually they were ready to stagger back to their motel a few blocks away. By the time Marta and I were ready to call it a night, we'd forgotten my mother's demands and both of us ended up squeezed into my old bed.

'Our day will be soon, my dear' I said just before drifting to sleep.

'It better be,' she said, 'or you will pay.' I knew she was joking, but there was something serious driving her joke. I bloody well would pay one way or another, but the level of threat in the words suggested a greater price than she actually meant.

***

It couldn't have been simpler. Six weeks after the wedding of my sister and Ian, we were back in the United States at our main base in Knoxville, Tennessee. We organised a date for the registry office downtown. Des and Barbara served as our witnesses, and nobody else was there. It couldn't have been more opposite to the wedding we'd attended in Adelaide, but it was exactly what we wanted. No fuss, no attention, just doing what was required to formalise everything. We both wanted nothing more than a commitment to each other for life.

We spent our wedding night in the apartment we'd moved into just a week earlier, before taking off to Jamaica for our honeymoon. We had less than a week, but it was all we needed. Marta was then into heavy training for the start of the season in late September. In the meantime, Des and I had our biggest ever opportunity. A live appearance on television across America, beamed from New York City. My personal life had just reached the ultimate peak and now my professional life had reached a similar height.

'Thank you. This has been the best day of my life,' she said before drifting off to sleep on our wedding night. As simple as it had been, the commitment to spending forever together meant everything to her. Just two months on from the worst day of her life, it was a reminder that there is always a sense of balance to everything. The world can seem a dark place at times, but it can light up quickly.

20 March 2020

AMBER

I'd sent Greta a message as soon as I got up, hoping that we could maximise our time together by meeting earlier than we had planned. I was meant to be meeting her at a café across the road from her place at midday. I was conscious that my shift could end up starting earlier, and I didn't want to be forced to leave too soon after arriving. When I hadn't got a response from her by 11am, I figured things would be staying as planned. She was working this morning, and clearly didn't have any chance to get back to me.

There wasn't a direct train to Hermanplatz, so I left early enough to ensure I'd have time if I missed a connection. When you are prepared for delays, they rarely eventuate, and this being the case, I arrived with plenty of time to spare. As I came up the stairs into the square, I got a message from Greta to say she was running late. I called her, offering to meet at her place but she didn't answer. Soon after she sent me a message saying she'd be coming straight from work, so I should continue to the café.

I thought I might be stuck waiting for a while, but she arrived no more than a couple of minutes after me, partly thanks to me taking the scenic walk around a few blocks. There wasn't the same enthusiasm in her greeting that she's shown the other night, but we were in a public place, and I assumed this was reasonable discretion.

'How was work? I don't even know what you do other than work in a supermarket.'

'Bits and pieces. Today was just watching the clock more than anything else.'

Her lack of detail had me wondering whether there was a reason for trying to hide things, but I didn't want to push. Whatever the reason, she didn't want to talk about it, so there was no point dwelling on a topic she wasn't keen on.

'How was yours last night?'

'Same,' I said, figuring it was better to keep the answer brief so we could move to a different topic as soon as we ordered.

'I did hear that the prospect of us having freedom in this city beyond the next couple of days are looking shaky. If there's anything you want to see or do, you might have to focus on doing it sooner rather than later,' she said.

'I think I'm already having lunch with my favourite part of Berlin.' It was probably a bit too corny line to use, but it was true. I was happy whatever we did, and just wanted to be spending the time together.

'That's sweet, but I don't think we should sit here all day staring at each other.'

'What do you recommend?'

'Ask twenty different people what's the best thing to do in Berlin and you'll get twenty different answers.'

'Berlin doesn't seem to have the same type of bucket lists sites that a lot of big cities have.'

'We're not enough for you?'

I explained that it was a compliment. Some cities told their stories through a small number of iconic sites. Berlin was better than that. It was the freedom and liberation that gave the city its feel. It was a city that was more than the sum of its parts, which to me was testament to how great the place was, not a reflection of any great lack.

'Well forget the other nineteen people, what would you choose to do on a day in Berlin? You know the city well enough. I'll trust your judgement.'

'What would you recommend if I had a day in your hometown?'

'The highway out of there,' I said laughing. 'Not really. It's a pretty town, but there's no attraction that you'd consider a must see.'

'That's the thing, when you live in a place, your favourite things are certain streets, shops, bars, restaurants and parks. They became favourites just through being in the right place and in the right way. You feel at home there. When you're exploring a city, you don't have that approach. You want different. You want new and unusual.'

'And you don't know anywhere new and unusual?'

'Well, there's the Reichstag, the memorials, the Wall, the Tiergarten, but I don't know what you've seen so far. One of the best spots is the Spy Museum. There's plenty of interactive elements. It's pretty good for that sort of thing, and there's quite a bit in the area nearby as well.'

'I guess there'd be nowhere better for a spy museum than Berlin.'

'Everyone was a potential spy then. It's never really changed that much either.'

'Now I understand your reluctance to talk about work.'

'I stand out too much to make it as a spy. Spies blend in more. Usually they'd have a cover story, like a backpacker working in an aged care facility.'

'I think that would stand out too much.'

Lunch arrived, and as we started eating, I noticed several people were staring at us, or perhaps more particularly at Greta. I suppose her looks were striking enough that such attention was understandable, though you really would think they'd be more discreet. It did seem to leave her with a blinkered approach, narrowing her focus on the food in front of her and me.

'You sure you wouldn't rather stay in this afternoon?' I was unconcerned how we spent our time together and was looking for an option that would be most suitable for her.

'I've got spies in my head now, so we have to go there.'

Berlin is known as the capital of spies. At the end of World War II, the four main Allies each took control of a section of Berlin. After years of unity against the Nazi's, the ideological divide between the Soviets and the other allies was arguably even greater. West Berlin stood as an enclave completely separated by East Germany. As the Cold War deepened, West Berlin was always seen as the most vulnerable part of the West. With 10,000 troops in the city while the Soviets had 300,000, it was only through information and espionage that the West could have confidence in its ability to keep the forces of Communism from driving further west.

Despite being just across the road from a U-Bahn station, Greta insisted on a car service, and it was no more than a couple of minutes before our ride arrived. There was no repeat of the hand reaching mine as there had been two nights earlier, and yet another sign that the magic of that night seemed a world away from what she was showing me today.

The car took us to Leipziger Place, a modern square downtown that looked to be a bastion of high-rise office buildings and shopping. The city had Museum Island filled with grand old buildings, but this was quite opposite. Espionage was always at the cutting edge, so it made sense for an espionage museum to be housed in the centre of modernity.

At the entrance, the CCTV cameras seemed excessive, but this was no accident, making the theme apparent from the beginning. What followed was a brilliantly put together museum with something for everyone. Children seemed to be loving it, with a range of hands-on displays that ensured no child would be complaining of boredom to their parents.

It's not unfair to say that the museum is a little gimmicky, but retaining its level of accessibility probably requires that. There is plenty of history, information and detail, but this all sits alongside participation elements that mightn't be so authentically matching the scenarios spies faced in the line of their duty. The most popular amongst these was a laser-maze. Said to be a standard training element used by spies, I think it looked more like something used in a Hollywood movie. You could use a range of settings compatible to your skill level before negotiating the room without breaking any of the laser beams. I didn't get far at all before failing dismally, but Greta unsurprisingly made it through, albeit not on the hardest level.

There was a bug detector for finding listening devices, a code cracking challenge, a safe-cracking exhibition, a message decoding display and a challenge in reconstructing files.

'The Stasi were famous for shredding everything,' Greta said. 'Even after all these years there is still work being done in trying to reconstruct information they'd tried to destroy. People from East Berlin can see the files that were created on them. Just ordinary citizens, but everyone was watching everyone. Maybe if you excel in this task, the cameras here may help you get a job away from the aged care home.'

'I think I'm happy staying where I am. Mind you, I'm now starting to wonder if I'm looking after a whole bunch of former spies. I might be working in my own mini-spy museum already.' I was thinking of Marta and her miraculous escape from the East. East Germany had been backed by the Warsaw Pact countries further east. In an era when World War III seemed more a question of when than if, West Berlin was always considered the most likely tripwire, creating the signal of a more resolute push from the Soviets and their allies. Could Marta have been connected in some small way?

While it was the French who had aided her escape, I wondered if it was possible that the East German's may have facilitated it. Could she have been an agent, sent to the West under the guise of an entertainer, but on a mission to report back to her homeland? I thought back to the costumes, the glamour and the general feeling she had of the restricted life that had been on offer to her in the East.

'It would almost be more of a surprise if none of your nursing home folk were spies. You might have to do a bit of spying on them yourself to get the real answers,' she said.

'Unable to speak their language, they probably think that's what I am.'

'Of course. That's your cover. You understand every word but just pretend not to speak our language.'

'*Ja, es ist wehr*,' I said with a laugh. I didn't laugh too long before wondering if the reverse was true. There was more to Greta than she'd yet told me. While I had no reason to suspect that espionage couldn't be her thing, I was hardly someone that had any secrets of value.

Whether the same was true of Marta and the people around her sixty years ago may just be another story.

***

'What have you done today,' Marta asked after the normal greetings when I first entered their room for the evening.

'I went to the Spy Museum this afternoon. I didn't realise the prevalence of espionage in this city.'

'Marta was a spy for the East. I was a big target, so they sent her to marry me.'

'Shut up Henry.'

'Why? The secrets out now.'

She shook her head and raised her eyebrows as she looked my way.

'I wasn't a spy, though I suspect that both sides had considered approaching me. That is why the East let me go to Paris, and it is why the West were keen to aide my defection. Eventually each side looked at my parents and couldn't feel convinced where my loyalties might lie, so they just let me skate. It doesn't mean that I was completely removed from the espionage that Berlin was synonymous with. Spies got me out of the East. At one stage I was hoping spies could get me back in.'

21

1 August 1968

MARTA

Sometimes there is a fine line between our greatest desire and our greatest dread. As much as I had seen America as my aim professionally, it never felt like home to me. Despite the opportunities drying up beyond World on Ice, Henry maintained that America was the best place for The Victors to remain, while Des was keen to head back across the Atlantic. With the next European season extended to cover a range of countries we'd never previously visited, eventually they agreed to sign on in Europe. They were a big enough drawcard that they could put provisos on their contracts. Chief amongst these was that Barbara and I would also be contracted.

We were back in Bremen, where Henry and I first met. The new seasons show was amazing. The routines more complex, the costumes more dazzling, and the four weeks of rehearsal seemed barely enough.

From the moment we'd re-joined the European company, my eyes were fixed closely on the second week of November. We were headed back to Berlin. As much as the pull of my hometown excited me, I was nervous of what could go wrong. I may have been insignificant in the scheme of the Cold War, but I was, nevertheless, an escapee from the East and a person that would remain of interest to the Stasi.

'There is nothing to be concerned about,' I was reassured by the tour manager Ernst. 'We will be flying in from Hamburg, never setting foot on East German territory.'

'But they have spies in West Berlin.'

'With no ability to act, just report. The East German government don't need spies to know where you are. You are a public figure. They will have no more ability to come after you there than they would anywhere else.'

I might be safe, but my greatest wish for my return was to see my mother, and I knew this wasn't possible. The East Germans had no concern with anyone crossing to their side of the border, but in my case, it would mean certain arrest and no prospect of ever getting back out. I would be just a few miles from her, yet still a world away.

After my escape five years earlier, I only saw a very small section of West Berlin, so when we arrived it was less of a homecoming, than an arrival in a largely unrecognisable city. Every city has variance between its different neighbourhoods, with ritzy areas that bear little resemblance to the areas dominated by the working class. In Berlin this was something altogether different. Both sides of the city had been heavily rebuilt at the end of the war, and while the East was done in a monotonous and cost-effective way, no expense had been spared in the West. The French, British and American forces ensured that West Berlin had the best of everything. West Berlin was designed to be a beacon of capitalism. They saw the threat of communism heading ever further west and held West Berlin as a strategic place from which to halt its progress. This demanded prosperity, and in both style and substance, West Berlin achieved this.

Stylish apartment buildings, new elite motor vehicles within the financial means of the working class, bustling shopping centres and entertainment precincts. None of this existed in my younger years in the East. We were fed the promises that everything in West Berlin was based on American propaganda.

'Once they have what they want, they will pull their money out. The city, like West Germany as a whole, will collapse. What we have may not look as pretty, but it is real. It is building a solid base that will ensure security and prosperity that will never fade.' My father's spiel was typical of what many in the East espoused. As the years past, the evidence against that type of thought continued to mount. If anything, it was the messages that were spruiked in the East that were the propaganda, with no legitimate basis.

There was no doubt that the Western powers had a vested interest in ensuring the strength and prosperity of West Berlin, but their role in its development didn't make the modern city less genuine. It had its own burgeoning culture, welcoming of foreign elements, but built on a traditional German foundation.

We had two free days on our arrival, and my desperation to see as much as I could meant Henry and I covered a great deal of the city, but only in the most public spots. The many reassurances I had been given regarding my safety had me feeling confident, but not certain. I was adamant that Henry must never leave my side, nor that we ever leave the safety that crowds offered us.

Usually on tour we saw little of the cities we were playing. We loved travelling at the end of a season and lapping up the highlights of destinations, but during a season, downtime was spent recovering and unwinding. Berlin was the exception.

'Would you ever consider living here after we retire?'

'Too many Germans,' he said.

'You can't have too much of a problem with them. You married one.'

'Yeah, that's my job done. I don't need several million more surrounding me.'

I didn't want to push the issue, but it was a thought that I couldn't completely divest myself from. Home is where the heart is, and my heart will always be with Henry, but it doesn't mean that there isn't another connection I would like to hold on to. It seems strange that I could feel such a connection to Berlin, for it wasn't the city of my birth, nor one with an array of happy memories. Hell, it wasn't even the same city I remembered, with the division in the city being in place as far back as I could remember. That didn't negate the feeling of home that I had. The Wall, if anything, strengthened my affection, as it so completely divided my life between past and present. All that I remembered was just beyond, but all that I looked forward to was on offer on this side.

We sold out the entire run in West Berlin. After our last show, I reminded Henry of how I had seen him perform all those years earlier at a World on Ice show.

'I must have made a hell of an impression. You trained for years, risked your life crossing the Wall and it was all just to pursue me.'

'Who pursued who?'

'You remember me from far earlier than I knew you.'

'Yes, but I barely noticed you. Just a couple of clowns interrupting the beautiful skaters.'

'Thanks for the respect.'

'It has grown over the years. Still, it's memories like that which will always make this city feel like home to me.'

I knew I wasn't going to change his view quickly, but it would be years before that became relevant. He acknowledged that he loved the city, and it was one that he'd always enjoyed playing, not just for the success the shows had there, but for the array of good times he'd had away from the show.

You don't always get everything you want in life, but with patience and persistence, you give yourself the best possible chance.

22

21 March 2020

AMBER

You don't always get everything you want in life, but with patience and persistence, you give yourself the best possible chance. I'm not entirely sure what it is I want from this situation. I am in the early stages of the trip of a lifetime. I want it to continue. I don't want to be finding a reason to stay here, and miss the rest of what I have planned, but I can't pretend that the excitement of my time with Greta doesn't make moving on seem easy.

My grandmother had been an artist. She specialised in painting landscapes. While she never reached any great heights, she sold enough works to keep the flame of passion alive. As a child, I had wanted to follow in her footsteps. It was apparent early on that I hadn't inherited her talent nor patience and so the desire quickly dwindled. Despite this, I've always dabbled in drawing, more as a means of relaxation than with any great desire to be creating legacies. In theory, I enjoyed portraits, but in practice I generally found myself disappointed at the result. I had done one of Andrew that I had felt proud enough of to give to him as a present a couple of years back. When he asked who it was meant to be, I was quickly back in my place, and hadn't shown anything I had drawn to anyone else.

I had bought a scrap book a few days ago and had spent some time doodling. Before too long I was into a couple of portraits, both of women on ice. The first was reproducing a picture that I saw each day on Marta's wall, of her at her glamorous best, in full costume performing with World on Ice. The second was of a picture so dominant in my mind, of Greta smiling at me as she helped me from the ice in the moment we met. I was far from satisfied with either portrait to be giving them to their subjects, but it remained my target. If I could eventually reach a point of satisfaction, I would give both Marta and Greta their likenesses. I had come to Europe to find myself, and to overcome the fears associated with being me. Andrew had heightened these in many ways. The reaction to my portrait of him may not seem that significant, but it crushed me. I didn't need grand validation, for it was no more than a hobby, but I was emotionally vulnerable enough that it was devastating to be mocked for something I put my heart into. I wanted to be stronger. Art was a small part of me, and it was one I wanted to set free. Whether it was celebrated or mocked by others, I had to be strong enough to accept those reactions. Once the artworks were ready, I would be too.

It felt like staying at the hostel was a waste of a day in Berlin. Going out for the sake of it sometimes seems just as wasteful. I felt the need for company, something that wasn't normally high on my priority list, so I decided to go downstairs to the hostel's bar. Working later in the day, I couldn't have a drink, but just sitting in the surrounds of others could possibly lead to conversation. If not, the buzz of people around me would at least take me out of the over-thinking that was frustrating me.

'Coke, *bitte*.'

The girl behind the bar was unfamiliar. I hadn't spent much time down here, so she may well have been part of the furniture. My scrap book caught her eye. As she was pouring my drink, she started the conversation.

'You are an artist?'

'No, far from it. I like to doodle, but I'm not good at it.'

'Let me be the judge.'

I didn't want to show her but accepted this was part of the challenge I needed to face. What if a stranger decided my drawings were bad? Who was she to judge? I had no reason to believe she had any expertise on the subject. I opened the book and let her see my attempts at capturing both Marta and Greta.

'Very good. You like skating?'

'Not really, but I am working at an aged-care home, and one of the residents was a champion skater. She has a photo on the wall that I see each day and it inspired the first drawing.'

'Who is the other one. She looks familiar.'

'Just someone I saw on the street,' I said, preferring not to go into details. 'I guess after working on the skates in the first portrait, I thought I'd put that to use in this one as well.' Having been so quick to bring up the topic, I wondered if she was an artist as well.

'Not really. Like you, it's a hobby, but nothing more. I used to paint but haven't since I've been here.'

'You're not a local?'

'No, but not from as far away as you. I'm from Amsterdam.'

'I hope to get there before too long.'

'You should. Great city, but I needed an escape. I haven't been back in a couple of years. You'd love the art scene if everything is open when you're there.'

I wondered if she'd been escaping something like me.

'Have you found what you came here looking for?'

'I don't know what that is. I just lost my direction at home. I had a bad relationship with my family, I'd lost my job, broken up with my boyfriend. I just felt like I was stagnating. Here works for now. Live upstairs, work enough shifts down here to earn a few Euro, and complete freedom beyond that to do whatever I feel like. It's hardly the forever option, but I've enjoyed the past year more than any other.'

'That's a good start.'

'What about you? Have you found what you're looking for here?'

My mind raced through a wide array of images. Greta, and the fact I followed through on my impulses. Henry and Marta, and the joy I got from helping them after spending so much previous time dreading work. The city itself, and all I'd learnt about how precious freedom is. The girl I was talking to now, who I managed to show my drawings to despite my natural fear telling me not to.

'I think I have. But I'm not ready to stop looking for more just yet.'

***

The television was on when I walked in to see Marta and Henry. Watching a news channel was awkward when you knew a small amount of the language. You captured enough to have an idea of the story, but generally got lost in the detail. When I'd seen Henry with the television on, he often ended up complaining about the story. This usually stemmed from misinterpreting what had happened, and the point he was making was exactly what was being said. This time we were spared, as Henry was sleeping soundly.

As had become standard, the news was dominated by talk of the virus.

'They were just showing Canada,' Marta said. 'The border has been closed to the United States. The situation there is getting very bad.'

'Yes, I know. It is a worry.'

'Are your family alright?'

'At this stage, yes, but the situation is constantly getting worse.'

'Don't you want to go home to them? You must miss them.'

'Sure, I miss my family, but you would know well enough that sometimes you have to take the steps that are right for yourself, even if it means leaving your family behind. It was right for me to come here, and it is right for me to stay.'

'I do understand. I never regret the moves I made, but it has always haunted me that I couldn't see my mother once I crossed the Wall.'

23

4 October 1969

MARTA

It was our last night in Amsterdam. To many, it was one of the world's most beautiful cities, but despite this being my fourth trip here, our itineraries had never left us with enough free time to get the opportunity to appreciate that.

We'd had a successful run here, but tonight's show was the perfect reminder that however skilled the cast may be, and however well-rehearsed we all were, there was plenty that could go wrong. Three of the corps de ballet were off sick, and while our understudies usually filled their places with aplomb, tonight there was confusion that led to several instances where the trained eye could see mistakes. There were also multiple falls. Nothing serious, and nothing that led to routines being ruined, but a high standard existed from our company.

'The audiences pay for professionalism,' our director Markus reinforced. 'That wasn't professional at all.'

Generally, we received notes individually on any imperfections in our performance, but tonight we'd been held back for him to lambaste us as an entire cast. Not quite entire, for the stars, even though they too had made errors, were not called in with us.

'What the hell was all that about,' Henry asked when I finally made it to stage door.

'Ten people screw up. Thirty people get the blame.'

'He's an arsehole. It might be worth considering the offer from Wiener Eisrevue.'

Weiner Eisrevue was a rival ice skating show to World on Ice that competed for many of the same artists. The company had formed on the back of the dominance of Austrian figure skaters before World War II. Having worked with both the Berliner Eis Revue and the Paris Eis Revue, I had felt that moving to a company like this would be a backward step, but Henry was adamant that the Austrian company was a good option.

'Similar venues, similar money, just less arseholes in the production company.'

Barbara and I were largely subservient to the decisions that Henry and Des made. They were a headline act, and all the ice shows, both in Europe and America were always after them. They'd worked with Ice Age in the United States before I'd met them, but had spent several years now with World on Ice. While their relationship with the company was strong, Henry constantly looked for something new. Convincing me to follow his lead was one thing, but Des was reluctant to leave the show that remained the biggest and best of its kind.

Most nights we went straight back to the hotel bar and had a few drinks before heading upstairs. I felt a little flat, so told Henry that I was going straight back to the room and would see him when he came up. As I made my way to the lift, I was called over to reception.

'There is a telegram for you Mrs Victor, as well as some messages.'

I'd missed calls from the French embassy in Berlin, and the telegram asked for me to call them immediately, any time. Despite knowing I was calling internationally, I was offered the phone at reception.

'*Hallo, das ist Marta Victor.*'

'*Marta, es tut mir leid.*' Hearing the ambassador's assistant say he was sorry, I knew what was coming, despite his extended pause.

'*Deine mutter ist gestorben.*'

The woman who had given me life had lost hers. Apparently, it was natural causes, but it was difficult to verify this. It had happened nearly a week ago, but it had taken several days before she was found. It took a few more days for the news to pass across to the West, where contact details for me existed.

I didn't shed tears, but I felt numb. I can't remember another word from the phone call. For all the selflessness she had shown throughout life, to end it alone seemed so wrong. The image of her lifeless body on the floor for days before being found was overcoming me. Not only couldn't I be there to say goodbye before she left this world, I couldn't be there to pay tribute afterwards. It was a reality faced by many before me, but its significance wasn't appreciable until you faced it yourself.

Minutes passed with me rooted to the spot, numb from the news. When I finally sought out Henry, I stood at the doorway to the bar. I was unwilling to step inside to the merriment of the scene and waited for him to see me. When he did, he instantly knew something was wrong. As he made his way towards me, the always stoic demeanour that I carried through any circumstance crumbled. The tears began to fall.

'What is it?' he asked.

I couldn't mutter a reply, but he knew. Other than he, Mum was the only person left who had ever mattered so much in my life. Although he undoubtedly had a myriad of questions circulating through his mind, he knew that the best he could do for me at this moment was hold me and stay silent. He took the time I needed before guiding me back to the room, at which point I was able to put the emotions into words that clarified what I'd been told.

'They had no details, just that she was found dead at home. She'd been there several days.'

'I am so sorry,' he said. 'It feels so wrong that I never got to meet the person who most made you who you are today.'

'When I grew up, people said how lucky I was that the war ended before my earliest memories formed. They lied. The war never ended. Sure, the bombs, the tanks and the concentration camps all ended, but they were replaced with spies who probably killed her, and a wall which kept me from her. The world isn't much of a place.'

'No, but it is why we have to do everything we can to hold on to the good bits.'

'Until what. You or I meet the same fate.'

'You don't know that there was anything untoward in her death.'

'And you don't know there wasn't.'

I was determined to find out what I could, but the prospects of genuine answers were not good. To those who had aided my escape, I was a finished case. They had helped provide initial contact after I had left, but now they owed me nothing. After the years that had passed, I had been lucky to receive this communication. It was unlikely that they would have any further insight into what had happened, and no more likely that they would pass this on if they did by chance know.

***

We arrived in Berlin in mid-December, for a two-week run. For the previous two months I had continued to make calls hoping to find out more details of my mother's passing, but to no avail. I had hoped that my presence on the doorstep may have led to greater transparency.

Henry accompanied me to the French embassy, his superior French language skills possibly required to assist. Irrespective, I was still sceptical about being anywhere alone in Berlin. On arrival we found that Cedric Lemaire was no longer in his position. Naturally, there was no record of me, for the nature of the operation involving me was one conducted with the utmost secrecy.

'How then did I receive contact about my mother's passing,' I asked.

'We have no details of that.'

I remembered the woman I spoke to had identified herself as Helene and was the personal assistant to the ambassador. I was told she was unavailable for the next few days, so left a message for her to contact me at our hotel.

I continued to work, as I had done since that fateful night in Amsterdam, with the utmost professionalism. Everyone who knew me saw the emotional baggage I was carrying, but every time my skates touched the ice that disappeared. In that instant, I transformed into the dazzling, glamorous figure skater my mother would have been proud of. I was flawless, show after show, only to smile through the final curtain call. After that, I'd disappear into the bowels of the auditorium feeling broken.

Henry was a tower of strength, just as he was professionally. He was at my side when I needed him. He gave me space in the rarer moments that I needed it. His presence in my life was the constant reminder that whatever hell we were exposed to, we could survive it together.

When I did get the call from Helene, it proved to be of little value. Cedric's replacement, Jean-Pierre Brochard, was the custodian of a file that had details of a small group of individuals. There was little information, just a reference point of people to contact in situations like these.

'It is humanity. A courtesy. We informed you of what happened as there was a need for you to know, and no other way of you finding out. I know from the information Monsieur Brochard provided me that there were no further details available about your mothers passing. We do not search for these. It would not be safe for us to be seeking such information. We are not willing to arouse suspicion. It is also, potentially compromising having you visit us here.'

'I am a West German citizen, seeking French diplomatic assistance before my trip to Paris for work.'

'Not to those on the other side of Wall.'

I had to accept that I would never know the truth. Mum was sixty-two when she died. It was perfectly within reason that a woman of that age could die of natural causes. It was also not unusual for any East German to become the target of the Stasi who had the power to deal justice on their own terms. It was estimated that nearly 5% of East Germans were Stasi informants. I have little doubt that my father was one of these. If this had been the fate she met, then perhaps the greater surprise was not that she had died, but that it had taken so long after my defection.

I learnt years ago that I could never have children. It wasn't a disappointment for me. I think having a mother who gave her children everything, perhaps even her life, had set a bar so high that I felt sure I could never emulate it.

The greatest gift we ever receive is life itself. Mothers give us that, and if nothing else, their legacy lives through us forever more. My mother continued to give to me right through life. The life I have now, one that has brought me a happiness that my mother never had herself, is courtesy of all she gave to me. Since leaving her to follow my dreams, I've often felt guilty that her existence was built around her children, yet she couldn't see and appreciate the results of what she'd given. I hope in her final moment, she knew the impact of her sacrifices.

24

22 March 2020

AMBER

I'd like to drive a knife through her heart. It feels like she has already done that to me. Maybe I was stupid. Certainly, I was naïve. I really didn't see this coming. I knew all along it was too good to be true, but I didn't think it was quite so untrue.

I never made it to work tonight. I called them early evening and said that I'd had symptoms of gastroenteritis and couldn't come in. They accepted that, happy that I would not be spreading anything. As a temp, I don't get paid if I don't work. It is a major problem in workplaces when people come in for the sake of pay when they are sick. Illness spreads like wildfire in nursing homes, and one person's illness usually ends up infecting countless more, both staff and residents. In the current climate, the stakes are far higher. I made sure that I specified it couldn't be COVID-19, though they insisted on me getting tested.

When I went back to the hostel after last night's shift, I was lying in bed thinking about Greta and wondering about the long list of things I didn't know about her. I started to wonder if there wasn't another life that she was living, with me as a secret on the side. Maybe she was married and had a husband who was ignorant of what she got up to when he was out of town. Maybe she was the one out of town, a little holiday pad in Berlin that she used to seduce foolish young women. Her apartment mightn't be homely, yet it wouldn't have been overly cheap.

How does a young casual worker afford such a place? Does she even have a job? She was usually available to see me, so she didn't work often. As my eyes got heavy and I drifted off to sleep I decided I would head over to her place before I went back to work tonight.

It wasn't gastroenteritis, but a far sicker feeling I had after my visit to Greta. I'd woken up mid-morning and decided I'd surprise her. She'd said she was working early in the morning, the reason why she told me not to come over after work last night. I'd assumed she'd be home around lunch time, so I aimed to get there soon after midday. I took some flowers so if I missed her, she'd at least know I'd been. I'd then have lunch at the cafe across the road, and hopefully spot her returning.

I knocked on the door and got no answer. After leaving the flowers on the doorstep I turned and headed back to the front of the apartment building. As I turned the corner there was Greta and another woman. Much older, I could have believed it was her mother or aunt, but her panicked state at seeing me suggested I had seen someone she wanted hidden. More likely, I was the person she had been hoping to hide.

'Amber. I didn't expect to see you.'

'Clearly,' I said.

'This is Leila.'

'Who is Leila?'

'She is Leila. I don't use labels, so I don't know what else to say.'

'Am I the woman you are cheating on her with?' I asked. I looked at Leila who looked puzzled by the altercation. It was unlike me to confront someone in these circumstances. I'd wanted to run away the moment I saw them, but now I felt I needed to know the extent of my gullibility and foolishness. I wondered if Leila understood a word that was being said. I felt sure that she would have a very good idea of what was happening, with or without knowing the language.

Leila said something in German that I didn't understand, which got a response from Greta that was barely audible to me. Following that, Leila continued towards Greta's apartment, or what I now understood may even have been her own home.

'It was all a fairy-tale right? Grow up. This is real. You've known me a week, you can't act like we're years into a relationship,' Greta said.

'You knew that this was new territory for me. You had plenty of chance to tell me where I stood. It wouldn't have stopped anything, but I could have avoided this humiliation. Did I deserve that?'

'Of course, that is not what I wanted,' she said. I wasn't sure whether I was starting to detect a semblance of guilt on her face or just another performance.

'Was I ever going to see you again? What has she thought you were up to the past week?'

'What difference does it make?'

I had to think about it. It didn't really make any difference now. I'd become instantly infatuated with an illusion. Yes, the physical attraction was real, but beyond that there was nothing more. It had seemed like there was so much more to her, but there was no way I could take anything else about her for granted. How was I meant to file the memories of my time with her. Passion or betrayal? Discovery of myself or loss of myself? I looked back at her and shrugged my shoulders.

'None I guess,' I said. I turned and began to walk away but I couldn't continue when I heard her again.

'I enjoyed every minute we shared. That was real, Amber. Hate me if you wish, but I think it comes from not understanding the whole picture. Some things you can't understand without knowing completely. Savour the best of the memories, because they were special to me, and I know they were special to you too.'

'Does she care?' I asked, referring to Leila.

'No. We have an unusual dynamic, one that works for each of us, and gives us the freedom to live our own lives. Usually, for me, that involves nothing. I didn't go looking for you, but I felt an instant connection when we met. Even if you can't see it now, I am certain you'll look back and realise you are richer for the experience.'

Why should I listen to an illusion? Everything she said made sense, but I wasn't ready for sense. I was hurt and didn't want to hear anything more from her.

'Be yourself and live well,' she said, as I turned to walk away from her for the last time.

As the tears started to well, I didn't want her to see me. Anger had been replaced by sadness. It was so much harder to have her know she'd hurt me than angered me. Anyone can make us angry, but it is the people deepest in our hearts that can really hurt us. I wanted her to think she didn't matter, which was impossible if she saw the hurt on my face. From the moment we met, I had been like a schoolgirl around her, and a schoolgirl can fall deep and fast.

I made it as far as the end of the street. A small park with a bench in the middle seemed the perfect spot to stop for a while and reflect. Mainly on the moment that had crushed me, but also on the week before it that had seemed like a rebirth.

Greta had been the greatest gateway to discovery for me. Now that the gate had closed, I wasn't sure what it was I'd found. Was I really someone who could be so driven by lust as to give myself to a stranger with no thought of consequence? Was I someone so easily hurt that I needed to be careful and protective of my heart, only slowly opening to the well earnt trust of a worthy partner? I understood that the two weren't completely exclusive and the truth was a combination.

'Be yourself and live well.' The last words I would ever hear from my first female lover. They kept ringing through my ears. I've kept saying that I came to Europe to find out who I was, but I don't know anything more about myself than when I began. I think part of the reason is that I already knew who I was, I just didn't feel safe and comfortable in being that person. Maybe Greta really did come into my life for a reason. Maybe the reason wasn't the physical experience, but just to pass on those words.

We don't get to choose what happens to us, but we do get some degree of choice in how we deal with what happens. Maybe not the complete ability to ignore the bad things, nor to pretend that all is good, but we can take different approaches to get different results. There are so many unknowns I have about Greta. Nobody can ever tell me I'm wrong in what I choose to believe about the time we shared. Was Greta even her name? Had that been part of the confused look Leila gave? When you meet someone, you take what you see at face value. You know with time, the perfection will give way to reality, but I now have no idea what about her was real.

'Be yourself and live well.' Be myself. She hadn't been herself. Or maybe she had, and I was too foolish to understand what that was. I thought I was being myself. I wasn't led, I was listening to my heart and running full steam ahead. Maybe we all step away from ourselves in moments, and that is what leaves us with regrets.

It was a chance meeting that started this. I wouldn't have been true to myself if I hadn't pursued things. Maybe the lesson was all about pursuing what I want. The pursuit itself needs to be the focus, rather than fixing my mind too much on the destination I hoped it would lead to.

After healing, I will be ready for whoever comes into my life whenever that may be. I won't reject desire, but I won't confuse it for more. I will welcome emotional connections, but I will wait for them to be proven, not jumped towards out of hope. Partners will not define me. I do not need a person in my bed or by my side to make me happy. If there is someone, it will be based on who I want, not who I think others would want for me.

As philosophical as I had been, I still wanted to cry. Greta had ripped my heart out. I knew I'd heal. I knew I'd be better for the overall experience. I also knew that I wasn't meant to be alright yet. It takes time.

With my head down I made my way back to the underground. Part of me wanted to leave Berlin immediately, and make another attempted beginning somewhere else, but it wasn't Berlin that had done this to me. I still had two and a half weeks here and I am strong. I may have hit the proverbial iceberg, but it's not going to sink me. I may need a day or two, but I am going to be myself and live well.

25

15 July 1972

MARTA

Dear Henry,

I love you, I love you, I love you.

What are you doing? Come fast to me, I am miserable without you. I miss you. I am hoping that after this, we are together always. I don't ever want us to be separated again.

Today was my second rehearsal. I am very tired. I am going to sleep for about twenty hours, I think. It is so hot here. With all the current workload, plus how much I am missing you, it is killing me. I am the understudy for Edie Charmaine, so I am doing all of the chorus work, plus additional sessions to learn her role too. The money isn't enough extra for the amount of work I am having to do.

Mostly things aren't so bad, except for missing you, and very badly at that. I hope you are here soon.

Collins asked me to convey his regards to you when I write. He is well.

How are you, my darling?

Hurry up. I need you! The opening is on August 8th, and everybody is asking me when you will be here. I said the beginning of next month. I hope it is even sooner of course. The show is playing New York from August 31st to September 18th.

I love you, remember that always.

Love Marta.

I would have continued far longer, but the greeting card I had bought him had no more space. It was just another in a collection that I was sending to him in our time apart. I needed him to know how much it was hurting me to be without him. I was busy, I was surrounded by people, including many I cherished as friends, yet nothing eased the heartache.

During the previous season Des made the decision that it would be his last. Several years older than Henry, he believed he'd reached the end of his capacity to live out of a suitcase. Both Barbara and he were ready to settle down.

'One more year, one more tour, that's how it's been for the past five years. We're not doing anything new, we're not getting the offers from anywhere else. The best we can hope for is another year of the same, which doesn't inspire me anymore. At this point, I'd be more concerned that we'll start deteriorating, and even if it doesn't end up leading to serious injury, it will impact our legacy and I don't want that.'

Henry wasn't ready for retirement, but his choices were limited. An acrobatics duo involved complete dependence on each other. Without Des, Henry had no act. He could try to find another partner, but the time involved in teaching someone all the routines was difficult and time consuming. Henry wasn't the most patient, and with his perfectionist streak, there was little prospect of him having anyone ready to partner him quickly. As the bottom man, the physical demands on Henry were greater, and as a best-case scenario, he knew he only had a couple of years left. The arduous task of bringing someone new into the mix seemed too much for that timeframe. When we finished our season in Munich in April, The Victors were no more. Henry was officially a former acrobat.

I was not yet thirty. With all that had been involved in getting out of the East, I was not ready to walk away from my career yet. Henry was supportive of my choice. There was no home to settle down in, though we did own apartments in Germany, the United States and

Australia. We'd never seen the one in Australia, using it as an investment that Henry's mother had acquired for him from the money he had sent home over the past decade. The others, in Bremen and Knoxville, had been bought close to the continental bases of World on Ice, the company we'd worked most regularly for. We'd never spent more than a month at a time in either apartment, but it had been handy to have a dumping ground for the possessions we'd inevitably acquire across each season.

Henry had initially seemed happy to continue life on the road without the pressures of working himself. However ideal that may have seemed to him when looking ahead, once the reality arrived it wasn't quite the utopian existence he expected. The glamorous life that people associate with entertainers is real, but it's a small part of a big picture. Henry thought without the time commitments and pressures of work, he'd have more time to appreciate the best side of the tours. More doesn't always mean better. Without the balance of professional responsibilities, the appreciation for his free time was nowhere near what he expected.

'How much longer do you want to keep doing this?' he asked, frustrated at the end of our European season.

'I don't know. You were happy for me to continue as long as I wanted. What is life going to be for us if I stop?'

I was already contracted for another season in the United States. When I travelled back to Knoxville, Henry decided to go to Australia, keen to see family, as well as to work on ideas for life beyond the entertainment industry.

'Why don't you wait until the tour starts? We can have six weeks together in Knoxville before that, enjoying life together. I'll miss you too much in the boredom of rehearsals.'

'You'll be committed more hours a day during that time than when you're on the road. It makes more sense for me to be with you then.'

I begrudgingly accepted his reasoning. I had thought it would be a taste of the life ahead of us, living for an extended period in our own place in Knoxville. In truth it wasn't where I wanted us to end up, though I felt that was where Henry would choose. He had always seemed more at home here than in Germany, perhaps through the greater similarity to the where he'd grown up. I also suspected that a return to Australia may prompt a desire for a permanent return. I'd had such limited time there, that I had no conviction either way on it, but I understood the importance of family well enough to know that it made sense if that was his preferred option.

In our respective careers, it was unusual to have such good fortune to travel with your loved one so much of the time. An acrobat and a figure skater, you would expect our paths to lead in different directions at some points. Other than the odd short-term jobs Henry had done on television or stage that had taken him away for a few days at a time, we'd spent very little time apart over the past decade. When you know an absence will be just a few days, by the time the loneliness sets in, you know you're halfway there. In this case, more than a month apart meant that I was immediately depressed by how long I had to wait to see him.

We had agreed to limit phone calls, the expense being so exorbitant, but writing letters and cards could never replicate the feeling that came when I heard his voice. The relief of this was only temporary, for the moment I hung up the phone, it faded into the memory like our time together. Minutes later, I missed his presence as badly as before the call.

Twice I had dealt with the loss of a loved one coming mid-season, and on both occasions, I continued to work. The challenge of retaining my composure while living a personal nightmare was surprisingly simple. The ability to switch off from heartache and channel everything into performance came naturally. Now my sadness was based on so much less, yet its impact was far greater. Rehearsal is critical in our business, but it is impossible to focus in the same way that you do for an audience. Trying to do this professionally while feeling emotionally compromised was a painful struggle. The less focussed I was, the more time tasks took and the more draining the whole experience became.

Henry arrived in Knoxville four days out from opening night. Lorraine had given birth last week to her second child, Alexander. I couldn't blame Henry for staying to meet his new nephew, knowing how little opportunity he'd generally had to spend time with family. Unfortunately, arriving at this stage meant that we had very little time together, for we had a dress rehearsal and previews in the next couple of days. We were also destined to be spending countless hours correcting any imperfections that had become evident during these performances.

'This is the last one,' I said ahead of opening night.

'What do you mean. You've got opening nights in sixty-three different cities ahead of you.'

'I mean season openings. This is my last season. I can't be apart from you again.'

'I'm coming on tour with you.'

'Yes, but how long for. Half of it? I've just endured six weeks without you, and it has made me see how little passion I have for what I do.'

'You love it.'

'I love it, yes, but only a small portion of how much I love you. Through all these years on the road, I have loved the performance because I have loved life off the ice as well. Without you near, I feel empty, and skating goes from pleasure to chore.'

'You are a long time retired. I made my decision, not because it was what I wanted, but it became too impractical to continue. You've given all you have following a dream, and to walk away from that before it is necessary may well leave you with a life of regrets.'

At his insistence, I agreed to shelve any plans until later in the season. I always maintained the belief that this would be the last season, but I kept that to myself.

Our New York season was at Madison Square Garden. Half-way through our run, star Edie Charmaine came down with a virus. I was her understudy, and suddenly in the most famous stadium, of the world's entertainment capital, I hit the pinnacle of my career. I had never been a nervous person, but in the hours between hearing that Edie wouldn't be performing, and the moment I took the ice, I began to understand the anxiety so many other people have before a major moment.

Throughout rehearsal, ninety percent of the time I spent was in my standard position within the chorus. I could skate my normal role with my eyes closed, but I'd had far more limited opportunity to learn Edie's role. I'd only had a couple of hours skating it alongside my co-star Albert Maxwell. That didn't matter. As soon as I was on the ice, I felt a sense of calm. Every moment of my life had led me to this point. The years of traipsing through East Berlin to spend hours training. The most dangerous hour contorted in the bonnet of a car as I escaped to the West. The love of my mother, of Lars and of course Henry. It was all leading me here. I didn't need to fear, for this wasn't a test. It was a reward, for the blood, sweat and tears of a lifetime. This was my party, and it was time for me to soak in every moment.

'You were better than Edie,' Albert said as we took our bows at the end of the show. I knew I had skated perfectly, but that reinforcement meant more to me than any comment I'd ever received.

Edie was off for a week, and I skated the role eight times before returning to my standard place in the chorus. I felt no disappointment when that time came, as I had already reached the summit. I didn't need to stay there to know that there was nothing left for me to do in my career. For many, there is an addictive quality to stardom, and the first taste leaves people wanting more. I didn't need more. I'd done it, I'd loved it, but like most things in life, the feeling of perfection could only be fleeting. I was more certain than ever that my time in the industry was coming to an end. When it did, I would now have a greater memory than I ever expected, and I would be ready to move on with no regrets.

26

23 March 2022

AMBER

'You look like shit.'

'*Danke* Hannah.'

'Are you sure you should be here?'

'Yes. It's emotional, not physical.'

'Heartbreak, is it? What's her name?'

'Her? Why do you think it was a woman?'

'OK, his name then.'

It was futile trying to pretend. I was still yet to acknowledge this part of myself to anyone. Although I didn't feel ready to be sharing it with the world, what better opportunity could I have. Someone with the understanding that stems from experience, and the intuition to have already worked me out for herself. My head was down, avoiding eye-contact as I responded.

'No, you were right. I'm just surprised that you would have realised.'

'I can read people. Don't worry, you're not that transparent. Most people would not pick it, but I've done enough people watching over the years to be able to spot what others miss.

'I never knew this was me. I was engaged to a man back home. He cheated on me, and it made me reassess life.'

'You thought you could change teams, and you wouldn't find the same type of players?'

'I guess, but that wasn't central to the change in my life. I had always just followed everyone else along the path of expectation. I suppressed so much of what I felt that didn't fit the right box. When I broke up with Andrew, I decided it was time to let the real person emerge from within me.'

'Good.'

'It feels like I would have been better to keep the real me hidden away.'

'No. The real you might get your heart broken, but that is part of the journey towards getting what you really want.'

She told me about her partner, Stef. They'd been together in a monogamous relationship for over a decade, but prior to this she'd had plenty of heartbreak from similar situations. She also acknowledged that as well as being the victim, she'd also been on the other side of the situation to.

'When you meet someone you like, you pursue them in the hope of finding just what you're looking for. It takes time to really know someone, and until you do, however perfect they may seem, they can be wrong for you. It might hurt, but more often, these situations give you something you are richer for. Enjoy the good memories and use the bad as lessons going forward.'

It was hard to appreciate the good from Greta, as it had been lost behind the pain of knowing it was all a game to her. The lesson came easier. If something seems too good to be true, then it probably isn't.

'When you see what you want, walk towards it, for it may be perfect,' Hannah said. 'Appreciate every step for what it is, but always retain the knowledge that it may be a mirage.'

'When did you know Stef wasn't a mirage.'

'It doesn't happen in any one moment, it just becomes clearer day by day. One thing is certain, love is more about accepting the worst of another person than appreciating their best. Nobody willingly shows you their worst in the early stages, so you only know it's genuine after considerable time. If you don't pursue relationships until you're certain about the other person, you'll never start one.'

All the wisdom in the world can only help so much. When you are hurt, words won't take the pain away. I know every word Hannah said is right, but it will take time for this wound to heal.

'You have very heightened emotions. You experience great highs and dark lows. I was the same at your age. The other day, you would have said the lows were worth having, in exchange for the jubilation at the top. Now you think the peak wasn't enough to justify the pain at the bottom. It's not about the power of the emotion, but the timing. What is most recent, drives your thinking. When you climb back, you will do so proud to be true to yourself.'

'*Danke*'

'*Bitte, Amber.* We better get back to work.'

***

It was almost a relief to get to have my dinner break without Hannah. As much as I appreciated her advice, I wanted to avoid thinking about Greta anymore, so sitting down alongside someone who didn't know me seemed preferable.

Johannes spoke very little English, so there wasn't likely to be much conversation. He did point to the television, and although I couldn't completely understand the words on the ticker at the bottom of the screen, it appeared the government had just made an announcement regarding further restrictions to combat the virus.

'No leave Berlin,' he said.

I didn't mind borders closing. I had no intention of cutting short my time here. The next few weeks may have changed from what I had wanted it to be a couple of days ago, but I had made a commitment to this workplace. I wasn't going to change that. If the city was to go into complete lockdown, my time here might consist of work and nothing else. I could live with that.

'*Ist die Stadt im Lockdown,*' I asked Johannes.

'*Nein. Beinahe.*' What did he mean by almost? Surely there was more to it than I was going to understand without decent translation. Hopefully Hannah would be up to speed with things later in the shift.

I put my dinner in the microwave and decided not to pay any further attention to matters outside of the nursing home. For now, it didn't matter whether it was the pandemic of the virus or the pandemic of my heart, nothing was going to make me feel better about walking out the door tonight. I almost hoped that absences did start impacting them here, so that I could get more shifts. If nothing else, it would kill more time, and for now that was the best I could hope for.

***

'What are you going to do now Maple Leaf?'

Henry and Marta had the television on, getting the latest news when I walked into their room.

'Well, I'm going to make sure you've both taken your tablets first.'

'No, I mean your trip. You're not going to be able to do much sightseeing.'

'What is the latest?'

'Pretty much everything is being closed. No congregations of more than two people. Restaurants must close. Anything that isn't essential won't be open.'

'You need to stock up on food,' Marta said. 'People are panicking and buying everything in sight.'

'So people aren't actually being locked down?'

'Not exactly, but if there is nowhere you can go, it is pretty much the same thing,' Henry said.

'You have to be one and a half metres from anyone else,' Marta added.

'I can still enjoy seeing different parts of the city. If the trains still run, I can venture to somewhere each day and explore it at my leisure. It isn't ideal, but there's always a way to make the best of things.'

In some respects, I could see an upside to this. There was no doubt that my options would become more limited, but many of the greatest sights in any city were out in the open. Having less people around would make it easier to appreciate these. At the same time, the prospect of eating microwave meals in the hostel each night offered little appeal.

If nothing else, the news was at least a convenient cover story for my less enthusiastic interactions with Marta and Henry. I don't think they'd really noticed anything, but I'd only seen them very briefly earlier in the shift. Now I was doing my best to hide my feelings. If they did pick-up on anything, the news could be a legitimate explanation. If I wasn't going to share the good news in my private life with them the other day, there was no chance of me sharing this. Sure, Greta may have been the problem, but it was my naivety that allowed it to end up the way it did. I had no desire to admit that foolishness.

'You're not even going to be able to go out for a drink,' Henry said.

'Maybe I should do that after work tonight. The restrictions won't change until midnight, I guess, so I better make the most of it while I can.'

'Oh, what I'd do to join you.'

'I've seen what's in your fridge.' They paid one of the staff members to buy them wine and spirits from time to time, and as incapacitated as they both were, they still enjoyed a drink. I didn't drink that often myself, but after mentioning the idea of going out for one after work just to humour them, I decided it mightn't be the worst idea. The only other option was returning to my room where I would do nothing but dwell.

'You know we used to run a nightclub in Kreuzberg?' Marta said.

'Really? I went to a club there the other night.'

'Well even if it was the same place, it wouldn't have resembled our days there. Berlin has always been a city dominated by its nightlife, but what that has meant continually changes. From one generation to the next, it is unrecognisable.'

27

3 May 1974

MARTA

'Welcome home Marta.'

Home. It was a difficult concept to understand. For most of my adult life we had lived out of suitcases as we traversed the world. There had been bases in Knoxville, Bremen and Paris, but we never spent enough time in any of them to have felt like home.

Berlin was the only home I'd ever known. Flawed and compromised, my youth here may have provided the reasons to leave, but within those times there was something compelling that was always drawing me back. When I escaped, it wasn't Berlin that I sought to flee, but the restrictions imposed on me that kept me from the career of my dreams. My memories had always differentiated between the home where my ideals were formed, and the regime that held power and manipulated our lives. From the times we had visited West Berlin on tour, I had seen that I could return to the city yet be saved from the dystopia across the Wall. The very existence of West Berlin seemed like an act of defiance. Freedom and individuality were celebrated. Everything that the Wall was built to stifle had ended up encouraged and promoted on the other side. I wanted to be part of that.

Henry had accepted my decision to end my career at the end of the 1973 season. We spent the next nine months travelling, spending time in America and Europe trying to agree on where home would become.

In theory, we may be equal partners in this marriage, but in practice, Henry made all the big decisions. With that I had always expected that we'd settle in his preferred location of America, or his old home of Australia. When we arrived in West Berlin, I was expecting to find that we'd be staying in our familiar hotel near Potsdam Platz, but as our taxi headed along a different route from the airport, I was in for a surprise.

'I don't know if this is forever, or just step one, but we are settling here. I have bought an apartment in Kreuzberg, so for a little while at least, Berlin will be home for you once again.'

He knew this was what I wanted, though it remained secondary to me. I had always maintained that my home was at his side, wherever that may be. If I had a choice of where that could be, Berlin would be it, but if it had to be, I would have followed him to the end of the earth.

Like much of Berlin, Kreuzberg had been destroyed late in the war and rebuilt in the subsequent years. In the initial phase, we weren't classed as East and West, but as belonging to one of four zones administered by each of the Allied powers. The Soviet zone was quite distinct from the zones administered by the Americans, the British and the French. All four powers knew it was in their best interests to rebuild and strengthen Berlin, and all of Germany, but the reasons for this seemed to differ.

I no longer felt concerned about the East German authorities. More than a decade had passed since my escape. There were many thousands of former East Germans now living in West Berlin, and they all seemed to live without any fear of repercussion from across the Wall. It was not based on any form of softened approach from the East, but rather a matter of priorities. Berlin was the epicentre of the Cold War. Victory couldn't be accomplished through retributions for the past, but in managing threats going forward. With a small public profile, I had never spoken of any political matter. Retired from that life, I was inconsequential to authorities on either side of the Wall.

'How did you escape East Berlin?' A reporter in New York had asked me this question when interviewing me after my brief starring turn with World on Ice.

'It all happened by chance. I hadn't planned or prepared anything. I entered a tunnel through taking a wrong turn when visiting a friend. It was only when I was half-way through that I realised where I was headed. I chose to continue and arrived across the river with nothing but the clothes on my back. At that point, it seemed safer to stay than to admit what I had done.'

Of course, this wasn't true, nor was it plausible. Even after all those years it was important to give the appearance that my defection was unaided. Giving up those who helped me would still have ramifications. Not only would it impact them, but it could lead to me being a target for retribution from their side. It wasn't the first time I had been asked this question in an interview, and my answer had always been the same. The stakes were high enough that any word I said publicly would be seen, analysed and used against me. I had always ensured that I gave no side reason to target me. This had ensured that I could return to Berlin, where I could live a routine, anonymous existence.

While we'd achieved a certain level of financial security through our careers, it was far from the kind of wealth that would sustain us forever. The sizeable pay cheques had always been offset by a lavish and expensive lifestyle, so once the former dried up, the latter needed to be addressed. We knew that cutting back on expenses was easier said than done, so we were far more interested in the idea of creating a new income.

Through our years on the road, food had become our second passion after the entertainment business. We'd eaten at restaurants the world over and had developed great insight into what worked to make particular establishments stand out above the crowd. As the years passed, we also spent a lot more of our free time creating our own meals, putting into practice the best of what we'd learned on the road. Setting up a restaurant seemed like the perfect idea.

Kreuzberg was a neighbourhood full of young people, seeking to enjoy life. It was the ideal place for what Henry and I had in mind. All our years in the entertainment industry meant we wanted to provide more than just a meal. We wanted to give patrons an experience, and we set to work on creating a new highlight to Kreuzberg's nightlife scene. A restaurant combined with a wine bar and a club for live entertainment, Henry set about building a business with the same gusto he had pursued his acrobatics career. The establishment would be called Victors. More than anything, he had taken inspiration from a club in Knoxville called JJ's. We ate and drank there regularly over the years. It was a busy, profitable venue, and it seemed reasonable to believe that taking a successful concept elsewhere should work well.

One of the adages people used with business was that location is everything. Kreuzberg was ready for Victors and Henry had no interest in waiting any longer than necessary. When a property became available to lease, he pounced. He spent no time identifying the pros and cons of the spot.

'It's the right size and the right price. What more could we want.'

'It's away from the main nightlife,' I said. 'We've got the type of establishment that people can drop in to, before or after dinner, not just people who will come especially and stay all night. That means being visible. It is important that we are easy to find, but who is going to find us here.'

'Offer people what they want, and they will come wherever you are.'

Marriage is a partnership, but it is fair to say that Henry didn't consider it quite an equal one. I was a part of everything, but when it came to decisions, I had little input into anything. Even the decision to move to Berlin was one that I didn't get a say in. It may have been a decision made based on my wishes, but it remained one that Henry made alone. If the decision on where to live could be made without my contribution, what was the likelihood of him listening to me about where we set up the business. Whatever else he may be, Henry was unbelievably stubborn. The more I urged caution, the more determined he was.

Proving people wrong had always been his greatest motivation, so I accepted that my uncertainty was serving a purpose by spurring him on. If I continued to doubt him. he would push harder to ensure success.

Victors opened to steady, but unspectacular customer numbers in late November. Customers enjoyed the food and the ambience, so I considered this to be a positive beginning, but Henry was never satisfied with average.

'We need to up the advertising.'

'Maybe. More importantly, we need to ensure that the people who come, keep coming back. Happy customers return, and they tell others to come. Word of mouth is the best form of advertising.'

'If you don't have enough customers to start with, there's not enough words getting into enough ears.'

'We're not in an international ice-skating show anymore. There were never going to be thousands of people counting down the days until we opened. The numbers are fine, and they will continue to grow.'

Again, Henry had no intention of listening to me. He was constantly altering menu's, working out theme nights and spending more on entertainment. He had sufficiently upped our costs to a point where anything less than full houses would see us losing money.

Henry had hired a chef that came with strong recommendations from people we trusted. Klaus was very good, but he became frustrated early in the piece by Henry's determination to remain the king of the kitchen. Henry's culinary expertise was remarkable for someone self-taught, but while we had been able to put on dinner parties that were beyond what our guests had ever experienced, the timelines that were essential for paying customers in a restaurant were different. And if there was one thing beyond all else that Henry was not equipped to deal with, it was unhappy customers.

'You can just fuck off,' he said to a young couple, complaining about their meal. Whether they understood his English expletives, his angry tone said enough. We'd had complaints about wait times on occasions, but this was the first criticism we'd had of the food. Both had ordered rare steaks but complained they had been overcooked. As far as I could see their complaints were valid. Justified or not, Henry wasn't going to accept such a criticism. Instead of ending up with an unhappy couple who wouldn't return, he'd got the attention of the entire restaurant focussed on him and almost certainly ensured that most of them would also be one-time customers.

'There is a reason I am out the front, and you are out the back,' I told him. 'The customer is always right.'

'That guy was an arsehole. Arseholes aren't right.'

'Everyone is an arsehole to you.'

This was not an isolated incident. While it was rare for him to cause such a scene, he never seemed to grasp certain realities of the business. A happy customer usually passes his or her experience on to someone else. An unhappy customer passes their opinion on to everyone they know. Getting it right 99% of the time earns a little goodwill, but that is lost in entirety when you get it wrong for the other one percent.

Klaus only survived three months before his ongoing feud with Henry became too much. He was replaced by a younger chef, Kurt, who was far more willing to play second fiddle. While Henry appreciated the lack of opposition, he was just as unhappy with the less professional and less capable replacement, and so Kurt was gone after similar a time frame.

'As soon as you have to rely on other people, you're screwed.'

'That is what our directors used to say. You want your name on the door, your job is to put the pieces together. If this was an ice-show, you would be trying to skate every role. It doesn't work.'

We had a twelve-month lease on the restaurant. By nine months, we had agreed that we wouldn't extend.

'We should just walk away now,' Henry said.

'No. I want to finish with something. If nothing else, lessons. What we can and should do in the future. We're paying for the next three months anyway, there's little more to lose by continuing.'

'Wages, stock, advertising. There is a hell of a lot more to lose.'

'Close for a week, change things around. Focus more on the bar, less on the food and you cut the chef's cost and the perishable stock. Don't advertise, just get the word to the right people.'

For one of the rare times, he listened. It wasn't a belief that I was right, but an admission that he had given up.

We had a range of cheap and unknown artists performing each night we were open. We sold only bar snacks, which Henry managed on his own while also serving as the security, giving him licence to let out his aggression if needed. Thankfully, it never was. I was behind the bar full-time. We hadn't cracked the formula for overwhelming success, but for the first time since we'd established, we were turning a profit. As October drew towards an end, Henry was back on to the landlord seeking a new lease. Unfortunately, after our initial decision not to re-sign, a new tenant had already been locked in.

After finally finding our place within the nightlife of Kreuzberg, our time was up.

28

23 March 2020

AMBER

'I'm going out for a drink,' I said to Hannah at the end of our shift. 'Fancy joining me? Won't be an option for a while after tonight.'

'Wouldn't it be better to hit the supermarkets and stock up on things you'll need for the period going forward.'

'They'll still be open. People can't go too many places, so they'll keep going there.'

'If there's anything left.'

'There will be. Money talks. When people want to spend it, businesses will find ways of making sure you can.'

'Maybe true. Still think I might pass on the drink. Life may look different tomorrow, but it's still another working day and I could get lumped with a twelve-hour shift at late notice. I need my sleep too much.'

'Alright. I will see you tomorrow.'

As I got to the door, she called out to me.

'Take care Amber. Believe in yourself.'

I hadn't thought too much of her when we first met, but she has proven to be so much more of a friend than I could have expected. Someone who understood me. Wise counsel and an ally. Over the course of the past four months, there were few people who'd been anywhere near as good to me.

On the most direct route, it is a fifteen-minute walk, but I decided to go the longer way. Up to and along Warschauer Straße, I would pass dozens of bars, and get a gauge of how immediate the impact of today's announcements had been. Everything had seemed to become quieter around the city each day as people get more cautious about the impact of the virus. Would today's announcements have accelerated that, or would the feeling of a last chance draw more people out tonight?

It appeared that it wasn't just the consumers who were lost in their efforts to keep up with the latest. Several bars and clubs were closed, despite the restrictions not yet being in place. Those that were open seemed busy for this time on a Monday night, though I didn't have much of a sample to compare it to. I kept walking, more intent on trying to understand the feel of the city in the strangeness of the circumstances than reaching any destination. As I got to the last few blocks from home, I took the opportunity to stop at the last available bar, an Irish pub of questionable authenticity called Molly Malone's.

'*Ich möchte ein pilsner bitte.*'

I wasn't sure if German would be necessary in an authentic Irish bar, but whenever a conversation wasn't likely to extend beyond a sentence, I went with it. Anything more and I knew I couldn't carry it. As he pulled the beer, he asked where I was from.

'Canada.'

'Wow, I'd love to go there. Whereabouts.'

'Toronto. I grew up in Sault Saint Marie, a town on the Great Lakes, just across the border from the USA. I guess in a way that's always felt more like home than Toronto, but my family moved there several years ago.'

'What's brought you to Berlin?'

'Always wanted to come to Europe. I had nothing tying me down so the time was right to come here and travel across the continent, who knows how long for. I've been in Germany since November, Berlin for a bit over a week. I'm meant to be here for another few weeks, but the way things are, who knows how long I'll be here.'

'What a time to have come to Europe.'

'I don't think it would matter where I was. This seems to be a world-wide issue.'

He gave me the drink and raised his own glass of water in unison with me. 'Prost!' I said, raising the glass to meet his. It was rare for me to order beer, at least when I'm on my own. In Stuttgart, I went out after work with colleagues on several occasions, and always drank beer, fitting in with the others. At the end of a long shift, I did start finding it an effective means of quenching my thirst. With that in mind, why not have one now?

He seemed to be a little too interested, so I dropped in the idea of meeting the perfect woman just to stop him from getting the wrong idea. I was enjoying the conversation but didn't want it turning into anything unwelcome.

It was out of my typically introverted character to seek interaction, generally preferring to keep to myself. One of the motivations of my time here was that I was destined to have the majority of time on my own, but one of life's realities is that we crave what we lack. I have limited conversation with colleagues at work and its only Henry and Marta that I really talk to of the residents.

As the barman became busy with other customers, I moved into a corner of the room, adjacent to tables with people enjoying their last taste of freedom. Before long, I was swept into a group of British expats. They got me talking about home, and several said how much they'd love to go there.

'Everywhere sounds exciting until you've lived there,' I said.

'I've spent five years in Berlin, and it hasn't lost its edge with me,' said James, the man who'd initially invited me to their table.

'Well give me five years and I'll know whether that's you or the city.'

'You're planning on spending five years here?' another of the group asked.

'No. I love new places too much to want to stay anywhere too long. I have a job here for the next four weeks, then it will be time to move on.'

'Where are you working?' James asked.

'A nursing home a few blocks away'

'Which one?' the woman next to James asked.

' *Senioren Fachpflegezentrum.*'

'Get out of here! I'm starting there on Saturday. What sort of a workplace is it?'

'You've worked in aged care before? No better, no worse than anywhere else. Not the most glamorous job, but I guess there's a rewarding side to it.'

'How do you do it without speaking German?' she asked, before introducing herself as Heidi.

I explained how most of my time was spent following the orders of whoever I was working with, so I had little or no direct communication with most residents. I then referenced Henry and Marta, and how he only spoke English, and that my language skills meant they could palm him off to me.

'The one nobody wants to deal with, that would be right.'

'He's great though. It's weird. Someone gets a reputation for trouble, so people treat them according to their reputation, and that treatment leads to them being more trouble. Because I can talk to Henry, I get to see the real person. He appreciates that, so he is good to me, which means I treat him better and the circle continues.'

Heidi and I were locked into a conversation of our own. She was born and raised in Berlin but had been speaking English since primary school. She was fluent with almost no discernible accent at all. She had met James when he was new to the city. They had fallen in love and were now engaged. It was good to know the limitations early, for she was gorgeous, and we had a similar rapport to what I'd first found with Greta at the ice-rink. I think I'm grateful that she is unattainable, for the last thing I want to do right now is meet someone else. The time for that will come.

Heidi had worked in aged care a few years earlier but didn't enjoy it, and left to pursue full-time study, but dropped out at the start of the year.

'Why are you returning to a job you didn't like.'

'Money. Depending on what happens with this virus, we want to get married later in the year and I want to be earning what I can in the meantime. I never hated the work, I just didn't see it as part of my long-term plans. Now I'm more focused on home than career, so a job that I can do well is enough for me.'

'Last drinks,' the barman called out, far earlier than I was ready to hear.

'Midnight all these restrictions take hold,' James said. 'It's ridiculous.'

I didn't want to get into a debate about it. Working in aged care, I understood the damage that a virus could do if not contained. We faced that with every strain of influenza, but while the current virus had so many unknowns, the consequences that normally are restricted to the particularly vulnerable, were now apparent to all of society. Locking down a facility was easy. Locking down the breadth of society was far more difficult, so it was understandable that governments around the world were unable to show uniformity of approach. Which was the right approach? Only time will tell.

James had bought me another beer and I said I'd hoped to be able to repay the favour soon.

'Take my girl under your wing at work, and that will be more than enough,' he said.

'It's a big home. We probably won't be working together. Multiple floors, multiple shifts. Even if we are in the same section at the same time, they probably won't have two newbies partnering up, but hope-fully our paths do cross.'

'They told me that Saturday would be orientation for six of us.'

'Yeah, they're paranoid about staff coming down with the virus and them not having enough people to cover it. I was already back-filling someone on maternity leave and they were still short staffed. With the virus they want a surplus of staff, but I think half a dozen more won't be enough to get to that point.'

Most of the group at the table had left as the pub emptied out. Finishing our drinks with the barman starting to speed us up, the three of us walked to the door before he started pressuring us too much.

'What shift are you doing Saturday?' I asked as we walked into the cold night air. They lived a block away from the pub, but in the opposite direction to my hostel.

'2 until 10pm'

'Awesome, me too. Do you want to meet up before and we can go to work together?'

'Yeah, that'd be great. Always feel anxious on the first day anywhere so it would be good to have someone to chat with on the way.'

Heidi pointed out their apartment building and said to meet her there at 1.30pm.

'We'll just make sure we stay 1.5 metres apart as we walk in. They're paranoid about everyone taking all the necessary precautions.'

'Ok. Have a good week 'til then Amber. I'll see you Saturday.'

After Greta ripped my faith in humanity apart, my instinct was to hide from people where possible. Gladly I resisted. Few of life's highlights come without others. People hurt us, but they also enrich us. Living in fear of what can go wrong eliminates the possibility of things going right. I love solitude and the peace it brings me, but that only has significance when it is offset by the good times that require others.

Marta and Henry made work easier to deal with, but if every room I walked into had English speaking residents with amazing stories, the impact wouldn't be the same. Life is about balance. We need the worst of people in order to appreciate the best of them. Berlin was the epitome of that balance. The home of tyranny for so long, it had evolved to the home of freedom. It had learnt just how precious that was. I was learning from the city, and the people in it, that when you want the best of life, you had to endure some of the worst of it.

29

3 January 1980

MARTA

Henry always seemed to be one moment away from pulling the pin and leaving Berlin for good. Fortunately, whatever bitterness he had whenever things turned against him, paled into insignificance alongside his love for me. Every time he talked of us selling up and moving, I told him that I was not leaving.

'I will miss you terribly, my darling. This is my home. I am not leaving.'

He would usually fire back that as his wife I should do whatever he says, but every time we went down that path, the debate ended quickly in my favour. For years I was waiting to jump when he said the word, but I had learned more recently the macho exterior was nothing more than a front. He needed me at least as much as I did him. He wasn't leaving, whatever he said.

West Berlin was an outsider, a progressive capitalist Western city completely encircled by communist East Germany. People who felt like outsiders were drawn here. It had shown in recent years through our arts scene. David Bowie, Lou Reed, Iggy Pop and numerous other giants of the music world had come here to seek the inspiration that the enclave offered them. Many artists wrote and recorded their greatest works here.

You didn't need to be an artist here, though it seems that many within that field thrived. The sense of being separated from the general way of life the ordinary person lives is definitively Berlin. Even in retirement, the lives we'd led probably helped shape us to feel this way. For all of Henry's threats, he belonged here as much as I did. It wasn't the past that tied me to this city as much as the present, and more importantly, the future. West Berlin was moving forward more dynamically than anywhere in the world. I still maintained a belief that one day, we could tear down the wall and remove the first part of that name. I believed this progress should be shared by all of Berlin.

Since the close of Victors, we had both gone through jobs and professions like underwear. I had worked in an array of bars and restaurants, while Henry had primarily worked in security, but had also had stints working as a chef's assistant, a bookmaker's clerk and had operated a couple of small businesses, most recently a car-hire operation.

'I shouldn't have retired when I did,' he said, returning to a familiar topic. Every profession has its own set of positive and negative elements, but the entertainment business is one that differs from most. While some people can't escape it fast enough, most who spend a decent time making their way to the top, never willingly leave. Circumstances had made our decisions. They had seemed right, but with life never reaching the heights we'd fed off for so long, it was understandable to look back with regret.

'You'd still be here now,' I said. 'There is no way you'd still be doing those tricks now, so what is the difference.'

'The difference is a few more years of earning those sums would have taken the pressure off us now. Also, if I'd seen the end coming earlier, I might have been able to find a way of pushing into some other role in the industry.'

'Teaching? There is nothing you would hate more.'

'Hell, I'd never have gone down that road. I don't know what I could have done, but there had to be some other avenue to use the experience I'd gained over all those years.'

While Henry found the idea of teaching acrobatics abhorrent, I had a different view of teaching figure skating. It had never been at the forefront of my desires, but it made sense to utilise my expertise and to make some sort of ongoing income from the lifetime of labour I had pursued.

High-level coaching roles existed, but these were all taken by people with lesser skating pedigree than me. They had, however, all been part of the local system throughout. For me to join their ranks, I needed to begin at the bottom, teaching virtual beginners at the local ice rink. The pay was minimal, but it was an opening. For me, the greatest pleasure was in putting a pair of skates on for the first time in several years. When we returned to Berlin, I had felt like I had come home, but it was only when stepping back on to the ice that the feeling seemed complete.

My work at the rink was three afternoons a week, totalling less than a dozen hours. It was children who were competent skaters, and just beginning to develop an interest in pursuing figure skating. There were no budding champions amongst them, but I did take heart in seeing the ongoing improvement in most of them. Perhaps it was the years of putting up with Henry that had taught me patience, for it wasn't a quality I was known for in my youth. This was essential working with children. I wanted to skip forward to work with talented teenagers who were already at national competition level. That is where I felt I could make a more significant difference, but the sport here was a closed shop. Those who had competed for West Germany at the top level were all that mattered. For all the heights I'd reached, I was an outsider. However much that tended to be the ideal of Berlin, it didn't play that way in the figure skating community.

While teaching had fallen short of what I had hoped it would be, I remained more positive than Henry. He continued to work odd jobs here and there, but none of them generated any sort of positivity from him. It was only the arrival of his sister from Australia that brought out any exuberance in him.

Henry and I had visited Australia the last two years. Henry's mother had come to Berlin last year, and he'd continually pushed Lorraine to bring her family across. Perhaps exposed to an inaccurate view of Berlin that may be commonplace in Australia, she questioned whether it was an appropriate place to bring her children.

'I thought it best to come and see for myself this time. All being well, we will come back as a family next year.'

'Bloody hell, what do you think we're doing here? If it was going to be dangerous here, it would be for the woman who escaped from the other side of the Wall. If she's safe here, everyone is.'

From that point onwards, Lorraine's week gave Henry an escape from the routine that he'd begun to slump into. He played the role of tour guide, taking his sister across West Berlin. He loved having her here, not just through spending time with someone he loved, but for the fact he had an audience as he told his stories as well as those of the city he now called home. He'd lived for the audiences for so long, and it was that, rather than the acrobatics itself that he missed.

While most nights we had cooked elaborate meals for Lorraine, giving her a taste of what we'd originally envisaged for Victor's, on our final night we took her to the restaurant which now stood where we'd originally been.

'I can see why the location didn't serve you well,' she said as we walked the dark street a couple of blocks from the main strip.

'It didn't help,' Henry said. 'There was more to it than that. What we had worked well for a certain type of crowd, but Berlin wasn't ready for it.'

Berlin wasn't ready for Henry perhaps. Henry might not have been ready for Berlin either, but I could feel that was gradually starting to turn.

30

24 March 2020

AMBER

I'm even more glad that I had a few drinks last night, as I slept much better than I otherwise would have expected to. The later night had seen me sleep in this morning, and with the limitations on available options before work today, that was destined to prove a good thing. I took a quick peak outside the window and notice no discernible difference from every other morning since I have been here. We're in a quiet spot, a few blocks away from the major arterial roads. It was there that any difference would be more obvious.

Where possible, the government is recommending people work from home. In my line of work that isn't possible. Supposedly many people can, but in our industry, there would only be a limited number of administration staff whose physical presence isn't essential. I think it's unfair if they get to stay home and work, while we must travel in each day, take additional risk with our wellbeing, and receive no bonus for doing so. Still, at what point does fairness ever enter the equation in situations like this.

I'd taken advantage of the time difference when I got home last night, ringing Mum in Canada. It was better to speak to her after a few drinks while feeling positive. She had been happy with the idea of me travelling but wanted it to be a short trip away. I'm sure in her mind, a trip to sight-see around Europe would be a good fun way of getting over the heartbreak I'd endured, but that missed the point of what I was pursuing. Once I explained I was coming here for an extended time to learn what I wanted in life, she was far less encouraging. Now with border closures and a world of uncertainty, she wanted me home. Anything less than enthusiasm in my voice would be met with a panicked plea for me to return.

'If you don't get out now, who knows how long you'll be stuck there.'

'You can't be stuck somewhere if it is where you want to be.'

'You want to be in a foreign land with restrictions on every aspect of your life and nobody you know or can depend on?'

'A journey of discovery won't uncover much if you're depending on others.'

'Germany has already been discovered Amber.'

'Yet every day I am discovering new people and new experiences. I'm learning more about myself than anything else. Good, bad and indifferent, each day is enriching me more than a month at home could do.'

'So, we just have to hope we might see you again one day?'

'Remember when you left Sault Saint Marie seeking a new beginning?'

When my parents divorced, Mum, Craig and I had moved to Toronto, with mum desperate for a new start. Effectively, she wanted to find who she was, and did this through starting a new life in a new city.

'Mum, I love you, but I need to continue this journey. I doubt I could get out now even if I wanted,' I explained. 'But I definitely don't want to.'

She missed me, and that was more a factor in her desire for me to return than any worries about my choices. I understood, for I missed her too, but I couldn't become the person I wanted to be while being chained to all that confined me into the person I had been. By the end of the call, she sounded more accepting and told me not to leave it too long before I called again.

'All the messages are great, but they don't mean as much as hearing your voice.'

I'd probably communicated more with her in the past four months than I did in the previous year at home. It's modern life, I guess. We often seem to be more in touch with those out of reach, while taking for granted those right at our side.

When I went to bed and reflected on the phone call, I thought about how nobody ever replaced my father in Mums life. She'd been on her own for eight years now and hadn't shown any inclination towards that changing. As I thought about her choices I wondered if we weren't more similar than I'd ever realised. Perhaps she'd had similar feelings to what I do, but while the end of the relationship with Andrew left me unwilling to suppress them any longer, she may have felt too uncomfortable to pursue her true self. Maybe the one difference between us was that I was ready and able to confront the fears that had held me down before now, while she was willing to let them rule her life.

Before I got up, I sent her a quick message, just to say how good it was talking to her last night. It didn't need saying, but it reinforced the positivity that the conversation ended with. I wanted her to understand that my time in Europe wasn't a rejection of her, Toronto or my life there. It was merely a way of gaining a different perspective of life, one that would hopefully lead to a beautiful new vision.

Gaining a wider perspective today wasn't likely. After a slow start to the day, there was less than four hours until my shift started. It was too long to spend in the room, but not long enough to make it far. With most of the city's attractions now closed, the only real options were the open spaces. The best of these was the Tiergarten, but it needed more time than I had. Following an online search for recommendations, I found Treptower Park.

Treptower Park was on the western bank of the Spree, roughly two kilometres from the Oberbaum Bridge, and stretching out for nearly twice that distance to the south-east. It was a tranquil park, with few people wandering. As a first timer here, it was impossible to tell whether the number of people reflected the pandemic reaction or a sign of normal crowd numbers here. Tourist numbers are down while locals are leaving home significantly less. Even with most attractions closed, it hadn't led to an increase in people seeking places like this. Home and isolated may not yet be compulsory, but it seems to be the voluntary choice of most people.

The most prominent feature of the park was the Soviet War Memorial. 80,000 Soviet soldiers were killed in the Battle of Berlin and this memorial honours them, as well as being the final resting place of more than 5,000 of these soldiers.

I wasn't enough of a history student to understand too much of the dynamics of World War II and its aftermath. In the space of a few short years, the Soviets had gone from the enemy of Germany, committing unspeakable atrocities against their people, to being the trusted allies in charge of the reconstruction of their country. A Soviet War Memorial may have made sense in the occupied era, but many suspected it wouldn't remain once Berlin became unified. Thirty years on it remains a tribute to the sacrifices of the Red Army, whatever else they inflicted on the German civilian population.

After wandering for a little over an hour, I'd had enough. I considered going to Tempelhof, the former airport site that now served Berlin as its biggest open community space. I think after last night I was probably keener for company than open space, but that wasn't an option, so I headed back to the hostel. If nothing else, I could at least go downstairs and do my washing, which would probably have me mingling with others as they came and went from the common areas.

***

As part of the routine to protect the home from the virus, Ada takes our temperatures at reception when we arrive at work. She was surprised to see me more than an hour early. When I got upstairs, Marta was equally surprised.

'You're not meant to be here yet, are you?'

'I came in early. I thought I'd take you outside. Get a little fresh air.'

'Really? I haven't been outside since I last went to hospital.'

'You have to wear this though,' I said placing a surgical mask over her face. 'They won't let you out of the room without this.'

She was already dressed and sitting up in her wheelchair. She hasn't left the room in my time at the home but makes the effort to get up as part of an ongoing mind-game with Henry. At this point, Henry was sleeping, probably the only thing that enabled Marta the freedom to go outside.

Getting out of the lift, we passed Ada, who was surprised to see Marta. I explained we would only be a few minutes, as I was just wheeling her up and down the block, and that it had been approved by the nursing director.

'*Wunderbar. Genießen Sie die frische Luft,*' Ada said to Marta telling her to enjoy the fresh air. There was no doubt she would. If it was true that the less you have of something, the more you appreciate it, then these few minutes would be golden.

As we got outside, we saw a man walking a dog across the other side of the road.

'Oh, how beautiful,' Marta said. 'Have I told you about Wolfe?'

'No.'

'Wolfe was our dog. A Deutscher Schäferhund, or what you would call a German Shepherd. You can never understand how much he meant to us.'

31

25 September 1986

MARTA

Henry never wanted children. That was fortunate, for I couldn't have them. I was far from maternal, and never saw it fitting in with my plans for life. Of course, not having children means missing out on a huge part of the human experience, but it also provides an additional level of freedom. The lifestyle we led in the sixties and seventies had always made this seem to be a great asset, but as life settled down, there was a level of emptiness.

Life always changes. The ideals we have at one point of time, often give rise to a whole new mindset later. We had moved out of Kreuzberg, buying a house in the well-to-do district of Charlottenburg. We had a house, not large, but with space surrounding us that we'd never known.

You slow down. We didn't regret what we could never have helped, but there was a part of us that wanted something more than each other. Although I'd never liked dogs, the more we walked around the suburbs, the more of my attention began to focus on those we'd pass. Henry never said anything about it, but for my fortieth birthday, he had brought home an Alsatian puppy. I named him Wolfe, after the dog that lived next door to us when I was a child.

Many people love their dogs as much as their family. I think Henry and I feel this way more than most. There's a certain amount of love within each of us. For most people, this was split between spouses, children and a wide range of other family members. For so long, Henry and I only had each other. We loved his family, but they were half a world away, save for the occasional trip. When Wolfe came along, our love had another being to share it.

A whole other side of Henry began to be released. The tough exterior gave way to a heart as soft as butter as he cared for the newest member of our family. It seemed that the move from Kreuzberg had given us a new life. Crossing the Wall had been an unimaginable change all those years earlier, but without anywhere near the drama, we had changed our lives nearly as much with this move across West Berlin.

Wolfe was unbelievably spoilt. He had the run of our house, and with few visitors, our house quickly became his palace.

Lorraine and her family came to visit us. They'd had a dog several years earlier who survived only until the age of three when he was hit by a car. Alex had not been born at that time, but Teresa had loved him madly. Ever since, she had wanted another dog, but her parents had been sufficiently scarred by the tragedy that they hadn't replaced him.

As soon as they arrived, Teresa seemed to forget about Henry and me. She immediately fell in love with Wolfe. Alex on the other hand was terrified of him, which was understandable for such a small boy facing such a big dog. Wolfe was only two, and full of exuberance, energy and excitement. He always had the attention and affection of everyone who he came into contact with. When he suddenly had a human that was trying to hide from him, it made him more determined than ever to win him over.

'He is just excited to see you,' I said, as he had knocked Alex over when jumping up to greet him.

'He tried to bite me.'

'No, he is just playing.'

It was futile. Alex spent the rest of the trip trying to hide from Wolfe. Henry ended up keeping Wolfe as separated from his nephew as possible, the only time our dog was ever kept from any part of our lives.

Wolfe continue to grow, as did his impact on us. We loved him every bit as much as we ever could have loved a child. We developed a routine, walking him every day in the grounds of Schloss Charlottenburg. We'd walk alongside the Spree, veering off at the point where there was an inlet through to the other waterways, the Karpfenteich, the Luisengraben and the Teichgraben. It was by the Teichgraben that we would sit, relaxing with a cigarette as we'd soak in the view and watch Wolfe run free.

Wolfe was rarely on his lead when we were in the park. While he was ready to strike fear into anyone who should come to our front door, when we were outside of our property, he never gave a moment of focus to other people. The same couldn't be said when other dogs were in his presence, and he was always ready to show himself as the alpha male. We didn't usually come across too many others, but when we did, we had to be ready to restrain him.

Yesterday was just another one of these walks, but with a few dogs in the park, he didn't have the freedom that he was accustomed to. As we were making our way back home, he was keen to get off the lead. He ran off ahead of us as we were getting closer to home, and despite Henry's shouts for him to come back, he continued ahead.

'Wolfe.' Henry screamed like I had never heard. He'd seen what I couldn't from behind the final bend. A car had been backing out of a driveway and had hit him. I was filled with fear, both at what may have happened to my beloved dog, and to what an overly emotional Henry may end up doing to the driver.

Wolfe was on the road, unable to move. In pain and in shock, but alive. Henry was far too concerned about fixing the problem than recriminations. He picked Wolfe up and was about to run back home to get the car.

'*Es gibt keine Zeit. Komm mit mir,*' the driver of the car yelled, offering to take Wolfe and both of us to the vets.

Henry would not normally have entertained the offer, but I had already opened the backdoor and insisted. The driver continually uttered his sorrow, explaining how it was a blind spot coming out of the drive-way, and though he'd stopped and checked as best as he could, he couldn't possibly see the dog running from down the street.

'A less careful driver and he would have been killed,' I said, but Henry didn't have the same attitude. He didn't care how or why. His dog was in peril and whoever had been behind the wheel would suffer his wrath. Initially I'd been relieved that the driver wouldn't have understood all of Henry's expletives, but he began speaking to us in English and I realised he'd known every word. He was a familiar face, living just down the road from us, but this was the first time we had met him. It couldn't be worse circumstances, but the man, Jonas, was doing everything possible now to help Wolfe be saved. He got us to the vets far quicker than we could have ourselves.

Henry was a hypochondriac, and that condition was reflected in his attitude towards our dog. As a result, the vet knew us very well. I'm sure when he saw us come through the door, he was thinking "not again," but only fleetingly. He could see the state that we were in. He immediately took Wolfe from Henry and disappeared out the back with him after finding out what had happened. We sat in the waiting room, overcome with fear.

'I swear to God if he doesn't make it, I am going to kill that arse-hole,' Henry said. Rather than berate him, I was merely thankful that he'd focussed on Wolfe at the critical moment and saved the anger for a better time. Later, when he was ready to listen to reason, I would explain why we should be grateful, not critical of Jonas.

'His injuries are serious,' the vet's assistant said coming out to see us and seek instruction. 'Dr Zeidler must operate, but he can't do that until Wolfe has stabilised. He was in shock, and that in itself causes dangers from fluids moving from the vessels to the tissue and cutting off the oxygen supply to his brain and other organs. That is now some-what under control. There is risk in what we need to do, and there is also great expense.'

'I don't care what it costs. Do what you must do,' Henry said without out a moment's contemplation.

We continued our wait, Henry pacing up and down the corridor, while I stayed firmly in my seat, my head in my hands thinking of the worst possibilities. I was desperate to see the vet walk back out with an update, but equally dreading the moment he did, knowing that news was just as likely to be a horror that I could not cope with.

It felt like hours, but eventually Dr Zeidler came out.

'He will be alright. He won't be the same dog for quite some time. He has a long recovery ahead of him, but he will be back to his best eventually.'

It was Henry, not I, who was in tears. I had never seen this before, but it highlighted the emotional bond he had with Wolfe. Mine was no less, though my tears never fell with relief, only in moments of tragedy.

We had to wait longer before we could take him home. We were advised that we'd need to return after he'd rested overnight for further checks. I held him the whole way home, and he stayed between us all night. Again, I held him for our return to the vets and Henry carried him in. Dr Zeidler gave him the all-clear, and after going through a recovery plan with us, we were on our way home with our sad and tired boy.

'He is just a dog,' Lorraine said when Henry relayed the story to her over the phone a little earlier.

'What the bloody hell does that mean? Should I say Alex is only a boy next time he's in hospital?'

'It's hardly the same.'

'It isn't that different. He means as much to us as your children mean to you. I know he doesn't mean as much to you as your children do to us, and therein lies the difference. But if you want to understand other people, you need to look from their angle. We have each other, and we have Wolfe. Anyone else is half a world away. Until you learn to see how that impacts emotional attachments, you can't understand what we've been through.'

Henry was right. She didn't understand, but it didn't warrant starting a fight. Lorraine was apologetic, and eventually Henry calmed sufficiently to end the conversation amicably.

'Nobody bloody gets it,' he said to me.

'Nobody needs to. We do. Focus on the relief. All is well and it's a time to be happy. I have Wolfe, I have you. I don't need anything else, do you.'

'You're right.'

Two words that he had always found nearly impossible to say.

32

24 March 2020

AMBER

'I am scared. He is everything and I can't bear the thought of living without him,' Marta said.

'You never know what is in store.'

'I do know. He has panicked without need for years. Now he is not panicking. He is resigned to the end.'

I'd never known a couple whose lives revolved around each other so completely. Without other family, the level of dependence they had on each other had grown progressively over their near six decades together. Now, there was little either could do for the other, but that didn't change the emotional needs that could only come from a life of shared love and memories.

'Let's go back up to him,' I said, turning the wheelchair back towards the door, then into the lift and back to the room.

'Where the hell have you been?'

Henry didn't like Marta being anywhere but at his side. While he didn't stir when we walked out of the room, he'd woken at some point while we were outside and wasn't happy that his wife wasn't there.

'I took Marta outside for some fresh air. It had been too long since she'd last had that. Don't worry, when you are up to it, I will do the same for you.'

'Next time I'm outside it will be in a coffin.'

'Not if you don't want it to be.' I genuinely believed it, as he was showing more life and fight now that he had something to be upset about.

'What if something happened?' he said.

'You'd have rung the bell.'

'I did. Didn't do any bloody good.'

'Shut up Henry,' Marta said. 'I put up with you all day and night, I deserve some pleasure when the rare opportunity comes along.'

'I should put in a complaint about you,' he said to me.

'Yes, it was wrong to do something nice for Marta.'

'Damn right. Each time my eyes shut, it's one time closer to them never opening again. I want Marta to be the last thing I see, not an empty bed.'

'You're such a drama queen Victor,' Marta said, using his surname as she did whenever she was angry with him. When we first left the room, she told me he would be like this. She knew every idiosyncrasy about him, far more than he knew them himself. Love doesn't always present in the same ways, but you'd never see a purer example than this.

***

The threat of Coronavirus on our workforce has failed to materialise so far. I still need to be on standby, but at this stage I have today off. Henry seemed to have forgotten our scrap by the end of yesterday's shift, but it still wasn't the worst time for a day away. Filling that time wasn't necessarily so easy. With sleep and work taking up three quarters of my usual day, it was manageable, but now there was sleep sandwiched either side of a long and empty gap with little in the way of options.

Before I snapped out of my laziness, the phone rang. Work. Frida. Always enough to have me on tenterhooks when I get calls on my day off. I needn't have worried. One of the staff has been placed in quarantine due to possible exposure to the virus at her home. She has no symptoms and hasn't been at work for the past couple of days, so it is unlikely to have any further impact on the workplace. The impact for me is far better, as I now would be needed for night shift.

I've been on afternoons since I've been here, so I'm likely to have different staff to be working with. Hopefully I'd be remaining on the 2nd floor, as I liked the residents. Marta and Henry are naturally top of that list due to our ability to have conversations in English, but even for those with whom communication is a struggle, the issue was known, making life easier. A new part of the building would mean a whole new set of awkward introductions. Manageable of course, but not ideal.

I was determined to make it across town today. From everything she had told me yesterday, Charlottenburg seemed like a beautiful, and very different part of the city. While the main attraction, the Charlottenburg Palace, would be closed, the area surrounding it was open space and there shouldn't be any issue with me passing through there. While I didn't know quite where Marta and Henry had lived, I drew a picture in my mind from all she said, and when comparing it with a map last night, I've worked out the streets to walk down that will feel like I'm walking in their footsteps.

'Not working today,' Erik said as I walked by the reception desk.

I had managed to avoid elongated conversations with him for the past few days, but now I'd reached the point where I was happy to kill time any way I could. I stopped, happy to give him some of my excess time.

'Yeah, but not until 10pm. I haven't done an overnight shift here yet, so that will be something different.'

'The things we do for money, right.'

'I'm enjoying it there. At the moment there's not too much else that I can do with my time, so why not make the most of it.'

'So where are you off to now?'

'I'm going to have a wander through the gardens around Charlottenburg Palace. One of the residents was explaining that it was where she used to walk her dog. She says she wants her ashes scattered there when she goes, so I figure it must be a beautiful spot.'

He'd proven to have an opinion on everything, so it came as little surprise that he spent more than ten minutes detailing every possible inch of Schloss Charlottenburg. I tried to take in what I could, not so much out of a desire to change my plans to fit them, but so that I could comment next time I ran into him. I didn't want to be too encouraging, but in these unprecedented times there was a value attached to any person you had contact with.

I sat alone on the platform at the station. Services were still running, as there was still a need for essential workers to travel, but few people were choosing public transport. I had spotted a few people waiting for trains on other platforms, reminding me that life continued, albeit a slightly different version. All of them were wearing masks, the first time I had seen people taking such precautions outside of my workplace. These hadn't been mandated by the government, largely it seemed due to the lack of available supply. One way or another, the people who were most likely to need them seemed to be adequately stocked up. By the time the train arrived there were two other people on the platform, but once aboard, I was alone in my carriage.

It was roughly twenty minutes on the train before arriving at the station by the zoo, where I had to change trains. I only waited a couple of minutes before the ten-minute trip to Sophie-Charlotte Platz. From this station, it was a walk along Schloßstraße, a wide boulevard with expensive high-rise apartments on both sides of the road. Although the road was only one lane of traffic each way, between these was a divider roughly fifteen metres wide. Two lines of trees to beautify the grassed section on the sides, split by a walking path and seats between these. It was the most beautiful street I had seen anywhere in Berlin. It made sense. Looking to the end of the street, the palace stood out from hundreds of metres away.

The palace is a beautiful building, and while going inside was impossible at this point, it was an extra place to consider returning to if things returned to normal. I walked across the first section of the courtyard to a statue of Friedrich Wilhelm atop a horse. I didn't know enough of the history from that era to know who he was, so it didn't hold my interest. I made my way left, headed to the western most point, then along to the river.

Consulting my map, I could see it wasn't the Spree that I had come across, but a stream called the Teichgraben. I remembered this was the spot where she said they'd always stop and sit down for a while before returning home. I walked along until I found a seat, which I could only assume was the very spot where they used to stop each day. I sat, and closed my eyes, thinking of them as they would have been nearly forty years ago when Wolfe was a young pup.

It was so tranquil. It probably would never be so peaceful in normal times, though perhaps this was closer to how it would have been a generation ago when it was part of their daily routine. Eventually a jogger passed, the first person I had seen since entering the park and serving as a reminder that despite the quiet, I was in fact in a prominent public place.

As I got up and continued my walk, a middle-aged couple were headed towards me from a distance. The man called out, and initially I had thought it was to me. Before I had time to wonder what the issue was, I saw a dog bound out from the bushes closer to the river and return to his side. It was a Labrador, but the sight of man, woman and dog together was as close as I could wish to see to the daily occurrence of Henry, Marta and Wolfe all those years ago. Part of me wanted to warn them of the dangers of cars leaving driveways, but even if they understood my language, expressing the reason for that message may have proven a little much.

The serenity of the estate at this unusual point of history made me contemplate. Almost 75 years to the day when the grounds were under bombardment, it was a picture of tranquillity.

There is nothing so beautiful that human conflict cannot destroy. There is also nothing so damaged, that humans can't restore, when they act with a genuine unity of purpose.

Berlin. Beautiful, unified Berlin.

26 December 1989

MARTA

Berlin. Beautiful, unified Berlin.

The Wall came down on November 9th. Not the whole Wall, for that remains a work in progress, but the significance of the Wall disappeared that night when the first sections were brought down. Easterners passed through to the West. People from both sides sang, danced and celebrated together. For a middle-aged couple with a dog in suburban Charlottenburg, the celebrations were a little more muted, as we watched the events occur on television. Naturally I was excited. I had hoped for this day for as long as I could remember. I wanted to walk through the area I grew up in, but I had no need to be the first to do this. This was the beginning of a new era.

While the world celebrated this end to division, the excitement wasn't shared by everyone. Removing the Wall didn't remove the separation between *Ossis* and *Wessis* as the citizens from each side were referred to. Many from the East sought revolution, but from within their country. They feared that a reunification of Germany would take them back to the first half of the century. In the West, the fear was that the wealth created in the previous four decades would be destroyed by a surge in people coming into their land. As a West Berliner who had been raised in the East, I couldn't understand any of this. To me, unity was everything. We were one people. The differences between us stemmed from belief, but most of this came from indoctrination through each side's propaganda. Unified, this would dissolve with time.

'When are we going?' Henry asked a week later.

'I have wanted this for so long, but now that the time has come, I feel less inclined.' People were flocking across the border by their thousands. East Berliners looking to purchase previously forbidden Western goods. West Berliners seeking to see if all the stories they'd heard about the East were true. Amongst them were people like me, those who had fled and wanted to see their past. I couldn't explain my reticence. Perhaps when you've yearned for the forbidden, it loses its appeal when it becomes available.'

'In time.'

Earlier in the year, Lorraine had told us that she, as well as the kids and Henry's mother, would all be coming to spend Christmas with us. She and Ian had separated the previous year. Teresa had moved interstate, and so with so much work to get most of her loved ones together to celebrate the festive season, she felt it right to go the whole way and have all her family in one place. We spent one Christmas in Australia just over a decade ago, but it didn't feel like Christmas to me, sweltering through a hot summer. When the plans were made, we really didn't believe they'd be arriving as history was being rewritten. Events were beginning to make it seem more believable, but even a couple of months ago, I still suspected we would be waiting several more years.

We kept the first day of their visit quiet, giving them time to get over their jetlag. Wolfe was happy to have the extra attention in our overflowing house. Several years since Alex had been here, his age and Wolfe's more sedate nature since the accident, meant that he was now getting along just as well with the dog as his sister did.

As an extended family, we took Wolfe on his regular walk through the Charlottenburg Palace gardens. Wolfe wasn't usually too excited chasing a ball, but it seemed that he and Alex had found an activity to share that helped them both bond. Once enough energy had been burnt, we headed home to prepare the feast we'd planned for our guests.

A block from home we made what had become a regular stop on our morning walks.

'Wolfe!' It was Jonas, the man who had nearly killed him, but also helped save him. Despite not owning a dog, Jonas probably spent more money on dog treats than just about anyone in Berlin. Initially it had stemmed from guilt, but in time it had become genuine affection. He loved Wolfe nearly as much as we did, and in turn we'd built up a better friendship with him than anyone else in the city.

Although Christmas Eve was the customary main event here, with an Australian family joining us, we split the celebration over it and Christmas Day. By Boxing Day, it was time to get out and see the sights. Having watched the scenes from a few weeks earlier, there was no question where they wanted to go, especially having seen most of the West Berlin highlights on previous trips.

'I can't believe you weren't there when it happened,' Alex said.

'You just would have seen the party mood and thought it was an opportunity to pick up girls,' Henry said. 'We're a little past that.'

'Nah, just the atmosphere. Witnessing history. It would have been incredible.'

'Different strokes for different folks.'

'At your age, atmosphere means excitement,' I added. 'At our age, atmosphere means hassle.'

Alex shrugged his shoulders. However much someone can try and put themselves in your position, there are limitations on how well they can do it. Only through shared life experience can you really understand the other side. As more people began to see what the other side of the city offered, they may have felt they were getting such an understanding, but it was like reading one line from a book. People were having beliefs reinforced, but they weren't accumulating knowledge.

With six of us in the car, we had to leave Wolfe at home, something we did no more than necessary. We drove into the city through the Tiergarten, managing to park our car not far from the Reichstag.

'It is cramped in here,' Alex said from the backseat.

'Not compared to last time I made this crossing,' I said.

While the famous scenes of the wall being toppled were more than six weeks old, the Brandenburg Gate had officially reopened only four days ago. Despite it being the symbol of the city for far longer than I'd been alive, I had never walked through them. In my childhood, crossing from the Soviet Zone to the Western Zones was permitted, but it was more rigmarole than my parents ever wanted. We had been across the border on several occasions, notably the night I first saw Henry perform, but never through the most famous point of all. In amongst the masses of people, tourists and locals from each side of the border, I felt like I was taking the most significant steps of my life as I crossed to the other side.

We spent the early afternoon wandering streets that Henry had never seen, and that were so far back in my memory, it was like my own first time in the city. The TV tower seemed to climb half-way to the sky, yet little else appeared to have advanced since I was last here. In my youth, the East never had the type of infrastructure and development of the West, and little had changed in the ensuing thirty years.

'Are we going to see where you grew up?' Teresa asked, the initial excitement of crossing into the once forbidden territory now fading.

'Of course.'

We returned to the car, then he followed my directions. More than a quarter of a century on, the trek lost none of its familiarity. Within ten minutes, we had parked the car outside of the apartment building that had been my childhood home. From there, we walked to Konrad-Wolf-Straße, and the vast land of the Sportforum.

'Over there you can see my second home, the Eisschnelllaufhalle. This was a state-of-the-art complex in my youth. The government didn't have the funds to give its people much in life, yet they spared no expense in having the facilities in place for athletes to conquer the world. This was where we all converged, trying to pursue our dreams while the authorities worked on any way of getting us there.'

'Doping?'

'Not me, but figure skating wasn't the sport for that. Nobody spoke of what was involved in their individual regiments, but I am sure within the bowels of some of the adjacent arenas, sports science was driving everything.'

Like everywhere we passed, I reflected on memories of this area as being a normal part of a normal city in my youth. Now it looked like a cold, soulless suburb, designed with objectives that had nothing to do with the best interest of its citizens.

As I had always done years earlier, we walked back via a different route, and I pointed out exactly where I had detoured on that last day in the East. Making it back to the car I looked up at the apartment. When we first got here, I saw the building and thought back on my childhood, but as I looked now, my mind turned to the last time I'd had reason to think of the apartment. Twenty-years ago, my mother supposedly passed away up there on the third floor. I had long since reached a point of acceptance that I would never know the full story of what happened to her. How and why didn't matter. What always upset me was the lack of a genuine opportunity to say goodbye, either when I left East Berlin, or when she passed.

A tear ran down my cheek as I looked up at the old apartment.

'Danke Mutter. Auf Wiedersehen.'

34

26 March 2020

AMBER

I hate night shift. That's not how I used to feel, but I didn't enjoy tonight. Normally it suits me, for it leaves the days free to explore new surrounds, but there's little of that to be done right now. It's also usually the least intense time workwise. Normally that's ideal, but in an environment where I feel like an outsider, I like to be as busy as possible. In my free moments, the one thing I do appreciate is spending time with Marta and Henry. While they might drift in and out of sleep at any time, they're not up for company at 3am.

None of that was such a significant dampener this evening. That came at 11.43pm. Well, the fateful moment was earlier, but it was at 11.43pm when I got the call to rush upstairs to assist.

Bettina Meier, a woman I had never laid eyes upon, had collapsed. The staff working on the top floor put an emergency call through, which saw us all rush upstairs to assist. The nurse was unable to resuscitate her, and when the ambulance arrived just minutes later, the paramedics had no success either.

Death is an inevitable part of this job. The circumstances that lead people into aged care may vary, but they always leave the same way. You never develop an immunity to feeling the impact, but the magnitude of this varies depending on your connection. I'd never met her, but as the third person to arrive at her room as she lay on the floor unconscious, I had become connected.

Travelling is a constant education. When you are lost and alone in a city where you don't speak the language, it builds character. My greatest character test was coming in my workplace. I was on a shift with nobody I knew, nobody who I could communicate fluently with, and in a situation where everyone was dealing with a testing crisis. Bettina may have been a stranger to me, but to others caught in the middle of the drama, she was a part of the furniture, adding to the emotion of the moment.

Closeness doesn't change the professional approach you take to work, but it is guaranteed to have some degree of personal impact. The panic tonight has been heightened, and the impatience shown to me as an outsider has been stronger.

'*Warum beschäftigen sie menschen, die kein deutsch sprechen*?' I heard being said when I failed to understand an instruction. I knew it was something derogatory about people who couldn't speak German. It wasn't ideal, but the current times had caused the need for less than perfect situations to prevail.

It was a sombre mood for the rest of the shift. I didn't know any of the other staff. There was one middle-aged woman I had seen a few times, and a guy of a similar age to me who was also a temp. I'd never spoken to them, so they were as good as strangers. Everyone seemed low enough that it wouldn't be the time to get to know them.

I'd popped my head into the Victor's room on a couple of occasions, but they were both sleeping each time. It may have been better that way, for I wouldn't have been able to hide how I was feeling and would have been unwilling to tell them why. They weren't oblivious to reality. They knew that someone passed away in here regularly enough, but bringing it up when it happened didn't feel right to me. They may have known her. She may have been as much of a stranger to them as she was to me. Either way, it would be another reminder of the inevitable end of the road they were getting closer to. Henry was declining rapidly.

***

The hostel used to provide a buffet breakfast for just €5. I only took advantage of it once. It was not just a good value meal, but a great opportunity to see the melting pot of people staying a here, a great reflection of the diversity that drives this city. There wasn't a compulsion to mix, but there was a feeling that everyone was welcome, and it took no effort to strike up conversations and form friendships. I needed that badly this morning, but in the new order of the pandemic, breakfast was no longer available.

The current restrictions haven't quite closed the hostel down, but it isn't the place it was a couple of weeks ago. No bar, no breakfast buffet, no new stays, no 24-hour reception desk. Instead of over a hundred people staying here, there is probably little more than a dozen, most of them on extended stays, working in Berlin like me. Yesterday I had spoken with Nikki, the woman from Amsterdam who had complimented my drawings. She couldn't leave, so she was just as dependant on me that the hostel stayed open, albeit in its restricted capacity. While she had a bed to sleep-in, she had lost her income. Like so many others, she faced great uncertainty of how long she'd get by. She had no way out, but before too long she'd also have no way of staying.

Whenever I had worked night shift at home, I always needed a couple of hours to unwind. Whether it was the fact I'd been spared it recently, or whether the toll of this shift had just been too great, I was feeling as tired as I was hungry. I really felt the need to talk, but that wasn't an option. There wasn't another soul to be seen around the hostel. Even if there was someone, would I have been comfortable going into such deep topics with virtual strangers. It was academic. We had reached a point in time where isolation had become normal. In the heart of Berlin's east, it may have been 2020, but I was getting a thorough insight into the East Berlin of several decades earlier.

I went back to my room and rummaged through the drawers in search of anything I could eat. A chocolate bar proved my salvation, and I was grateful for the fact that I'd overbought the other day. I should be better prepared, though I knew there was other food in the room. At this point it was more about the comfort of something sweet than any nutritional value. While still savouring its milky flavour, I laid down. The physical and emotional fatigue I felt after the long night at work meant I would be asleep before the taste had disappeared from my mouth.

I was wrecked after dealing with the loss of a stranger. How would I be if it had been someone I cared about?

35

6 August 1998

MARTA

Love is the best thing in life, until it is the worst. Love eventually ends. I experienced the pain of the end with both my mother and my brother. In both cases, there was a feeling of a little piece of my heart breaking. For the horror of that pain, neither ending impacted my day-to-day life, such was the distance that circumstances had put between us. This time, it is so much harder.

We said goodbye to Wolfe this morning. He had been deteriorating for a long time. In recent months, his suffering had become unbearable. We knew there was only one decision to make. Understanding this and doing it were two very different things. Looking in his eyes, how could we do it? At the same time, how could we look in his eyes and have him suffer any longer? Eventually, we conquered the selfishness. It wasn't about us. We had to do what was right by him. It seemed counter-intuitive, but after giving us so much through his life, the only way we could reward him was with an end to that life. As I kept reminding myself, it wasn't an end to life, but an end to existence. Wolfe's life had been wonderful, but more time was not adding to this.

It has been crushing us throughout this final period. Making the decision was heartbreaking. Saying goodbye was the worst moment of my life.

No doubt people will ask about us getting another dog. How could we? You cannot replace the irreplaceable. We didn't have *a* dog. We had *our* dog. There is no substitute. He meant the world to us, and that is what has made this so painful. I never want to go through that again.

Either Henry or I will go through something similar. One of us will outlive the other. We have both always said we want to be the one who goes first, as death is nowhere near as terrifying as living without the other half of who you are.

Tomorrow we will walk the same route we always took Wolfe, alongside the Spree, through the grounds of the Charlottenburg Palace. We will scatter his ashes in the river.

Ever since the fateful day when he was hit by a car, he never ran off ahead of us. It had been done the hard way, but he had learned the lesson. In the park where we visited each day, he'd run around and enjoy the freedom and space available to him. He was like the youthful puppy of years earlier, until he finally reached the point where there was no longer any run left in him. At that point, we'd let him off the leash and he'd immediately sit, looking up with his big brown eyes to say, '*I've had enough.*' It was the beginning of the end.

From that point on, he'd spent more time at our feet as we sat at the table or on the lounge. I hated leaving him when I went to work at the restaurant where I was waitressing, but the absence was kept to a minimum as Henry drove me and picked me up each shift, with Wolfe loyally sitting behind us. His ears pricked up at the sound of noise outside, but the body no longer jumped up to make his presence felt. All he wanted was to be close to us. Life became more one-dimensional for us, as we never wanted to leave him. It wasn't just age, but circumstance that had seen us transition from a life where home was an occasional resting spot, to a place we barely left by choice.

They say that dogs are man's best friend. That doesn't go far enough to explain the love we had for Wolfe. We gave him a wonderful life, and he repaid us with a level of loyalty, trust and affection that could never be matched. He would have followed us into the gates of hell if it was where we led him. He would have laid his life on the line for us, and to be honest, we'd have done the same for him.

We have had plenty of time to prepare for what was coming. We knew last Christmas time that Wolfe was near the end. We talked about what would follow. For as long as we had been in Charlottenburg, it was home to the three of us. Without him, it would never feel like the home we had loved. We agreed that when that time came, it would be time for us to move on.

'I'm too old to leave Berlin,' I had told Henry.

'I don't mean leaving Berlin, but this house. I think it will be time for a ground floor apartment. Low maintenance. No hassles.'

In the months that followed, we'd been alerted to a couple of opportunities to manage apartment buildings. These wouldn't be the hassle-free options Henry had discussed, but they would solve other issues. Henry wasn't working, and I was continuing at the restaurant out of necessity. Our savings had dwindled every year, and we needed some income to keep our heads above water. Managing a building seemed ideal. We would work side-by-side from home, exactly how we wanted.

'When the time comes, it is something to consider, Henry said.

The more time passed, the less we discussed it. Knowing that any move would come only after we'd lost Wolfe, we couldn't think of the future without thinking of the precipitating moment, something we were both determined to avoid. Eventually, we could escape the thoughts of that moment no longer.

'I can't do it, Henry.'

'We can't not do it. He has given us everything. There is only one thing left we can give him. Peace.'

We were both emotional wrecks when the decision was made. As he had done all those years earlier, Jonas provided the transport to Dr Zeidler's. He understood that Henry would be in no state to drive. He did everything possible to ease our burden in the build-up, never over-stepping the line, but offering any form of support we might need.

Today, he was worth his weight in gold, even if we were incapable of showing our appreciation.

Jonas offered Wolfe one last treat in the waiting room, but he didn't take it. I sensed he knew why we were here, and it wasn't a time for treats, but relief. With Jonas waiting outside, we walked out the back, Henry carrying him before I gave him a final cuddle. Placing him on the table, we each kept one hand on him, holding each other's spare hand tightly. Dr Zeidler proceeded, and we watched Wolfe's eyes close. In moments, it was all over.

For the second time in my life, I watched my husband crying. The stoicism of my youth kicked in, retaining a demeanour of strength for him. It was, of course, an illusion. I was as broken as I had ever been.

There was silence the whole way home. We said a brief thankyou to Jonas as we got out of the car, but whatever he said in response failed to register. We spent the evening in silence, trying to drink our way through the pain, but only adding to it.

'The real farewell is tomorrow,' Henry said.

'It's only his ashes.'

'That may be true, but it is where he will be for eternity. What's more, it is where we will join him for eternity before too long.'

36

27 March 2020

AMBER

For God's sake! Over the past week I'd had three texts from Greta, seeking to apologise again. Why the hell can't she leave me alone? There is nothing for anyone to gain by ongoing contact, but perhaps her conscience wasn't going to allow her to rest without some sort of sign on my part. It was for that reason, rather than any genuine forgiveness on my part, that led to a quick response to the third of her messages. "I'm OK thx." I had thought that would be the end of it, but now I had another message from her.

Get a look at today's Die Welt. We are in a photo together on page 15!

What the hell was she talking about? Nobody had taken a photo of us together at any point. What the hell could we be doing in a national newspaper? It seemed like a strange attempt at getting my attention. Why she felt she needed that attention was a mystery. At least it gave me something to do between now and the start of my shift, so I wandered down to the supermarket, needing also to stock up on a few other essentials to get me through.

As soon as I got out of the shop, I flicked through to page fifteen. I'd expected it to be the social pages, but as with the fourteen previous pages, it was news stories connected to the Coronavirus and its impact. This article was on the Eisstadion Neukölln which had closed, accompanied by a photo. It wasn't so much a photo of us, but a photo of

Greta, with some clumsy person on the ice beneath her. Sure, I knew it was me, but I would be unidentifiable to anyone else, thankfully. Underneath the photo was a caption I couldn't understand - *Schauspielerin Greta Loch hilft einem gefallenen Freund auf der Eisbahn im Eisstadion Neukölln.*

Getting back to the hostel, I asked Erik to translate the article for me. Apparently the rink was running at a loss and there were doubts on whether it would be able to survive the forced closure, one of many businesses across the city that were vulnerable to the government's current actions.

I pointed myself out in the photo to him.

'Wow, you just arrive in a city, and you make the papers. You met Greta Loch!'

'Who is she?'

'An actress. I guess you don't get a lot of German TV or movies in Canada.'

'Is she a big star? I spent some time with her, and she didn't seem to attract attention from anyone.'

'Not really. She was in a show called *Rotlicht*, which I loved, so she's very familiar to me. I guess to those who don't watch that, she'd be pretty much unknown. So, when did this happen?'

'A couple of weeks ago. Bit strange that they had a reporter and photographer there before any of this happened.'

'Clearly whatever pressures they're under aren't really based around the current closure.'

'Never trust the media too much,' I said, conscious that what gets reported is usually based around truth, but only the segment of truth that suits those delivering it.

'How was the Tiergarten?'

'I still haven't been. Might go today,' I said.

I returned to my room and decided to reply to Greta. Curiosity had gotten the better of me.

Saw the paper. Lucky we went there when we did, I suppose.

Within a minute she responded.

It was! How are you coping with the restrictions? Finding enough in our city to keep you occupied?

I continued.

I am going to explore the Tiergarten. If you want, you can meet me at the Victory Column at 1pm.

It was ridiculous to be willingly meeting her, but between the tragedy at work last night, the loneliness I felt, and the inability to do much in the current climate, bad company seemed better than no company at all. And in truth, I didn't consider it to be bad company. From the moment I met her, she'd been amazing to be around. Yes, she'd hurt me, but maybe it was time to get a little bit more understanding of how that came to be. If she turns up. She never confirmed one way or the other.

I got off the train at Hansaplatz. Despite taking the wrong exit, it wasn't long before I spied the giant Victory Column and was headed in the right direction. This was always high on my list of 'must-sees'. Years ago, it had served as the first thing I knew of Berlin, courtesy of the music video *Faraway, So Close*, and the film of the same name. My brother loved the song and watched the clip repeatedly before making me watch the film with him. The column featured heavily in both. 'I'd love to go there one day,' I had said at the time. A decade later I hadn't thought much more of it, but now with each step I was getting closer to finally fulfilling that wish.

As I walked, I began an internal monologue, pretending I knew how Greta would respond to everything I said. I wanted her to feel bad, as though there was a certain amount of negative feelings that should exist from the situation. Every bit that she carried would be a little less left within me.

As I climbed the steps from the tunnel beneath the road, I saw Greta sitting, waiting. Normally you can climb an internal spiral staircase to a viewing platform at the top of the column, but like most things, that was closed, and it had meant the area was largely deserted.

She looked up slowly and smiled. 'Hello Amber. It is great to see you.'

She stood up, and though she shaped to hug me, I was unresponsive, so she stayed back.

'I wasn't sure you'd see me, but I'm glad you did.'

'Why?'

'To explain everything. Let's walk. It's beautiful around here.'

'Can we sit here for a bit first?' I said. It was not so much my preferred option, but a desire to break the pattern of our previous interactions where I followed her lead in every instance. 'I want to soak this spot up.'

'Sure,' she said with less conviction in her tone than the word would indicate.

I looked at her, trying to work out how best to ask what was on my mind.

'Who are you, Greta?'

'What do you mean?'

'When we met, I took you at face value. I was honest with you and took for granted that you'd been the same with me.'

'I was.'

'You didn't tell me you were a celebrity.'

'I wouldn't say I am. I was a cast member in a show that didn't get picked up for a second season. I haven't had a role since. That is hardly celebrity status.'

'You told me you work in a supermarket.'

'I have been. Researching a role.'

'Who is Leila?'

'A producer. She has me lined up for a role in a new show.'

'And you're sleeping with her?'

'We've had a relationship of sorts for the best part of six months. It's hardly normal. It's open. No commitment. I guess largely I'm a plaything for her.'

'You're alright with that?'

'Everyone has dreams. My reality is a long way from those dreams, but it might help me get closer to them.'

'The casting couch?'

'If you like. When people hire and fire, the decisions are always based in some part on their personal opinions. My mother worked in the government for decades. Every time an opportunity came along, she was passed over for someone who was less qualified, but a bigger part of the social fabric.'

'There's a difference between being friends with someone and sleeping with them.'

'The principle is the same.'

'What did you stand to gain by sleeping with me?'

'The same as you.'

'I don't think so.'

'You enjoyed every moment we spent together just as much as I did.'

I couldn't deny that. I suggested that we go for a walk through the park. We went back through the tunnel under the road and headed to the southern side. We walked along a path that led to a beautiful small reservoir.'

'How did that photo end up in the paper. If it's only news now, how did they have a photographer there two weeks ago?'

'That's why I was there. My agent wanted to get some extra shots of me. When she knew they were running a story on the rink, she forwarded a couple through to the paper.'

'Did you just approach me as part of getting some publicity?'

'No. The photographer was shooting me skating. We'd basically finished, as far as I knew. I'd spoken to her, and said I was staying out on the ice a little longer, and it was at that stage I saw you'd hit the deck and helped. I didn't realise the photographer was still there.'

'Was she taking photos when we were having coffee?'

'No. Why would she? She was paid to do a job, and that was capturing me out on the ice. I'm not significant enough that my every move is of interest to anyone.'

'Coffee? Our date? What were they about?'

'I liked you.'

She began to tell me more about her past. She'd been in a relationship with another actress a few years earlier, but after her partner hit the bigtime, Greta was left behind. She hadn't been in a meaningful relationship since but was now in two sham-relationships. Not only was she involved with Leila, but she was also involved in a form of relationship with a man.

'That is not a relationship of any kind. Wolfgang is my flatmate. He is gay, but its better in our business to keep that private, so we played along with the idea that we were a couple. We are the best of friends, but absolutely no way there's anything more to it.'

'Was that Leila's place we went to?'

'Yes. I spend more time there these days.'

'Seems like the woman I was getting to know wasn't really you at all,' I said.

'Yes, it was. Much of my life is an act, but you were seeing the real me. I was so comfortable talking to you and being myself. I rarely get to interact with someone who wasn't judging me based on my public profile. I felt attracted to you instantly, and I could sense you felt the same.

'I'm not getting into anything serious at this point, not with anyone. It doesn't mean I shut myself off from my feelings. I felt something special for you, so I pursued it.'

As we walked on, we found a couple of scooters and she suggested we ride them to see more of the surrounds. As if I hadn't stepped far enough out of my comfort zone, I agreed to do this for the first time in my life.

'Are you hoping to rekindle the moment? Help me up when I fall and make a fool of myself?'

'You'll be fine.'

'Where's the photographer.'

'Enough, already.'

I quickly felt comfortable on the scooter, and we made our way through the park, passing manicured gardens, extravagant statues and a range of animals in their natural habitat. Following what seemed like a miniature version of Stonehenge, we reached the end of the park, just across the road from the Memorial to the Murdered Jews of Europe.

'Have a look here,' Greta said. 'This is the Memorial to Homosexuals Persecuted under the Nazi's.'

It was a single block of stone with a small window to look in, showing footage of two men who kiss. I didn't really get it, for it seemed that their sexuality was still being hidden inside.

'Yes, but this is remembering the persecution that forced such things to be hidden.'

'Who didn't they persecute.'

'That's why we're such an open city now. Free and diverse.'

'Yet still hiding in sham relationships,' I said, referring to her and Wolfgang.

She shrugged her shoulders. 'It isn't necessary, but we were already flatmates anyway, so it made sense to play along.'

We left the scooters nearby and began to walk towards the Brandenburg Gate.

'What do you want now?' I asked.

'Right now? Our options are limited.'

'No. What do you want at this stage of life?'

'To be true to myself as much as possible. Enjoy life and spend as much time as possible with people who make my life better. What about you?'

'I want to be true to myself too. And that truth mightn't be the same as yours.'

We stopped at a park bench and sat down, keeping the appropriate one and a half metre distance from each other. My approach to her had softened. I was grateful that we'd had this time together. I felt like I was beginning to understand who she was, and from that point it was easy to process everything that happened between us. I wasn't her victim or her conquest. I think, in amongst the complicated web she has weaved, she craved something genuine. I was a glimpse of that. Her intentions weren't bad, but they were impossible. I couldn't be a part of a game, however genuine my place within it might be. Right now, I needed everything, or I needed nothing.

'Before today I had regretted ever meeting you. My mother always said that people either come into your life for a season, a reason or a lifetime. There might be many false alarms before I find someone who will be with me for a lifetime, but to be with someone, I need to have some hope that's who they are.'

'So did I come into your life for a season or for a reason?'

'I thought a very short season, but I now understand it was a reason. You've taught me something I've never accepted. It is alright to be me.'

'It is.'

We talked more about the future. I told her that all being well I would be heading to Hamburg next before making my way to the Netherlands, Belgium and France. She told me that the production she was hoping to be starting mid-year would see her moving to Munich. We swapped notes on the different cities, and like our first ever interaction, the conversation was natural and fun.

We sat there for nearly an hour before she said it was time for her to leave. She told me that she wouldn't keep messaging me if I didn't want. She thanked me for an enjoyable day.

'I hope you look back on all of this happily.'

'I will. Thank you.'

I kissed her on the cheek and watched her turn and walk away. It wasn't what I wanted, but until I'd reached a stage where I wasn't so emotionally vulnerable, I needed to take smaller steps than I ever could with Greta.

One day the right person will coincide with the right time. Hopefully it doesn't take until I'm in need of a nursing home myself.

37

2 March 2018

MARTA

It would have been inhumane to allow Wolfe to suffer any longer than he did. It seems exceptional irony that we use that choice of word. Henry and I are now at the same stage of suffering as Wolfe was. Humanity doesn't extend to ending human suffering, for extending a human life in any circumstances is a matter of course. I couldn't choose an end for Henry, nor could he for me, but it is only the presence of each other that leaves us with a semblance of desire to continue. If I lost him, I would choose an end to my pain if such an opportunity arose.

When Wolfe left us, we both expected it wouldn't be too long before we joined him. We'd lived far from healthy lifestyles, and a wide array of health issues were having significant impacts by our early sixties. We never thought seventy was possible, then somehow eighty came on the horizon and Henry still survived. Through it all, we retained our independence, struggling though we may have been to survive on our own.

We'd spent a few years managing property, before we became eligible for pensions. It wasn't much, but with the proceeds from our house at Charlottenburg, we had sufficient. Our needs were few other than the vast quantity of medications that kept us going. Renting, we were always one landlord's decision away from being forced to find a new home, and this happened several times before we got some stability in a ground floor apartment in Kreuzberg. It wasn't much, but at that point we needed little more than a roof over our heads and no stairs to climb.

I had a major heart operation two years ago. While it was a success, the same couldn't be said for my overall rehabilitation. I couldn't get back on my feet. Henry continued to make all the decisions, and while I should have been pushing harder, he continued to force me to rest. He took on increasingly greater responsibilities for everything around the house, which had a dual effect; it continued to see me weaken through a lack of activity, while he weakened through doing too much. We felt we were in a race with each other to the grave, but life doesn't always follow the script you write for yourself. There was little life left in us, but death still didn't come calling.

Eventually there was no alternative. Henry couldn't get me to the toilet and into the shower. As hard as he'd battled for us to reach the end on our own terms, he had to admit defeat. We needed permanent care.

Sandra, one of our neighbours, had been a valued friend in recent years. Her patience and tolerance were admirable, for Henry had become progressively more difficult and showed very little appreciation for her. Despite this, she continued to go above and beyond being neighbourly, doing numerous chores for us.

'I don't trust her,' Henry would say. 'I'm not giving her the grocery money until she gives me a receipt.'

'She is doing us a favour. You think she's going to leave the country to cheat you out of a couple of euro?'

'You blindly defend her through anything.'

'I defend her because she has never done anything wrong.'

Henry had managed to alienate people over the years. For a couple of years after his mother passed away, he refused to speak to his sister. Eventually the rift healed, but only after the constant attempts of Lorraine to reconcile. While it was a relief to everyone that harmony had been restored, there was little that the family could do for us from half a world away. Lorraine was too old to travel now, and while he'd had visits from both Teresa and Alex, these came only every couple of years.

Jonas had continued to be a friend after we moved out of Charlottenburg, but eventually that crumbled after a fight that had no obvious origin. Sandra was now the only person who was both willing to help and physically close enough to do this.

Henry was taken to hospital a fortnight ago. I was taken with him, there being no possibility of me surviving even a night on my own. As his recuperation began, a social worker came to us and told us the words that I, and more particularly Henry, dreaded ever hearing.

'You cannot stay in the hospital, but you cannot go back to your home. You need permanent full-time care. There is no alternative.'

She gave us a list of potential options. We would have had nothing to go on, but Sandra offered to take us to each of the homes for inspections. Henry couldn't leave the hospital, but they organised a wheelchair for me.

Only one of the homes had a double room available, the *Senioren Fachpflegezentrum*. As unappealing as the establishment seemed, by allowing us to share a room, it satisfied the one essential requirement I demanded.

Henry had never ceded to my opinion on any issue, but after more than half a century of marriage, he was willing to let me make the decision. I guess this was similar to the last few months at the club in Kreuzberg, an indication that he had effectively given up. Options were few, and time was of the essence. He would hate it, and I wasn't sure that I felt any better about it, but necessity reigned supreme.

Henry and I were still at the hospital for a few more days. We heard that Theresa and Alex were coming from Australia to assist us with the apartment. In the meantime, Sandra was a saint, packing everything we may need in our early days in the home.

'I hate it,' Henry said, as he arrived here for the first time.

'Naturally. You hate everywhere. You don't need to like it, there is no alternative,' I said.

'I would rather be dead than living here.'

'That'll be soon enough.'

'I know. Life ended before death arrived, and this place fills the gap in the middle.'

Sharing my life with this man had been my life's great pleasure but sharing a confined space with him for my remaining days was going to be infinitely more difficult than all the years which had preceded it. His attitude never improved, even if it wasn't on display all the time. His humour came out occasionally, but mostly he seemed like someone for whom existence had continued for too long. He'd lived such an amazing life only for it to twist towards a sad and unrecognisable final act.

After fifty-five years, I was finally back living in East Berlin. The city's landscape may not be dominated by a physical barrier anymore, but the distinction between the two sides has never completely disappeared. It is roughly four kilometres from our previous home, and a similar distance from the home I grew up in. The similarities to the latter are evident every time I look from the window. It may be a return to my heritage, but the view from the window doesn't have a feeling of home.

***

Two years on and we're still here. I could easily say that it won't be much longer, but we've been saying that for so long that we have proven that these things cannot be predicted. Young and supposedly healthy people drop dead in the most unexpected manners, then here we are, inexplicably surviving against all odds, with little to be gained from this additional time. The length of life is no great measure. The quality of that life is everything.

There is little dignity left at this point of life, incapable of doing even the most mundane tasks. Existence seems cruel in so many ways, yet there are still brief moments when I can appreciate being alive. Henry may not have many of these moments, but when he isn't complaining, just the sight of him conjures the greatest of memories, and it is then that makes me accept that this is just another part of our shared journey.

When we came in, the staff were reasonable to us both. Henry's lack of German wasn't a problem, as most staff were able to speak a little English with him. As they got to know him better, and found him constantly argumentative, they all seemed to lose this skill and refused to use anything but German to communicate. Ever since, it has been a race to the bottom, with Henry getting harder to deal with, which has led to being treated worse. I have remained the peacemaker, ensuring the staff know not to take him seriously.

In his days as an acrobat, Henry often had to lay on the ice to perform his lifts, before remaining in a wet tuxedo for more than an hour until the end of the show. He always said that it wasn't the risks of the performances he did that would end up killing him, but the impact of body temperature changes on his respiratory system over the years. It has impacted his health for decades, but in the past couple of weeks, his deterioration has accelerated rapidly.

As his energy levels have dissipated, his fights with everyone around him have eased. There have been times when I have felt that any desire he had to continue living, has been purely to spite those around him. If that was the case, then the spite has now gone. Perhaps the end really is getting close.

38

28 March 2020

AMBER

Heidi was ready and waiting out the front of her building when I arrived at 1.30. Unlike me, she already had a mask on, and seeing that, I decided I should follow suit. For the sake of the workplace, I was the one who should be setting the example. I may be a short-term temp staff member, but I've been there long enough to know their demands.

'How's the week been?'

'Not good. We had a death Thursday night.'

'Sorry.'

'It's all part of the job. It wasn't on my floor, but because it was night shift, it was all hands-on dealing with it. I didn't know the woman, so there wasn't any impact in that way, but I also didn't know anyone else working the shift. And there was pretty much nobody who could communicate with me, so the whole experience was horrendous.'

'Well at least you'll have someone there today who you can talk to.'

'I will. Good to have you onboard.'

It was a fifteen-minute walk to work but seemed even shorter with someone to talk to the whole way. It was interesting hearing her experiences in the industry, but more of the time was spent talking about life under the restrictions and her happy home life with James. I didn't have similar experiences to draw on, but irrespective of the topic, I was happy that for the first time, I was doing this walk with someone else.

She mentioned her frustrations with the current pandemic rules and empathised with how much harder it must be for me.

'You must feel ripped off being here at this time. What do you do in your time off when everything is closed?'

'It's hard to say. I've never lived through a pandemic at home, and I've never known Berlin without a pandemic. Maybe it's less of an adjustment when you're already dealing with a whole new world. It's like there is no sense of normality for me here anyways, so it's a different type of adjustment.'

'But what do you do when you're not working?'

'The options are limited. Still, when you think of the history of this city, the options were far worse in times gone by and there was far more than boredom to worry about. I think I can appreciate the history more by experiencing the restrictions now.'

'It kind of feels like we have a new wall. This one isn't unique to Berlin though. Doesn't help me feel any better about it.'

'I know, right.'

'This is worse than the Wall though,' she said with the certainty of youth. Only time would tell, but I doubted that this virus would become as memorable a part of human history as the Berlin Wall had been.

'You think? I was trying to be non-committal. I felt it was a little self-indulgent to compare the current inconvenience with the long-term horrors the people of this city had endured, but in fostering a new friendship, I didn't want to be actively disagreeing with her.

'For sure. Any situation in life is only as hard as our preparation makes it. When the Wall went up, the people of this city had dealt with fifteen years of occupation, five years of war before that, a revolutionary government stifling freedoms before that, and not long earlier, the previous world war and the recovery from it. Berliners were prepared for what the Wall meant in their everyday lives. Nobody is prepared for the impact this virus is having on our lives.'

I couldn't argue with that. Equal does not mean the same. The situation that this city faced now couldn't be argued as comparative to the darkest days of its history, but the impact on the individual wasn't so dissimilar.

'It's certainly not the ideal time to be a tourist.'

'Don't call yourself that, or they won't let you stay.'

'That's right. I should say it's not an ideal time to be a new resident.'

'It's not ideal for anyone, but at least most of us have the creature comforts of home to return to. I can't imagine life in a near empty hostel would be so comfortable.'

I nodded but said nothing more, as I wanted to get off the topic. The more you focus on the negative elements of a situation, the more they tend to override everything else. The restrictions were a reality. Nothing but time would change them, and the more I thought about what I was missing, the less I would be able to appreciate what I was having. I'd come to Europe to experience a different world, and I was getting something far more different than I could ever have anticipated.

Millions of people love to travel, but there aren't too many who enjoy the ordeal of the airport and the long-haul flights. The journey is often a chore, but the more difficult it is, the more you appreciate the destination. The pandemic wasn't a new world that society had arrived at, it was a part of the journey to the future.

80% of Berlin's population couldn't remember life in isolation behind the Wall. It doesn't matter how much you see, hear or read, there is no substitute for living history. The constant reminders of the Wall throughout this city had only marginally increased my understanding of what life would have been like in that era. The restrictions brought on by the pandemic have done far more to teach me this.

We learn more from defeat than victory. We learn to appreciate more through struggle than ease. Berlin had developed into the city that celebrates freedom more than any other in the world, and it did so through the appreciation of its earlier defeats and struggles. I wasn't going to tell Heidi to enjoy and appreciate the privilege of experiencing such a unique moment of history, but I felt that society would be better for what we'd endured. Perhaps not many people would notice that, and far fewer again until the benefit of hindsight kicked in.

We arrived at work a few minutes ahead of schedule, largely thanks to the speed and ease in which we could cross Karl Marx Allee in the absence of normal traffic. Masked up and socially distanced, I brought Heidi inside and headed to the front desk to deal with the new formalities associated with the beginning of a shift.

'*Guten Tag Ada. Das ist Heidi. Sie ist neu.*' Ada spoke no English at all, so my very basic German was put to the test whenever I dealt with her, ensuring our conversations were always short. She wasn't the friendliest, even when greeting visitors, so my lack of language skills proved to be a convenient excuse.

Heidi and I both had our temperatures taken before I said my farewells as she was taken through to the conference room for induction with the other new starters.

'If I don't see you through the shift, I will meet you out the front just after 10pm. *Ja?*'

'Sure,' I said, looking forward to the company. Whatever difference in views we had, there was something about her manner that really appealed to me. I'm not stupid enough to start falling for her, but I can't pretend that I didn't find her company more engaging courtesy of a genuine attraction. In most cases, unrequited affection was painful, but at this time of my life it was perfect. It built enthusiasm for life and for the future without the potential negative consequences of disappointment and heartbreak that accompanied a more realistic interest.

Heidi was on my mind as I wandered upstairs for the pre-shift briefing, but when Frida pulled me aside, my thoughts transferred instantly.

'*I know you have become close to Marta and Henry so I must vorn you. His condition deteriorated very badly overnight. It is not about if, but ven.*'

My head dropped. I knew this was coming, but not this quickly. Henry knew it better than anyone, and despite not necessarily saying it,

I think he was at peace with the reality. Marta would be another story. As hard as what was coming would be, it may be better now with me being able to devote more time and care towards them than they would receive once I'm gone.

'You still need to work your shift as normal, but at least we are fully-staffed this afternoon. You may be able to get relief on the floor, leaving you with a bit more time to focus on them.'

I looked at her and nodded. There was a sign of compassion in her eyes that seemed far removed from her standard demeanour. Death is a familiar theme in aged care homes, and at times there are people within them who become desensitised to it. In most cases, we shed a quick tear and move straight on, but from time to time the impact is far greater. Most of us develop relationships with some residents that are far closer. When we're forced to say goodbye to those people, the ability to concentrate on the rest of our jobs is compromised.

Marta's presence adds another rare dimension to the situation. There are few married couples in places like this, for people's acceptance of the need for full-time care usually eventuates only once alone. For her sake, my tears will need to be shed in my own time. While I'm here, my responsibility is to help her in any way I can. She is a tough woman. She has lived through infinitely more than all the staff here combined, but that is scant preparation for losing someone who has been her world for most of that life.

It was a good thing I'd been warned of what I'd find when I entered the room, for it allowed me to retain composure and be the support Marta needed. Henry's organs had begun to shut down.

'Look at the lazy bugger. Won't even say hello to you,' she said, holding herself together better than I had anticipated. This in turn had me working harder to fight back my own tears. I'd known him for a fortnight. How crazy it was that I had developed a kinship that had me so upset at what was happening, but in life, timing is everything. At a point when I felt most isolated and alone, it was these two people who gave me a value. The attention I gave Henry meant enough to him that he reciprocated, giving me something I needed now. A feeling of worth. A feeling that I did make a difference, however small and briefly it may have been.

I usually crossed paths with the registered nurse on duty just once or twice in a shift, but today it almost felt like we were partners such was the time we were both in Henry's room. Marta was sitting in a wheelchair at his bedside, never moving from the spot. She'd drift in and out of sleep, looking for the most part barely more alive than her ailing husband. It was heart-breaking to look at the scene. I hoped it wouldn't take too long. We often think that each day is a blessing, but at this point there was nothing more that was gained in each passing moment.

When my shift ended, Henry looked exactly as he had eight hours earlier. I didn't really want to leave but knowing that the nurse had said he could continue like that for a couple more days meant that staying was futile. I gave Marta a hug and told her I'd see her early tomorrow, not waiting until my 2pm start time.

'Thank you, Amber. From Henry too. You brought out the last sparks of joy in him. They've been very rare in these last couple of years. It meant so much for him to have those moments and even more to me to see them.'

I rushed downstairs and found Heidi waiting for me. There was still a tear in my eye, and I explained the situation to her. She gave me a hug, which I really needed. I was certain to be giving so much support in the next few days as the inevitable came. I was desperately going to need every bit of support that I could get in return.

39

29 March 2020

MARTA

It doesn't matter how inevitable it is, nothing can truly prepare you for the end. The moment itself is irrelevant. His breathing had got progressively slower until there was no more breath at all. I didn't even notice, and it was only through the nurse, Nina, that I knew he had gone.

'*Mein herzliches Beileid.*' I would hear these words over and over as people came offering their condolences. One by one, all the staff on night shift came and saw me. By the time the last one came in, the day shift arrived, and the process continued. Through it all, the tears didn't stop as the reality set in. I was now alone in the world. I may be getting more attention than I've known since we've lived here, but that was an illusion.

I always wanted to go first. I never believed I could cope without him. We'd both been in sufficiently bad health for so long, that it seemed certain one or both of us would have met our maker long before we reached aged care. Now at least there were people to do everything for me, but nobody could give me the reason to live another day.

Amber walked in early in the morning, and again I started crying. She immediately followed my lead.

'I didn't think you were working.'

'I'm not, I just wanted to be here for you.' Her kindness was overwhelming. She knew there was nobody else who'd be coming, other than the staff. Like her, they cared, but as part of their professional role. Change jobs, and I'll never see them again. Amber was a friend. It may have stemmed from her job, but it was beyond that now. Her presence may be temporary, but her legacy would be permanent.

Henry's sister, nephew and niece would be devastated to not be here, but with borders closed, it was impossible. All the staff here will do everything they can, but in the main sense it is Amber alone who is sharing my grief.

Throughout the morning, staff I didn't even recognise had all gone out of their way to see me, from our carers to kitchen staff and cleaners. Everyone knew '*der Australier*' so his passing had a real impact across the building. As much as Henry had been the bane of some of their existence, they did have a special affection for him. They knew the life he'd led, not for him ever seeking to make a deal of it, but for the sheer amazement they had at what he'd achieved in the entertainment industry. Once he'd got close to the end and was no longer the source of their frustrations, they began to appreciate the full story of the man. A great man had died. Not just the man who was the centre of my universe, but a man in his own right with his own legacy.

For all the kindness they showed, I'm sure they saw it as the passing of a man who they imagined was special in his day. For Amber, it was the loss of someone she considered special for her own experiences with him. While others were sad for my loss, she was sad for who she had lost too.

'Would you like me to call Henry's family?' she asked.

'You are so kind. I don't think I can talk to them now.'

Amber checked for the time difference and said it was mid-evening in Australia, so I told her to proceed.

'Hello, is this Lorraine Reed? My name is Amber Megan. I'm calling from the *Senioren Fachpflegezentrum* in Berlin. I am sorry to have to inform you of this, but Henry passed away early this morning.'

I could hear Lorraine crying at the other end of the phone. Although I wasn't ready for the conversation, I had to talk to her. I motioned to Amber to pass the phone over to me.

'Lorraine. His suffering is over. Now it's my turn,' I said. I struggled to get much else out, as did she. I told her that I'd ring tomorrow and hung up just before breaking down again. I wanted to ring when Amber was here. It made life so much easier. I didn't want to be dependent on an individual, but when someone goes so far above and beyond, you want to utilise their kindness without using it inappropriately.

Today everyone is remarking on what a character he was. I'm sure the same people were using the word *Arschloch* before today, but it is amazing how quickly people turn from contempt to respect at a time like this.

I know he was difficult to everyone here, but that isn't uncommon. People at this stage of life often can be difficult. With many of the residents in a place like this, dementia is at the root of their problems. Henry never lost his mental capacity. Even the standard deterioration of memory that most people experience in their twilight years failed to materialise.

For well over twenty years, he believed his time was nearly up. In his last forty-eight hours, that belief transitioned to knowledge. He had almost experienced a renaissance in the past couple of weeks, the additional stimulation that Amber had evoked in talking about his life had seen more positivity stem from him than I remember in years. That dissipated in the last two days, but in the brief moments of lucidity he had, I knew he was saying goodbye.

'I'm going to see Wolfe,' he told me yesterday. 'Make sure they know where to put me.'

'You're staying with me until I am ready to go there with you.'

'I never wanted to be anywhere without you. Not in this life or anything that follows.'

'You never will be Henry.'

He drifted off to sleep straight after this. His breathing was laboured, but constant, and not noticeably different from what I was seeing regularly. Over the hours that followed, he stirred many times before the purr of a gentle snore begun again. Everything was sufficiently normal that I too slept on and off, all the time remaining in my wheelchair at his side. At some point, my hand had slipped from his, but I stirred as Nina came in and placed our hands together again.

Nina told me that he was ready. He'd been waiting for my hand before he took the final steps, and she was now going to leave us in private for a few minutes. I had no idea whether he'd hear me, but I guess the words that came out were as much for myself as they were for him.

'I always said you were the most important thing in my life, but in truth, you were my whole life. Everything else just led me to your side. My family, my career, my city, they were all just pointing me to you. When the Wall kept me in, I found a way out. Now another wall is coming between us, but again I will be patient and wait my time. We will be together for eternity my darling. I love you, in this world and beyond. *Auf Wiedersehen* Henry.'

His breathing had been so slow that I never recognised the moment. We always think about that terminal breath, as though it is a monumental instant when we leave this life. When the end comes like this, it is unnoticeable. It was several minutes before Nina returned and confirmed what I suspected.

'*Er ist in Frieden.*'

My head dropped and my eyes closed. The tears took a while to start, but once they did, I wondered if they would ever stop.

I knew it was for the best. His suffering was over. He was at peace. In time his ashes would be there, but I chose to believe his soul was already down by the waters flowing through Schloss Charlottenburg, Wolfe at his side, beginning his wait for me. It didn't matter if it was days or years, eternity awaited us. Together.

40

April 2, 2020

AMBER

When a person passes away, one of the first things to do is the organisation of the funeral. For the past week, that has disappeared from the agenda. The government has imposed a temporary ban on any gatherings of more than two people, right across Germany. Not even funerals have been spared.

A funeral is meant to be the ultimate final tribute to the departed. A celebration of their life. Usually, the celebration is lost behind the sadness of their departure, for the people who have lost a loved one are at the stage where grief transcends all else. Marta would have been unable to do anything but shed tears. The fact that a service couldn't be held, further upset her.

'I don't know why it bothers me. Who would have come? I would have been sitting in the chapel alone.'

'That's not quite true.'

'Well, you would have sat with me. Who else?'

'Other staff would have been there.'

'They hated him.'

'No. They admired him greatly. It was more of a game they played with him as they tried to wrestle the power of their dynamic.'

'Some game.'

She probably wasn't too far from the truth. What did that mean? Some people tend to think that the number of mourners who attend a funeral is a reflection on the person, the quality of the life they have led and the popularity they held. It was an overly simplistic way of looking at things, even if there were times when there was merit in such measurements. If Henry survived for half a century less, he'd have been mourned by a crowd that wouldn't have fit in the Berlin Cathedral. Had his life been emptier for having lived longer? Of course not. His life had changed. It had moved out of the public eye. Rather than sharing his life with the world, his life became more directly focused on the one person who made his world. In life, he needed nothing more than Marta. Why should it have been different in death?

Staff shortages have meant that I am working for the eighth straight day. Normally such a stint would be destroying me, but now I couldn't be more grateful. I'd come in even on a rostered day off, but that currently isn't allowed. I was meant to be off the day Henry died, but Frida rostered me on specifically to care for Marta that day, as a special favour both to her and me.

There is so little that anyone can do under the current restrictions, that I feel like I would go insane without the daily escape that work provides. Not only that, but I also feel an overwhelming need to provide Marta with support at the moment. She is broken, and though I can't put her back together, I can take care of all the pieces and prevent the damage getting worse. I know other staff are looking out for her through this vulnerable period, but they are doing little more than their jobs. Marta isn't someone I provide care to, she is someone I care for. There is a world of difference between these definitions.

While restrictions prevented staff coming in when not rostered on, no such limits had been placed on coming in early, nor staying back late. Most days I was spending an additional time at the home before and after each shift. While working, I was obligated to be wherever the calls took me, but I could direct all of my extra time to being at Marta's bedside. While today's shift had given me plenty of opportunities to check on her, now that I was off the clock, I could give her a little more quality time.

'How are you feeling?'

'I miss him so much. What am I going to do?'

'You are going to do what he would want you to do. Live the best and most positively you can, knowing that he's waiting for you at the end of it.'

'If he is waiting, it would be best that I join him as soon as I can.'

'No. It's eternal, so time is irrelevant.'

'For him perhaps, but not for me. Every minute seems like an hour. Time never seems to move.'

There was no way to make her feel better, but I knew it was healthier that she was saying these things than to be silently contemplating them in solitude. I never doubted my presence was helping, even if it couldn't be reflected in anything she showed me. Every now and again I would bring up something about Henry that would generate a smile, yet it was soon followed by more tears. Nothing was wrong with that. The tears were healing, therapeutic and inevitable. Only with time would they become less frequent. It wasn't just my job to be aiding this, it was my responsibility as a friend.

Marta drifted in and out of sleep a couple of times, but I stayed by her bedside. I had nowhere else to be. I did have an idea of something I would do when I got back home, but there was no need to rush for it.

'You're still here,' Elena, the night shift coordinator said to me, when she came to check on Marta.

'I'm just about to leave.'

Marta stirred again and I decided it best to say my farewell.

'I have a meeting with the bosses tomorrow. You know I only have a few days left on my contract.'

'I can't bear to have you leave, but I know you have so much more to see and do.'

'Not yet. They are too short of staff, so I am sure they will extend me. I can't go anywhere else while all these restrictions are on.'

I pulled down my mask and gave her a kiss on the cheek.

'Try and sleep. I'll see you tomorrow.'

***

My appointment with Hans and Frida was less of a meeting, and more of a quick formality. They thanked me for the special attention I had given Marta and Henry and said they were very happy with my work in general. They asked if I was willing to continue for another four weeks, to which I obviously said yes. I wasn't going to leave Marta at this point by choice, so even if the borders were open, I would still be signing on to stay. It couldn't be that way forever, but hopefully the next month or so would bring a little more clarity and stability to the world, and a little more comfort to my favourite resident. When I'd finished with the managers, I raced upstairs to Marta to give her the news.

'I couldn't have lost you. Not now.'

'There was never really a chance they'd let me go in the current climate. Still, you can never take these things for granted.'

I reached into my bag and passed over the contents to her.

'What is this?'

'Turn it over. What do you think?'

'I love it. Who did this?'

'I did.' It was the drawing I had been working on over the past few weeks. I wasn't completely convinced about it, but the timing forced my hand. After a couple of touch-ups last night, I felt it was the best I could do. Marta was going through such an incredibly painful time, that anything which may lift her spirits was priceless. I didn't expect the drawing would have much of an impact, but any moment with a smile felt like a little victory.

'You never told me you had such a talent.'

'I can draw better than I can skate, but I wouldn't call it a talent.'

'I would. Thank you, my friend.'

'Thank you for the inspiration. Do you want me to put it up on the wall next to the photo it captures.'

'No. Not yet. I want it close to me. It may be a drawing of me, but I see you when I look at it. I want it by my side when you can't be.'

It was such a beautiful sentiment and validated every bit of extra attention I had given her. Some may wonder why I have given so much of my time and energy to her, but I don't feel anything that I have done has been unwarranted.

We don't all have the same needs, nor do we all have the same means. There are times we need to give a little more, other times we need to accept more. Marta wasn't getting a moment more attention than she needed or deserved, but circumstances meant it couldn't come from anyone else. Friends couldn't visit. Lorraine, Teresa and Alex were stranded in Australia. Staff gave what they could, but the balance had to come from someone. I happily took that role.

I had received just as much. I am a richer, fuller person than when I arrived here. That wasn't solely Marta's influence, yet she was intertwined with everything that had helped me grow.

41

30 April 2020

MARTA

A month without the love of my life. It feels like an eternity. I miss him every day and I have no doubt that I will continue to do so forever more. They say that time heals all wounds, but that isn't true. Perhaps it gets a fraction easier each day, but the time it would take to feel close to recovery is longer than the time I have left.

'Good morning my dear,' Amber said as she walked in to start another day at the home.

Amber has been the most remarkable support through this time. I feel so sorry that her life has been thrown into chaos by the events of the world. She was meant to be on a trek through Europe, stopping only briefly here. Now she is stranded, and there is so little that she can do. For me this has been such a blessing, as she's devoted countless hours to me, with nothing in return. The selfish part of me wants this to continue, but I know at some point she will have to go. She deserves to. I hope she'll carry forward some good memories of us.

'I missed you yesterday,' I said. I couldn't complain. She has had very few days off in the time she has worked here. As staff have been forced to isolate in so many different situations, those who have been available have been rostered on far more than would normally be allowed. Amber requested to work as much as possible, her options with her time being so limited due to the lockdowns.

'There's a few more signs to life around the city now. Shops are starting to reopen. I heard this morning that the zoo and most of the museums will be reopening in the next week. Most people are in masks everywhere, but that is a step ahead of where we've been.'

'It must be getting closer to you moving on, I suppose.'

'Don't worry about that. They've extended me for another four weeks. You might find I am hard to get rid of.'

'I hope so.' When Henry died, Amber was spending hours a day with me. Gradually this had decreased because I genuinely was coping better. It is like watching a child grow. When you seem them only once a year, the growth seems so rapid. When you are living with them, you don't notice the progress. I hadn't felt the improvement each day, but I can look back a month and see just how far I have come. It couldn't have happened without Amber.

'You know, religious services are going to be allowed to recommence tomorrow. Have you thought anymore about having some sort of small commemoration for Henry?'

I shook my head. Henry certainly didn't want any sort of religious ceremony. He had no desire for a funeral, though in different circumstances we would have no doubt held one. Now that a month has passed, there seemed little point in any sort of formal event.

'The only thing I want, is after I have gone. I want our ashes scattered together.'

'Yes, in the grounds of the Charlottenburg Palace.'

'That's right. In the waters of the Teichgraben.' There was nothing else either of us wanted after we'd passed, but this was very important to us. We scattered Wolfe's ashes there, and it had remained a precious place to us as a result. Though we'd moved from the area soon after, we kept going back there regularly. We always felt his presence and felt closer to each other as we returned and reminisced. We continually reiterated our plans for spending eternity there.

'How will it happen?' I asked.

'What do you mean?'

'When Wolfe was put down, we had his ashes. Who is going to be responsible for Henry and me?'

'There would be provision in your Will for someone to be in charge of your Estate.'

'I don't think it mentions our ashes.'

'As long as your beneficiaries know, I am certain they will make sure your wishes are taken care of.'

I had told Teresa and Alex about our wishes previously. They'd been to Schloss Charlottenburg with us, but only back when Wolfe was alive. We'd never shown them where his ashes were scattered, and therefore where ours should be. I didn't know if it would be at the back of their mind and possibly forgotten, but even if they did remember, how would it be managed when they were so far away. I asked Amber to help me write to them.

'You know Marta, you said that Henry and you were closer because you only had each other. You said that you loved Wolfe so much as there was nobody else. I think it's probably true for your niece and nephew. If they have so little other family, I am sure, despite the tyranny of distance, they have an especially strong love for you both, and will do anything you wish.'

'They will, but only if they can. What if they cannot come to Berlin?'

'There will always be a way that things can be organised. I have their email addresses and have been in contact back and forth with them in recent weeks. If they need help, I will provide it. If I cannot help, I will direct them to those who can.'

'What would I do without you Amber?'

'Probably get more rest.'

'The one thing I get too much of already.'

I thought a month ago that I would never smile again. Amber manages to make me smile every day. It isn't a mask, but a genuine feeling of positivity. It may be comparatively small amongst the ongoing sadness, but it is something. In the darkest moments, a light, however dim and distant, is essential. Amber shone that light on me every day.

She has given so much to me, and I feel remorseful that I have given her nothing in return. I feel there are troubles lurking beneath the surface, but she has been either unwilling or unable to share more of herself with me. I have felt it best all along to respect her privacy, but it feels like in the helplessness of my position, the only thing I could ever give her is advice. When I don't know what the issues are, there is little advice I can give.

'Is there anything else I can do for you Marta? I must make my way downstairs to clock on.'

I shook my head and smiled at her, saying I would see her later. Once again, she had spent an hour with me on her own time. Since Henry passed, most of the time she spent with me was her own, not her employers. I couldn't be more grateful for her. Most of her colleagues are good to me too. Whatever troubles they'd had with Henry, they never had with me, and every member of staff has been kind and generous with their time in this past month. It may not be quite the same as the way Amber has been, but it has all helped.

You never know when your number will be up. With this new virus, one person could walk into this home and start a spread that would see us all done for. They are being exceptionally cautious, but that minimises risk rather than eliminates it. The stories I see on television make me feel that it is only a matter of time. Other homes have already had cases go through them. It would be foolish to think that we won't suffer the same thing eventually. I don't have the immune system to cope with anything like that, so I'm sure if it strikes me, it will be a quick end.

I am not afraid. Fear strikes when you have something to lose. There is nothing left in life for me, so there is nothing to lose when the inevitable comes. I am not in a rush for it to end, but neither do I have any desire to elongate my existence.

How do you measure a life? I am seventy-eight, though my body looks like I am fifteen years older than that, perhaps a measure of how much I put it through over the years. I don't think the time is relevant, for I lived so much through those times on the road, that I squeezed more life out of individual years than most people did in a lifetime.

I was a national champion. I starred at Madison Square Garden. I escaped across the Berlin Wall. I spent two-thirds of my life married to the man of my dreams. Could any life have been more fortunate?

I was born in the time and place of the world's most brutal ever conflict. I lost the person who was my childhood hero, after seeing him once in his last six years. I never saw my beloved mother in her last decade on earth. I've spent the last quarter of my life with little physical capacity for any joy. Could any life have been more unfortunate?

Henry always said life balanced out, and I guess mine has. The tragedies and the triumphs combined to make my life no happier or sadder than most others. This balance has come from extremes, and there is no doubt my life has been fuller and richer than most because of these.

From my bed, my view out the window is limited. Trapped inside, you can be anywhere in the world. It makes little difference. The one clear image I can see outside is the distinct shape of the Fernsehturm reaching up towards the sky. Nothing symbolises Berlin more than a tower built in the East, with the intention of being seen by everyone on the other side of the Wall, hoping to create a false vision of progress.

Berlin's story was a balance of incredible highs and unspeakable lows. The fullness that comes from a rich array of experiences that is unparalleled anywhere else. It doesn't make it better or worse, but it makes it incredibly special and unique. The story of my city couldn't be more like my own, though eventually they must diverge. As my time comes to an end, the story of Berlin will continue to be added to. Whatever comes after this life, I like to think that my soul will live on here, hand in hand with Henry, and with Wolfe at our side.

I am ready and willing to face my fate, whatever that may be.

42

14 July 2020

AMBER

It had meant to be four weeks, but four months had passed before the time came to make my next move. Ironically, Greta had left Berlin before I had. We'd caught up several times in the past couple of months, and after the pain she had caused me, we'd ended up with a solid friendship. She wasn't seeking more. It was good in amongst the loneliness I'd felt here to have someone to spend time with.

She had won a role in a television show that would be produced in Bremen. Of all the places, she would be moving to the same city that had been Marta and Henry's base for years during their career in entertainment. We had lunch last Tuesday, the day prior to her move. I finally gave her the drawing I'd done a few months ago.

'You said I had kept things from you when we met, but clearly you kept a few things too. This is absolutely brilliant.'

She got a little emotional. Clearly when I had the right subject, I could produce something of value.

Greta had ended both of the so-called relationships she was involved in. Wolfgang was ready to come out, and she moved out of his unit a couple of weeks before a well-crafted media article discussed their separation. She had already separated from Leila, soon after the Coronavirus outbreak had led to the cancellation of the show she had been set to produce.

'However much you thought you could learn from me, I feel that I got the lessons. In telling you to be your best self, I realised the changes I needed to make to be my best self. I was trying to be too many things to too many people. Now I'm ready to be myself. On my own, and more than happy with that. I am ready for whatever comes next. Professionally and personally, I'm being myself and living well.'

I can't pretend there wasn't a part of me wondering what might have been. There was so much about her that attracted me, but I knew we were both at a certain place in our lives where we had to follow our own path, not someone else's, whatever appeal that might hold. Life is full of miracles, and maybe one day in the future our paths will cross again. Far more likely that won't happen, but the roles we've played for each other will leave us better equipped to be ready when the right opportunity arises.

Saying goodbye to Greta wasn't difficult. While I'd learnt to value the friendship, I only saw her occasionally. Her move would have no impact on my day-to-day life. Saying goodbye to Marta would be a very different story, our lives having been so intertwined through the whole of my time in Berlin.

I worked my last shift at the home yesterday. I'd asked Frida if I could hang on to my identification card for an extra day. I didn't want my goodbye with Marta to be in the confines of my final shift, and said I'd come back the following day when I could spend some time with her. She wasn't used to staff having such close bonds with residents, but she understood that Marta was alone in the world now and granted my request.

As I made my way to Marta's room, I ran into Hannah and Heidi. They'd been the only two staff members I had developed any affinity with throughout my time here. They often worked together, though neither ever seemed too pleased by that. Hannah often told me that she found Heidi lazy, while the younger lady struggled to cope with Hannah's demanding nature. I could empathise with both views. Having got to know and like each of them, I wasn't willing to play sides.

I was grateful for the role that each had played, not just for me in the workplace, but in helping me through the struggles I faced in this part of my life.

'Thank you, Hannah. I can't tell you how grateful I was for your support when I first came here. I've always felt like an outsider, but you really changed my thinking.'

Her expression never changed, but her words were warm. She'd seen deep within me when I was doing all I could to hide. I wished her on-going happiness and made my way further down the corridor where Heidi was just walking out of a room.

'I'd give you a big hug if I could Amber,' she said, but of course such contact wasn't possible in the current climate. Restrictions were no longer as severe as they had been, but such close contact was still forbidden in the nursing home. 'I will miss having someone normal in this workplace. Make sure you keep in touch.'

'I will. Maybe I can come back for the wedding.'

I shouldn't have said that. I didn't really want to come back here, not through a lack of love for the city or the people who'd become part of my life, but because I felt that my departure was a line in the sand. My life was at a stage where I was taking steps forward. Looking back wasn't part of my plan.

The relationship I've built with Marta has been hugely significant for both of us. I really hope that saying goodbye to me isn't going to have too much of a negative impact on her. I don't think many people fully appreciated the significance of her loss when Henry passed. Hopefully she understands the nature of the role I played for both Henry and her. I was never here to become part of their lives, I was here to play a role in a transition. That transition is done now. Henry has gone, and Marta has adjusted to the new reality, however hard it may be. There is nothing more I can do now to make that any easier. Anything I can give, I have given. The time is right.

'I thought you'd gone,' Marta said as I walked in. She was up, dressed and sitting in a wheelchair. She had an appointment with the hairdresser who visited the home once a week.

'Without saying goodbye? Not a chance.'

'I will miss you enormously Maple Leaf.'

'Likewise.'

'The level of care you have shown me, and Henry when he was still with us, is something I'll never forget.'

'Just doing my job.'

'No, you did so much more. I know your time here hasn't been the perfect experience you hoped it would be, but those times are coming.'

I initially assumed she meant the restrictions that the virus had placed on my trip, but I was also aware that she was wise enough to piece together the things that I hadn't said.

'Broken hearts heal,' she said.

'Has yours?'

'No, but Henry was my life. He became that after we'd been to heaven and hell together. You might find your heart broken by people who aren't worthy of it. You don't know if someone is worthy of your heart until you've been through the worst of times together, for anyone can seem ideal in the best of times.'

'My heart is much fuller for the time I have spent here. Balance, right. There will always be good and bad.'

'No better place than Berlin to understand that.'

I poured her a half-glass of white wine as I had each day since I'd been here. It was her one treat, giving a small positive against the physical and mental struggles she faced. She may remain in her current state for some time, or fate may reunite her with Henry soon. Either way, it would be a tiny postscript to an amazing life.

'Don't worry,' she said. 'You've trained Heidi well. She will be looking after me, maybe not quite as well as you, but close enough that I know I am in good hands.'

I gave her a hug and a kiss and told her I would write to her regularly. She could expect a postcard from Hamburg within days. I knew it wouldn't stop her missing me, but I made sure she knew that would be a feeling that we both would experience equally.

'Thank you,' she said, as a tear ran down my cheek, and I turned and walked out the door for the last time.

I came to Europe as a lost soul looking to find myself in a world full of knowns. As the pandemic has torn at the certainties around us which we take for granted, I feel far more confident within myself of who I am. I don't need a policy statement that defines every thought and every belief. I don't need labels to tell the world everything there is to know. I am me. My dreams, my hopes, my desires, my opinions. All of these are valid. I don't need to fit anyone else's ideals. I will be moving on to the next page with an understanding that I am the director of my own story.

Throughout life we are shaped by the people around us. Good, bad or indifferent, the influence of those in our lives is always significant. We understand this when we are young, with our families and as we grow, our friends. This never stops throughout life, even when it isn't so obvious. Although with age each influence has less new ground to break, I know that I had an influence on Henry in the last weeks of his life. Unquestionably the influence that he and Marta had on who I am today, was even greater.

The final goodbye will be to the city of Berlin itself. I consider every city to be an entity of its own accord, just as each living creature is, but our connection with a city is so different as the relationship is almost entirely one way. Berlin is no different for what I have brought it, but I am changed for what the city has given me. Germany is defined by efficiency, precision and stoicism. These traits are on offer throughout the nation, but in Berlin they are coupled with the distinct cultural differences that history has thrust upon it.

Half of the people living in the world today were not born when the Berlin Wall fell. Despite this, the era of division is what the city is synonymous with. The Wall trapped people in a physical place, but we are all trapped behind walls at some points of our lives. When the Wall was torn down, freedom of movement became a reality. Our own personal walls can be far harder to pass. Seeing the results of what this city has transitioned to, serves as the ultimate reminder that we must always seek to find a way through.

I'm on two different journeys. The physical one stagnated for longer than I intended in Berlin, but a global pandemic will do that. The inner journey has seen me take far greater steps in Berlin than anywhere. That doesn't mean I've reached the end, and it is the reason why I can't let the journey end here. If this is the place for me, it will still be the place once I've travelled further and seen more. I'm not in a race to reach the end of the journey fastest, I am striving to get to the end of the journey in the best possible way. I know there is more to see, more to learn and more to experience.

Marta and Henry travelled the world. They found everything they needed in each other, but they still felt lost in many different places. Berlin was right for them, but was that more about the city or the mindset they were driven to along their journey? I don't know, but I do understand the wisdom that comes from seeing so much of the world.

Tomorrow, I head to Hamburg and a new stage begins. Every step I take, I'll be doing with the extra enrichment that my love affair with Berlin has given me.

FROM THE AUTHOR

Bedside in Berlin was conceived a few months after my return from the city, when the COVID-19 pandemic had seen lockdowns commence around the world. In my workplace, an overseas backpacker had started a short-term assignment with us. Rather than exploring the city and moving on to the next, her experience was one of work, return to the hostel, then repeat. It couldn't be further from how I would want travel to a foreign land to be, but it was the reality of the time. I felt like she was stuck behind a wall, and the connection to Berlin was formed.

Berlin had never been at the top of my travel bucket list. The decision to go there was based on a desire to better understand the life story of my aunt, Hella. She had been raised in East Berlin, escaping across the Wall to forge a career as a professional figure skater. The character of Marta was obviously inspired by her, though the character evolved into her own unique entity. Hella and my uncle Marty lived such full and exciting lives that I could never do justice to their stories. The snippet I sought to focus on was the link to Berlin. They symbolised Berlin; the union of East and West, the artistry, the rebellion, the fight for something better.

Despite initial uncertainty, I loved Berlin. Berlin is multi-dimensional. Some destinations are loved for their history, but from my perspective, Berlin's appeal comes despite its history. The capital of the Nazi empire and the epicentre of the Cold War, Berlin doesn't hide its history, it displays it as a lesson for humanity. Its strengths come from these lessons. It is welcoming, accepting, forgiving and inclusive. It is a city that is essential to experience in order to fully understand the best and worst that we can seek in life.

Bedside in Berlin exists thanks to many people. To my mother Patricia, whose letters when travelling inspired me not just to travel, but to document my experiences. Not only did it help to entertain and inform others at the time, it consolidated the stories in my mind. Every day I have spent on the road remains fresh in my mind thanks to the lessons she taught me.

To my wife Alison who has travelled far and wide with me in search of these experiences. I love sharing the journeys with you, not just to destinations around the world, but on our journey through life together. Many thanks also for the design of the cover.

Thanks to my sister Leonie Page for her inspiration and advice, and to my family, Clyde and Jule Milner, Jon Fearn, and Sally, Darian, Hugh and Ella Crouch for their love and support.

Thank you to the many friends and supporters who have helped with ideas and support as I've pursued my dream of turning the stories from the road into novels that celebrate the people and places that have played such a role in my life.

Most importantly, thank you to my late aunt and uncle, Hella and Marty, for inspiring this story, and my life in general.

PARADOX IN PARIS

Available May 2023

'With rich and decadent delights on every block, how is it I never see anyone overweight?'

'That is just one of the many paradoxes about this city,' John told him.

Paris is arguably the most alluring city in the world, yet it also gave rise to Paris Syndrome, a psychiatric condition afflicting people deeply affected when the city fails to meet their expectations. For all who love the wonders of Paris, there are many who remember it with disdain.

Twenty-three-year-old Elliot Martin arrives in Paris to see the sights while hoping to build a relationship with John, his estranged uncle. When John was Elliot's age, he visited Paris for a short trip. He fell in love with the city and never left. He wrote a best-selling novel and was as seen as the hottest new property in world literature. Thirty-five years later, he has not tasted success since.

Like his uncle a generation earlier, the trip was seen by others as Elliot running away from his problems. He maintained he was running towards the solutions. Will Paris give him the inspiration to get life on track? The possibilities are endless in the City of Light.

HURDLES IN HOBART

Available July 2023

Hobart and its surrounds in Southern Tasmania are often over-looked on a tourist itinerary of Australia, but it is a unique region where natural wonder combines with history, cuisine and the arts to be a traveller's paradise.

English journalism student Zaniya Fergusson isn't excited at the prospect of a week with her family in Hobart, but a chance encounter with recent widow Helen O'Shaughnessy sets a new agenda for her trip. Helen's late husband Lucky was the world's worst jockey. Having fallen in all of his forty-three hurdle races, he spent more time in hospital than on horseback over his career. Fifty years on from his last race, a man once famous for failure had passed away without attention, until a newspaper article titled The End of Hobarts Biggest Loser.

Against the backdrop of Lucky's life story, the Fergusson's discover the richness of Hobart's myriad of unique experiences. For Zaniya, the transformation of her view of Hobart mirrors the change in view she wants her article to bring for the legacy of Lucky O'Shaughnessy, from loser to Hobart's Biggest Hero.

SURVIVAL IN SAINT PETERSBURG

Available September 2023

Saint Petersburg is arguably the world's most beautiful city, but beneath the beauty lies a city that has known trauma and tragedy like nowhere else.

Ekaterina Komarova has experienced it all. Born in the city in the 1930's, she lost her family through Stalin's Purge and the Siege of Leningrad. As an orphan, she was a victim of systematic rape and abuse. She escaped and found happiness with a husband and son before tragedy again left her alone.

Australian tourists Adam and Louise visit a Soviet era doughnut shop, but in amongst the throng of customers, their attention turns to an old woman hobbling between tables. Neither a customer, nor an employee, the tourists are determined to find out more about her.

Through interpreter Yuri, Ekaterina tells her life story. Intermingling with their experiences in the attractions of the city, Adam and Lousie discover what she and the city did to survive. Ekaterina is the essence of survival in Saint Petersburg.

ABOUT THE AUTHOR

C.R. Page was born in Adelaide, South Australia. He graduated from the University of South Australia with a degree in business before working for many years in the South Australian public sector.

A love of travel led to him writing articles and short stories, planning to begin a travel blog, but in time the greatest elements he was seeing in places warranted a bigger canvas. The concept of the travel novel began to take shape.

In 2022 he won the Port Adelaide Writers Festival award for his short story, Sanctuary. This was followed by the release of his first novel, The Ride to Work, a story of mental health set on the morning commute to a workplace.

Follow him on Facebook at CR Page - Travel Fiction.